RED MAN DOWN

The apparent suicide of an ex-cop leads Sarah Burke to investigate three bizarre deaths in three years in the same family. What are they hiding?

When a criminal shot by a rookie cop turns out to be an ex-cop and Red Man, Sarah Burke becomes embroiled in a murky investigation into three bizarre deaths in three years in the same family. She quickly turns to the family for answers, but why are they so secretive?

Further Mysteries by Elizabeth Gunn

The Jake Hines Series

TRIPLE PLAY
PAR FOUR
FIVE CARD STUD
SIX POUND WALLEYE
SEVENTH INNING STRETCH
CRAZY EIGHTS
McCAFFERTY'S NINE *
THE TEN MILE TRIALS *
ELEVEN LITTLE PIGGIES *

The Sarah Burke Series

COOL IN TUCSON *
NEW RIVER BLUES *
KISSING ARIZONA *
THE MAGIC LINE *
RED MAN DOWN *

★ available from Severn House

RED MAN DOWN

Elizabeth Gunn

Severn House Large Print
London & New York

This first large print edition published 2014
in Great Britain and the USA by
SEVERN HOUSE PUBLISHERS LTD of
19 Cedar Road, Sutton, Surrey, England, SM2 5DA.
First world regular print edition published 2014 by
Severn House Publishers Ltd., London and New York.

British Library Cataloguing in Publication Data

Gunn, Elizabeth, 1927- author.
  Red Man down. -- (The Sarah Burke series)
  1. Burke, Sarah (Fictitious character)--Fiction. 2. Women
  detectives--Arizona--Tucson--Fiction. 3. Ex-police
  officers--Fiction. 4. Police shootings--Fiction.
  5. Detective and mystery stories. 6. Large type books.
  I. Title II. Series
  813.6-dc23

  ISBN-13: 9780727897503

Severn House Publishers support the Forest Stewardship
Council™ [FSC™], the leading international forest certification
organisation. All our titles that are printed on FSC certified paper
carry the FSC logo.

Printed and bound in Great Britain by
T J International, Padstow, Cornwall.

ONE

I'll just have one quick go at the crossword, Sarah Burke told herself, and then I'll get my lazy buns out of this chair and take Denny shopping.

A mall run on the first Saturday after Christmas had never come close to making her Favorite Treats list. In fact, it was near the top of her secret WOO list, composed of things she usually tried to Weasel Out Of. But she had promised this trip on Christmas morning, when gift money fell out of cards and began burning a hole in her niece's pocket.

No question, Denny had earned the favor. Ever since they moved into the house on Bentley Street, she'd been doing more than her share to support this improbable household. Several times in the hectic months since Sarah and Will Dietz had cobbled their family together under one roof, Sarah had thought, *My lover, my mother and my niece? Even the French wouldn't try to make this movie.*

5

But against all odds, it was working pretty well. And eleven-year-old Denny's helpful hands, especially in the kitchen, had been a big part of that success. Abandoned by her addicted mother after years of neglect, she had bounced back from the self-abusing waif Sarah had adopted last year and shown how much juice and humor a willing pre-teen could contribute to the lives of striving adults. So if a mall run today felt like pulling teeth without a sedative, Sarah had made up her mind to suck up and do it anyway, with a smile.

But just a little self-indulgence first, to help me stay patient, even if Denny sets a new desert southwest record for the number of jeans tried on in a single day.

She poured a second coffee, yawned and stretched. Around her, the house on Bentley Street hummed with Saturday morning sounds – Aggie's mixer whirring in the kitchen, Will running a power drill out in his shop. And down the hall from the breakfast table where she sat, Denny's favorite hip-hop music rattled her bedroom door.

Sarah was counting the letters in 'ebullient' when her cell played the opening bars of 'On the Road Again.'

'Looks like we might be growing some new brand of stupid,' Delaney said. Her sergeant was still at home too, she could tell:

6

his background noises were TV cartoons and a barking dog, definitely not homicide division. 'Some numbskull all by himself, stripping copper wire in full view of heavy traffic. Ripping it out of the power hook-up in front of an abandoned warehouse on Flowing Wells and stashing it in his pick-up.'

'Easier to see what you're doing in daylight, I guess,' Sarah said, waiting for the real news. She knew he hadn't called to talk about wire theft.

'No doubt. And then deciding to shoot it out with the officer who caught him at it. That was brilliant, too.'

Ah. Well, there goes Saturday.

'Officer's name is Spurlock. He called it in and he's waiting at the scene for you. Should be three backups covering the scene by now, and the ME's on his way – I caught Greenberg before he started his morning run. I'll be along as soon as I get everybody else called.' She was starting to hang up when she heard him say, apparently from a little distance, 'Oh, say—' Then he came back on, in full voice, and added, 'The IR guy's running a little late, too – he wants to meet us downtown. So will you secure our shooter's weapon and shield until I get there?'

Oh, sure, boss. Why wouldn't I be glad to be the one to strip him of his most important

7

possessions? All she said was, 'OK.'

On her way to gear up, she stuck her head in Denny's room and said, 'I'm sorry but the mall's got to wait, babe. I just got called to work.'

'Drat,' her niece said. But then quickly added, 'Oh, well, the sales will still be on tomorrow.' She'd been living in Sarah's house long enough to adopt a cop's-kid attitude: stuff happens; work can't wait; live with it. Anyway, she had fresh Christmas loot – a new iPad that was never out of her sight and shared the bed with her now – so she had plenty to keep her occupied.

'Got a call, huh?' Dietz said, coming into their bedroom while Sarah was dressing. It was the closest he would come to offering sympathy. The good thing about two-cop couples was they both had plenty of experience with wrecked weekends, and knew bitching only made things worse.

Will Dietz was a nondescript man, noticeable only for the scars left from a firefight he'd inadvertently walked into a couple of years ago. They had fallen passionately in love during his recovery, just as her obligations to her abandoned niece and ailing mother were threatening to overwhelm her. His efforts had rescued them all, doing most of the work to move everybody into this one old house near two good schools. Now

Denny was powering through middle school and Sarah's mother had a nice guest house in the backyard and the assisted living she needed. Undemonstrative, stoical and steady, he had quietly become Sarah's North Pole.

As for the Saturday night date they had planned, they could see the movie later, Will said. 'And should I cancel the dinner reservation?'

'Guess you better,' Sarah said. 'Officer-involved shooting and a fatality, so I'll be gone a while.'

'Well, nice to have known you,' Dietz said, their standard black humor for these times. He kissed her neck and went back outside to prep the new lumber he'd been cutting – he was fixing the crumbled wainscoting in the hall.

On her way out, she stopped at Denny's room again to ask her to keep an eye on her grandmother. 'I heard her mixer going; she's cooking up a storm out there. If she starts to fade she might need some help with the cleanup.'

'She said she was thinking about banana bread.' Denny giggled and hopped off the bed. 'I'll go ask her if she needs me to lick the bowl.'

Dietz had taught her how to light the old gas oven, because Aggie got dizzy bending over. Denny would do that first, Sarah knew, and then find a spoon and clean out that bowl till it hardly needed a rinse. How could you not make a trip to the mall for a kid as good as that?

Although, maybe by tomorrow ... if she found something on the internet ... Would she think it was fun to have something delivered by UPS?

Officer Spurlock looked unusually pale for a Tucson street cop, Sarah thought. A little sweaty, too, despite an ambient outdoor temperature of fifty-seven degrees. He was standing very straight by his black-and-white squad car in a trash-strewn gravel parking lot that surrounded an empty warehouse on Flowing Wells. Two of his fellow officers were stringing crime-scene tape around the entire lot. A third patrolman, whose name badge read, 'T. Garry,' had set up a surveillance post across the lot's driveway, holding a clipboard inside a posse box. Inside the tape, a police photographer carried two bags of camera equipment toward a tarp-covered mound that lay near a pickup in the otherwise-empty lot.

Sarah said, 'Hi, Tim,' signed the sheet on the clipboard Garry handed her and timed herself in at 10:03 a.m. Walking carefully to keep out of dog poop and some prickly-

10

looking weeds, she approached Spurlock, showed him her badge and announced herself the first detective on the scene.

'Glad to see you,' he said. 'Glad to see anybody at all, actually. Felt like forever I stood here alone with that body.'

'How long was it really?'

'Twelve minutes till the EMT team got here. Took them about two minutes to pronounce him dead and be on their way. Then a hundred years or so went by till these two guys,' he nodded toward the two men working on the tape, 'showed up and told me to stand over here and wait. I did that for another century till this photographer walked in and said the same thing. Been standing here like a dork since before I was born, it feels like...' Hearing himself begin to babble, he stopped and swallowed. Then he quickly added the one other thing he simply had to say to somebody. 'This guy didn't leave me any choice at all, you know?'

'You'll have a chance to tell me all about that, and anything else you want to tell me. But we have to take this one step at a time. You were the first responder, is that right?'

'Yes, ma'am. First and only, for what seemed like a long time.'

'OK. Detective is probably better than ma'am for this occasion. Or you can just call me Sarah. Do you know if the items in the

11

pickup were stolen from this building?'

'Beats the hell out of me – I never had time to find out.'

'I see. Did you just happen across this scene or did somebody call in a complaint?'

'Alert seniors drinking beer over there in the bar called it in – see the little sign on the second floor of that warehouse? Somebody converted that room to a bar, I guess, and all the patrons were having fun watching this guy work for a while. Then they talked it over and decided that even if this place is abandoned, this mutt probably shouldn't be wrecking it, so they called nine-one-one.'

'You get their names?'

'No. The minute I got here I saw that guy pulling wire out of that power box and called for backup. He wasn't moving very fast but I saw him spooling out wire, and I could see that the back of his truck' – he licked his lips, as if his mouth was dry – 'was full of those fixtures that looked like they'd just been ripped out of *somewhere*, and I thought, I gotta *stop him*, so I—'

He stopped and made a small hissing sound, like somebody who's just been hit in the gut. Following his stare, Sarah saw that the photographer had pulled the tarp off the mound. A dead white man lay there, face up, with a bright smear of blood under his head.

'Officer Spurlock,' Sarah said, 'are you sure this is a fatality?'

'Well, the ME isn't here yet, but the head guy on the EMT team said he was qualified to call it and he did – no use transporting a dead body, he said, and he called the ME to take care of it. Take a look if you— Do you think he's still alive?'

'No, but I'm puzzled – where's all the blood? Just hang on here a second while I take a look, OK?' She hurried toward the motionless body on the ground. She had recently had a corpse at a crime scene begin to move. It was not an experience she expected to forget, or wanted to repeat.

Buddy Norris was the police photographer today. A methodical man who didn't like distractions, he said sharply, 'I'm not done yet, Sarah.' Which meant *get the hell out of my crime scene*. And the rules said he was right. An iron-clad rule at a crime scene was to *take a picture of everything before you touch anything.*

'Buddy, I'm not touching anything, I just have to get one look. Because if this is a fatality where's all the— Oh.'

Spurlock's first shot must have been a thousand-to-one successful crime-stopper that entered just below his chin. It appeared to have kept going straight back, probably through his spinal cord. Or was buried in it?

13

Either way, there wouldn't have been much bleeding after that bullet found its target. This man was probably dead when he hit the ground. *Nice shooting, Officer Spurlock.*

She walked back and stood beside the young officer. 'Looks like your suspect died really fast,' she said. She glanced through her notes and found his first name. 'Daniel,' she said, watching the nerve twitch in his cheek, 'is this your first shooting?'

'Yes, it is,' Spurlock said, 'and I gotta tell you, it does not feel good.'

'It never does,' Sarah said. 'I would be quite alarmed if you said it did. But you and I are going to have to walk this scene together while you tell me everything you can remember about what happened here. And then, once the rest of my crew gets here, you and I will go downtown and meet somebody from Internal Affairs. I'll sit in while he interviews you and we'll make out the preliminary report. First, though,' she said, pulling on gloves, 'I have to ask you for your badge and your weapon. As of now you're on paid investigative leave, Daniel.' She watched his eyes darken for a couple of seconds and got ready for an argument, but the moment passed and he pulled his badge off his belt.

'Call me Dan – everybody else does. This doesn't feel so good either,' he said, unclipping the holster that held his Glock.

'I know. Think of it as a nice paid vacation with the family.'

'I'll try. When does it start?'

'As soon as you finish talking to me and Internal Affairs.'

'How long does the investigation take, usually?'

'On average? Three or four months. But you won't get that much time off – just three working days, usually. Though you can request one or two extra if you feel you need it. What shifts are you working?'

'Saturday through Tuesday.'

'So you might get back to work on Tuesday, if all goes well. Check with your duty sergeant. Meanwhile a dozen or so people will be writing their reports – I'll write one, and Delaney, and the Chief of Police after he walks the scene with one of us. Internal Affairs will review the scene and write a report, too, and somebody from the County Attorney's office—'

'Jeez,' he said, 'everybody gets to comment but me?'

'Oh, you'll get interviewed plenty – more than you're going to like, probably. But the more you help me right now, the easier the whole thing will go.' She turned to a fresh page. 'Did you talk to the men who called in the complaint?'

'No. Like I said, the minute I got here I saw that guy and called for backup. I walked over to that bar as soon as the other two patrol cars got here and asked the guy who's running the place to show me who called it in. He said they left right after they ended the call, said they didn't want to get involved.' He shrugged. 'People are funny about that sometimes, aren't they?'

'Yes.' The ME's car had just parked beside hers and she saw Moses Greenberg, a.k.a. the Animal, get out of it and stride impatiently toward the tape. Sarah removed the ammo clip and the last bullet from the chamber of Spurlock's gun, then dropped it and his badge into an evidence bag, saying, 'Will you wait here, please, while I have a word with Doctor Greenberg? Then we'll take a stroll around this lot before we go downtown.'

She walked over and stood beside the doctor, who was already hurling questions across the eight feet of space between him and the photographer. How come the scene was only just getting photographed? Greenberg wanted to know. Where were all the detectives who should be here by now? Had the photographer rolled the body yet? How much longer did the doctor have to wait? Moses Greenberg had a Type-A personality augmented by a fanatical fitness regimen.

Running marathons, biking mountain trails and swimming a mile or two a day, he stayed fit and ready to cope with the next crisis, which as often as not he would create himself.

Dr Greenberg was not easy to be around. Sarah liked him anyway, because his standards for himself were even higher than for everybody else, and he had a nice, respectful way with bodies.

Buddy Norris flung back short answers without looking up, making it clear he didn't give a crap about the doctor's anxieties. 'I'll be done here in about five minutes,' he said, 'but then I gotta do all that junk in the pickup and a bunch more in the warehouse. Plenty of time for questions later, Doc.'

'Good morning, Doctor,' Sarah said, and waited through a couple of loud, well-phrased sentences describing everything that was wrong with the way this scene was being handled. His curls and high coloring grew more dramatic as he described the several catastrophic mistakes it was probably already too late to prevent.

When he paused for breath she said, 'Yes, well, you know this is an officer-related shooting? So we'll need detailed descriptions of the number and placement of bullet wounds.'

'Ah. Yes, I suppose you will be quite

anxious for that,' Greenberg said, 'considering how little blood I'm seeing. Looks like the poor sap died while he was still falling down.' He looked at her sideways. 'No witnesses, huh?'

'No. Spurlock called for backup but everybody was on another call. It took a few minutes for anybody to get here.'

'Well then,' Greenberg said, 'let's hope all the entry wounds are at the front.'

Not needing any more of Greenberg's black humor just then, Sarah walked quickly back to Spurlock and said, 'Let's take a hike.'

They started at the street. Standing in the driveway in front of Officer Garry's makeshift check-in desk, Spurlock had distance from the body and better concentration. 'Take it from the top,' Sarah said. 'You were on Flowing Wells when you got the call? Heading north or south?'

'Just crossing Wetmore, headed south. Dispatch asked if there was anyone in the vicinity, said witnesses reported somebody burglarizing an abandoned warehouse on Flowing Wells. I called in, said that I was just north of there and I'd take it.'

'So you were approaching from the north, you arrived at this address and turned in right away?'

'No, I stopped right there at the curb' – he

pointed to a spot ten feet from his foot – 'to eyeball it for a minute. I had a good view across the empty parking lot. I suppose that's why he thought he could score some wire here today,' Spurlock said, indicating the bleak, boarded-up windows and long-neglected parking spaces with their headers askew. 'Christmas break, Saturday, the street is busy but all the action is at the malls. This is a pretty dead area normally. Today, you can see, there's hardly anybody in the buildings on this side of the block.

'The only vehicle in sight was that old Dodge pickup a few feet back from the power box. The driver's-side door was open and the driver had the cover off the box. I didn't have to get any closer to see what he was doing – he already had a small spool of wire started.

'I got on the radio, told Dispatch what I was looking at and asked for backup ASAP. But then nobody came! All while I was on the radio, he had that auxiliary motor turned on and was rolling copper wire around the spool. There was one big shriek when the wire tore loose at the far end and then he just kept rolling it up, neat as can be.'

'You were still paused on the street?'

'I was right here in the driveway' – he pointed to the ground by his feet – 'pulling in. I wanted to wait for backup but I saw

19

that wire coming out and I thought, *I can't just sit here like a doofus and watch taxpayers' property being destroyed.*' The pulsing tic reappeared in his jaw as the stress of the decision replayed in his mind. 'So I pulled into the lot—'

'This way?' She started them moving, under the tape, back toward the body. The rest of the detective crew began to arrive – all at once, it seemed. They all pulled up to the driveway, saw the tape and then backed out and pulled ahead to park at the curb. Soon there were three more Impalas lined up nose-to-tail in front of hers.

Ollie Greenaway nodded to Sarah, signed in and ducked under the tape. He strode silently toward the doctor in his rock-solid, old-street-cop way. Jason Peete was right behind him, talking fast to Ollie's back. He wore a watch cap pulled down to his eyebrows, covering his shaved head, and a fleece-lined jacket with the collar turned up; he hated the cold. And Oscar Cifuentes, pressed and pomaded as always, got out of his Impala and added his stiff macho presence to the scene. When they had all signed in and were talking to Delaney, last of all came Ray Menendez, flashing his handsome smile at Sarah – 'Just always so *cleaned-up* looking,' said the tech staffer who had the biggest crush on him. To no avail – he was scrupulously faithful to the beautiful girl he would soon marry.

Spurlock was still speaking. 'I turned on my flasher as I drove toward him—'

'You did?' Sarah said. 'So there'll be a recording in your camera.'

'Well, yeah,' Spurlock said. 'Come to think of it, I never thought to toggle the camera on, but ... it starts saving the recording when the overhead flashers come on, doesn't it?'

'Sure does. Picks up the last thirty seconds before the lights came on, too. You might have a video of the whole event.' The camera was rigged to compensate for the under-standable tendency of street patrolmen to forget to hit the 'record' button during their most stressful times. Always running, it would start to save the video if they acti-vated their warning lights or siren, or when their speed exceeded seventy-five miles an hour. Smart camera; lucky Spurlock.

'What next?'

'I turned on my outside speaker too, and I said, as loud as I could, 'Put down your tools and stand up with your hands over your head.' Spurlock's voice grew stronger as he remembered that. Sarah thought it helped him to see the lot filling up with police personnel. His personal nightmare was turning into a civic event, and he could deal with that. Soon it would be in the

21

newspaper and belong to everyone.

'Did he respond promptly? Or seem to think about flight?'

'He stood up when I told him to but he never seemed to think about running. I had my eyes on him the whole time and it seemed to me that as soon as he heard my voice he accepted being caught. All his moves for that next minute looked calm and easy, like somebody who's been arrested before. You know what I mean?'

'Yes.' First year on the street, you learn to look for the difference between beginners and the ones who've been around a while. Often the first-timers are the dangerous ones; nobody knows what they'll do. Experienced thugs accept the occasional arrest as the price of doing business.

'I stopped in front of him and watched him straighten up before I opened my door. When he was all the way up, I said, 'Step away from your vehicle,' and he did. When he was standing on the asphalt, away from everything, I drew my weapon, opened my door and got out of the car. I still had the door between me and the suspect but I never took my eyes off him. He'd put his hands up nice and easy, held them just above his head. I opened my mouth to tell him, "A little higher," but just as I stepped out from behind my door his right hand dropped behind his head, and quick as a snake he pulled it forward holding that gun, the Sig you see on the ground there, and started *firing*. He's got a holster pulled up tight behind his neck, you'll see.'

'That must have been quite a surprise.'

'Tell me about it. Tricky bastard.' She was watching Spurlock curiously now because despite his sweaty upper lip and the jumping nerve in his jaw, this rookie patrolman had apparently put three bullets – three was his own guess, but it might turn out to be more – into the kill zone of the moving man he claimed had shot first. He'd hit his target every time. He might be a little nervous but if everything he was saying was true, Gerald Spurlock was one hell of a shooter.

'You believe he only got off one round?'

'That's all I heard. There could have been a second shot covered by the noise of my firing, but I don't think he had time for that.'

'Where did his bullet go, do you know?'

'No. Not into me was what I noticed.' They each gave a small, humorous snort. Spurlock had already learned that you didn't carry on about these things. 'As soon as I saw that gun in his hand, I returned fire three times. He went rigid for a couple of seconds and then dropped like a stone.'

'So it was all over very fast?'

'Yes.' Dan Spurlock turned his boyish face toward Sarah, raised his eyebrows and said, 'The whole incident took place in less than a minute.' He made another small sound, like a hiccup.

They had walked and talked their way back to the body, where everything had changed and was still changing for the man on the ground. Copper wire had no value for him now. He had been photographed many times, front and back, from every angle. His temperature had been taken and his eyes were closed. And he had found security at last – he had his very own toe tag now, with its own incident number, so there was no danger of his being mistaken for some other aspiring copper-wire dealer who might lie beside him on a shelf in the morgue.

His body bag was coming out of the transport van and he would lie inside it, growing colder and stiffer and then softening again while police detectives learned everything there was to know about him – except, perhaps, the answer to the question they had all begun to ask each other, looking around them at the multi-use buildings which, while not at the top of the heap commercially, were not entirely empty either – some had traffic coming and going, and every one had dozens of anonymous windows that blinked transparently down on his bagging-up.

So the whole crew of detectives had begun to ask each other, 'What was he thinking?'

And before very long, from wondering that they went back and took another look at the dead man as if his face might hold the answer. And then another question began to circulate.

Ollie Greenaway asked Sarah, as soon as she walked up to him. 'Doesn't this guy look familiar?'

'I kind of want to say he does,' Sarah said. 'But I'm not sure ... number-five male, maybe forty, give or take? Thinner than average. And missing several teeth ... maybe a tweaker, what do you think?'

'Could be. Or a far gone alcoholic.'

'Medium brown hair going gray, nondescript clothes. But he doesn't look homeless, does he?'

'Not quite dirty enough for that. Very shabby clothes, though.'

'Looks like any guy down on his luck, and with a couple of bad habits.'

Cifuentes said, 'Yeah, long-time unemployed is how I'd peg it. I know I've seen him, though. I just can't say where.' When the sergeant ended one of his many phone calls, Oscar repeated Ollie's question to Delaney. 'Doesn't this guy look familiar?'

'Kind of,' Delaney said. 'Probably got a local sheet.' He turned to Spurlock. 'You looked for ID?'

'Yes. I couldn't find any.'

'He must have a driver's license on him somewhere.' A couple of them gloved up and searched the body. 'Nothing, huh? How about the pickup? No? Did you look in his shoes?'

A stiff breeze had sprung up. Greenberg said he wanted to bag up his John Doe and get out of here before he turned stiff himself. For once Sarah agreed wholeheartedly with the doctor. She had her warm coat on and didn't care about the cold, but she wanted to get Spurlock downtown. He had calmed down considerably during their walk but now Delaney's rapid-fire, impatient questions were making him nervous all over again.

The crime-scene specialists were still going over the lot but the fingerprint lab tech was finished. The impound guys were working on the Dodge, getting it ready to tow. All the detectives had closed notebooks – there was nobody around to canvass – they were making phone calls, turning toward their cars. Then Jason Peete, who had been making an inventory of the items in the truck, came back, walked around the body one last time and said to Delaney,

'Boss, I can't remember his name but I think I know where I saw him last. Man, he's really changed, though.' His face crumpled into a huge grin and he crooned, 'You are so going to hate this!'

Delaney, who did not appreciate Peete's lapses into street behavior, said fiercely, *'What?'*

Suddenly serious, Jason said, 'This man used to be a sergeant on the Tucson Police Force.'

'What? Nah. Come on, Jason, that's crazy.'

'Can I help that? He musta been around for a while, too, because he was on the training crew for recruits when I went through the academy.'

'Jason, now, that can't be, I'm sure you're wrong.' Delaney hustled over to where Greenberg had just zipped up the body bag. A crime-scene specialist was standing ready to help him hoist the body onto the gurney, and as Delaney approached they squatted, Greenberg counted to three, and together they settled it onto the narrow cot. 'Wait a minute,' Delaney said, as they began to raise the securing straps, 'I need to take another look.'

'Oh, Sergeant, for God's sake, what now?' Greenberg yelled.

Delaney raised one hand in magisterial silence, bent, grasped the metal tab and pulled. When the bag opened enough to reveal the face, he motioned all his detectives over to stand beside him. 'Once and for all now, anybody else think he looks familiar? Because I've been in this department a lot longer than you, Jason, and I certainly don't remember this man around the academy.'

Leo Tobin, who had been on a hike far up in the Tortolitas when the call came, had just parked in front of the half-dozen other department cars. Getting out, he saw the entire detective squad lined up in a row, bending forward and occasionally straightening, like toy birds by a water dish. Curious, he strolled up to their backsides and said, 'What's going on?'

'Oh, Leo, you made pretty good time down the mountain, huh?' Delaney said.

'Yup. This the alleged thief?' Tobin peered at the weathered face. 'Aren't we being a little extra punitive on this poor hard-working wire stripper?'

'He drew down on Officer Spurlock, who did exactly what he was supposed to do,' Delaney said.

Beside her, Sarah heard Dan Spurlock suck in a breath.

'But now, Leo,' Delaney said, 'stand over here by me and take a good look, will you? Jason claims he remembers this man – used to be a Tucson cop.'

'Jason is right. Just this once, of course.' Leo turned his crusty half-smile on Jason Peete, who flipped him the bird. Leo turned back to Delaney. 'Come on, you remember this guy. Man, he's really gone downhill, though, hasn't he?'

'Downhill from what? I don't remember him at all. You're sure he was in the department?'

'Think a minute. You'd have been long out of training by the time he joined that crew. But before that, he worked graveyard out of East Side for years and years, so you must have known him there. Name is...' he clasped his forehead, '...come on, brain, you can do it ... Ed Something.'

'Yeah!' Jason said, lighting up again. 'Ed Lawson ... Lewis? No, Lacey.'

'That's right, Ed Lacey. Whose specialty on the training crew was putting on that red padded helmet and beating the bejeesus out of dozens of would-be street patrolmen.'

'You see? Now I'm not so crazy, huh?' Jason grinned around the circle of his fellow detectives. 'That's why I remember him! Because the year I trained, Lacey was a Red Man, one of several who beat my black ass around that gymnasium more times than I can stand to think about.'

TWO

Thinking about the first time she met the Red Man, the most feared and respected trainer in the academy, Sarah felt the wind grow colder. It was almost ten years ago – no, longer, closer to eleven. *Man, time really rips along.*

She'd been warned. Recruits in the class before had told her, 'Watch out for the Red Man. He's not kidding when he says you have to fight.'

But she was a ranch kid, raised to think townies were softies. And this was law enforcement, right? There might be some tough tests to pass, but they weren't going to chain her in a dungeon and turn the ravenous dogs loose. And it wasn't as if she'd never felt pain – growing up, she'd fallen off a horse plenty of times and, as her father always insisted, got right back on. A steer had knocked her down once, and she'd broken her arm calf roping on her junior rodeo team.

None of that had any malice in it, though

– animals just did what they did and you learned to live with it. It was a whole different thing, she found out, to be attacked by somebody who really intended to hurt her. She'd held her own in her first fight test – paired off with another student, kneeling on the mats in the exercise room with gloves and helmet on, whaling on each other. Each of them secretly thought they'd won, and nobody got a broken nose.

But the man in the red helmet was a whole different can of worms – one of the elite. She'd walked into the gym and confronted him as she'd been told to do. The man on the door had said, 'You're in a fight for your life now, you understand?' When she'd nodded, smiling, a little cocky, he'd smacked her lightly on the rear and said, 'Good luck.'

She remembered walking across the mats, aware of the several observers standing around the walls. The Red Man had stood in the middle of the space, his face showing nothing through the mask. He hadn't worn a red padded suit any more by the time Sarah did her training – just a padded red helmet and gym clothes. But they still called him the Red Man – partly, she suspected, because it made him sound more awesome. Playing policeman as she'd been told to do, she'd said, 'Put your hands above your head and turn around!'

He'd hit her in the face. It hadn't been a little tap; it'd hurt like hell. And the force of it had knocked her down. Lying on the floor at his feet, she'd felt her confidence drain away like water down a sink drain. It was all she could do at the time to get up, and as soon as she was back on her feet he'd hit her again. The merciless man with the toneless voice had landed two more solid punches and a hard shove before she'd suppressed enough of the fear to begin to fight back. She'd yelled, 'Stop resisting!' and swung a roundhouse. He'd deflected it and hit her again, in the ribs, hard. She'd kept punching at him, but it was like punching a wall, hard and unyielding. Soon she'd been on the ground again, with the hard man on top of her. A couple of ludicrous minutes had followed in which she'd yelled, from underneath him, 'Stop resisting!' There'd seemed to be no way to get at this monster, who'd clearly been bent on taking away the career she'd set her heart on.

The other thing she hadn't known much about till that morning was rage. She'd learned a great deal about it in the next five minutes. Red hot rage had flooded her brain and helped her to go on fighting till she'd somehow rolled out from under him, jumped up and landed a couple of well-placed kicks she'd learned in Tae Kwon-Do. They'd been good enough to earn a welcome grunt of surprise and appreciation from the Red Man, and one of the observers had said, 'That's more like it. Now get the cuffs on him, Sarah.' She'd been awkward with that, too, but she'd done it, and finally got to walk out of that terrible room, past the observers with their straight faces and amused eyes.

It hadn't been pretty, but it must have been good enough, because she'd got to stay and try it again later. He'd been patient the next day when he said, 'Let me show you what you missed at the beginning...' and began pointing out the behaviors to watch for: the tense shoulders, hostile or dead-looking eyes – 'And if he turns like this, making a wedge shape, see? That's to protect as much of himself as possible when he clobbers you.'

Before she was done she'd had to learn how to respond effectively without the anger – to fight like a savage while staying perfectly calm. Rationalizing the battle had turned out to be one of her strengths, and she'd graduated with high marks from the academy. But she'd never forgotten the pain and terror of that first day's battle.

'And that's what it's for,' Dietz had said when she'd told him about it. 'Every time you ever think about it, you'll remember that you didn't curl up in a ball and try to hide. It costs a lot of money to train a cop. We have to spend it on people who aren't going to quit in a fight.'

A homicide detective when she met him, Dietz had been on the training crew earlier and taken his turns as the Red Man. He had put in many hours pondering the best ways to train a cop. 'Every time you think you've got all the answers,' he'd told her, 'something changes.' Training would always be a work in progress, probably, especially in border cities like Tucson with constantly shifting populations – and now with technology that never stopped evolving.

They tried to spend the money on people who could keep their wits facing firearms, too.

'You can't just point and shoot,' the Red Man had said to Sarah. 'You gotta stay focused, but you don't have time to hesitate.' If Will Dietz hadn't kept his head and fought back quickly in the totally unexpected gun battle he happened to walk into two years ago, he would have been dead in the first two minutes. No question, he had told Sarah, that his many hours of training had saved his life. All that drilling, over and over and over again, fixed target to moving target to running gun battle with a trainer shouting in your ear, was to develop the quick reaction to a threat that Dan Spurlock had displayed today.

Spurlock told Sarah and the IA man, Jeffries, everything he could remember about it that day, after she took him to their headquarters at South Stone. First they listened to the recording from Spurlock's car, and the other side of the traffic from his dispatcher at the West Side station. Then they asked him to review the shooting as he remembered it.

'Everything seemed to slow down,' he said. He looked like he might be going into shock, not quite ready to puke but not in the market for snacks either. 'All the rest of the world went, like, *away* someplace – there was just me and him with that gun in his hand. Like we were alone together in a tunnel – even the traffic noise went away.'

Sarah nodded and saw Jeffries nod too – involuntarily, she thought; he didn't mean to be encouraging, but like her he remembered how it felt. There was never going to be anything again quite like the first time you saw a weapon aimed at you and knew this was it, The Big One, your ultimate question about your ability to do this job, getting answered *right now.*

'Over and over during shooting drills they tell you, "You don't have any time to think." And oh, man is that ever true...' He looked at Jeffries, whose square face showed noth-

ing during these interrogations, and then at
Sarah, who nodded, wanting to keep making eye contact so he'd know she was paying
close attention. 'You see the threat, pull your
weapon and fire. It doesn't take thought, it
just happens. I mean, what else are you
going to do?

'In class, the trainer always says, "And
when you shoot, you shoot to kill, understood?" Like we might be tempted to fire a
warning shot over somebody's shoulder. But
shit – you're never going to fire that Glock
unless you have to, so if you have to fire it
you sure as hell aren't going to dick around.
I mean, what? Knee-cap this bad guy while
he shoots your head off? I don't think so. I
didn't think about it at all. Soon as I saw
that gun in his hand I slid sideways to get
behind the door again, and I aimed for that
kill zone each time.'

'You hit it, too, didn't you?' Sarah said,
letting a little glint of admiration show. They
didn't have the autopsy report yet, but they
had retrieved the digital recording from the
camera in his squad car and were playing
it, over and over, on Sarah's desktop. It
showed Lacey standing beside his truck, his
right hand pulling a weapon from behind
his head while his left hand followed it forward, getting ready to support the gun he
was already firing. He'd got his feet apart,

almost braced, before the first of Spurlock's bullets slammed into his throat. The video showed just the tip of Spurlock's Glock firing, at the left edge of the screen.

There was one electric moment, after Spurlock's first shot caught Lacey under the chin, when the man stood perfectly still – stopped in his tracks by that first bullet. His inertness lasted long enough so Spurlock's next two shots went through-and-through in his upper chest, the bloody spray of the exits showing plainly in the video.

Immediately after the third shot Ed Lacey's knees buckled and he fell backward onto the asphalt where he lay without moving, his dead eyes staring at an empty sky.

The young officer, taking no chances, apparently maintained his shooting stance for twelve seconds (Sarah had timed it, thinking, *I bet it felt longer to him*). Actually it felt longer to the officers watching the video now, too – an incredible taut stretch of time while the nose of the Glock stayed motionless at the edge of the screen and Lacey lay on the asphalt, little motes of dust rising in the sunshine from the body heat his wounds gave off.

Then the edge of the Glock disappeared and Spurlock moved cautiously into camera range, his gun lowered but still not holstered. He walked stiffly to the side of the fallen man, leaned down, and with his left hand touched the spot behind the ear where the pulse should have been. Finding none he straightened up, holstered his gun and walked slowly, like a much older person, to his vehicle.

Out of camera range, he could be heard on the dispatcher's recording, calling to report the shooting and ask for an EMT unit. It was extremely poignant, after that textbook performance with the Glock, to hear his young voice ask plaintively, 'Am I ever going to get any backup here?'

Spurlock's face flushed brighter at the sound of his own voice. He had been spooked and sunburned, standing so long alone in that lot with the corpse. Now, his knees were starting to jitter in his chair; his cheeks and nose and even his eyeballs got redder and redder. He looked about ready to light up like a box of fireworks and fly into space.

Sure glad his weapon's put away, Sarah thought. She found herself hoping he had no guns at home for personal use.

'Let's watch it again from the beginning,' Jeffries said. They had sent Spurlock home, telling him to expect a call from somebody on the counseling staff no later than Monday morning. 'If you don't hear from them by noon,' Sarah had said, 'you call me, you hear? And I'll light a fire under somebody.'

'Sure,' he'd said, not meeting her eye. 'But I'm all right, Sarah.'

'I know. But it's very important that you talk this through with someone who's trained to help.' She'd watched him walk away, hoping he'd do as she'd asked. He was getting a ride home – his squad car was impounded and his personal Prius had been chauffeured home after Jeffries checked his blood pressure. They were treating Dan Spurlock with every consideration, which little by little was stripping him of his newly-formed identity as an authoritative officer of the law.

'I asked Counseling to get to him as soon as they could,' she said. 'But they're so busy – they might have to make him wait.' She did an anxious dry-wash.

'He'll be all right,' Jeffries said. 'I had bad dreams for a couple of weeks after my first gun fight, but I survived it and he will too.'

'Tough to have it happen in his first six months, though.'

'I know. But right now our job is to clear him and the department of culpability. Let's take another look at that recording.'

They locked the door and asked the support staff to hold calls. With all the building sounds at a distance, they watched the four-minute film again, rolled it back to the beginning and started over. After they'd watched it twice more in silence, Jeffries said, 'OK, I'm ready to review, are you?'

'Yes.' She got her mouse ready. Seven seconds in, she stopped the video. 'First thing I noticed is here.'

'Yes. The suspect moved around to the far side of the box he was working on. Getting his back out of sight, right?'

Sarah nodded. 'Yes. And then I think I saw something a few seconds later...'

'Wait,' Jeffries said. 'Back up a—There.' It was just a flash, but they both saw it: the whites of Lacey's eyes when he peeked to make sure the black-and-white was moving toward him. 'This is what, fifteen seconds in?'

'Eighteen. Twelve seconds before Spurlock turned on the flashers. Don't we love that retroactive recapture?'

'Oh, yes.'

'Lacey wasn't surprised by Spurlock's approach, was he?'

'No. He pretended to be caught off-guard by the flashing lights, but I think this shows he set himself up to get caught.'

'I agree.' After they'd both looked at their shoes for a while, Sarah said, 'Of course, this opens as many questions as it answers—'

'I know. But we're waiting for the autopsy anyway, so...'

'And the crime-scene crew were still working on the lot when I left. It'll help if they find the bullet Lacey fired.'

'Yeah. Delaney will have Spurlock's jacket, right?' Jeffries spoke absent-mindedly; he was packing his briefcase, a chore he performed with complete absorption, as if the integrity of the entire force depended on his keeping his notes in good order. He snapped it shut finally and said, 'I'll find out what shifts Lacey worked at the academy, talk to some of his crewmates there.'

'Yeah. My crew'll be doing that too, and talking to Ed's family, of course.'

They both said at once, 'If you get anything useful—' and shook hands. Sarah watched the tidy way he walked out of the office, carrying the shiny black briefcase that had become an object of fear and loathing to so many people.

OK, he's a neat freak. But he seems reasonable. As he closed the door she thought, *I wouldn't have his job for a million bucks.*

She went home feeling dissatisfied, wishing she knew either more or less about the man Spurlock had killed. Her instinct was telling her to follow the evidence, find out what happened to change Lacey, learn why he'd set himself up to be killed. But if Jeffries cleared Spurlock, she knew, that would be the end of it for her section.

* ★ ★

'Denny,' Sarah asked while they ate breakfast Sunday morning, 'have you thought about shopping online?' The prospect of taking her energetic niece to the mall to watch her lay waste to racks of clothing was no more appealing today than it had been yesterday.

'I already did,' Denny said. 'I know exactly what I want.'

'Oh. Well, then ... do you need any help with the ordering?'

'I don't want to order online. Everything's on sale here in town right now. Soon as you help me decide on a couple of things and I make sure of the discount I'll be good to go.'

'So you want to go see it in the store?'

'Yes, please. If it's not too much trouble?' She had on her nice blue top, her hair was combed and her nails clean. Life with an often-reluctant mother had taught Denny how to be irresistible.

The parking lot was already crowded but they were both good walkers and it was a beautiful day. Sarah smiled, getting out of the car, and said, 'You want to start in Macy's? I saw some nice tops advertised.'

'No, I think Penney's or Sears will have what I want,' Denny said. She skipped inside, looking pleased, paying no attention to the crowd all around her, pushing and yelling. Maybe she was more confused than she looked, though. She was passing shoes, jeans and sweaters, hopping on the escalator...

'I think you've passed all the junior sizes,' Sarah said.

'I know. I think ... yeah, there's what I want.'

'That's Housewares.'

'I know. Now, if they haven't sold all the ... no, here they are.' She stood like a pointer in front of a shelf.

'Honey, those are toaster ovens.'

'I know. Have you noticed how hard it is for Grandma to bend over now? Even when I'm there to light it, she still has trouble getting a dish in and out of that little narrow oven. I know you and Will want to remodel the whole kitchen, but that won't be for quite a while yet, will it? And one of these could sit up on the counter. I think Grandma would enjoy it quite a bit, don't you?'

'Denny, these things cost at least a hundred dollars.'

'On sale right now for $89.95. See?' She showed Sarah the tag. 'The ad says it'll cook a whole chicken. And I know it'll bake four potatoes – I saw that on TV. What do you think?'

'It's very nice. But you don't ... Surely you don't have that much money, do you?'

43

'With this week's allowance, yes, I've got enough and a little left over.'

'How did you get so much?'

'I saved up all fall for Christmas. But then you all said only small gifts, so that's what I did. Hankies for grandma and that little bottle of cologne for you ... Will's Dreml head was the most expensive thing. So I still had most of what I saved, and then Uncle Howard sent me a check, remember? And Mom sent money in her card...'

Janine had certainly done that. The limp, stinking twenty, smelling of hemp and sorrow, had fallen out of a cheap card that arrived two days before Christmas and temporarily silenced all conversation in the house. Denny had put it away somewhere and never spoken of it again until now.

'I see,' Sarah said. 'And this is how you really want to spend all your money?'

'Yes.'

'All right, then. Let's see, this one has a broiler...'

They examined all the features available and picked the one that seemed best. Sarah managed to get a salesperson to help, in the madhouse that the store had become, by standing on tiptoe and turning on her Officer of the Law expression.

The clerk pulled a ready-boxed one off a back shelf. She showed them the numbers matched the model they'd chosen, said, 'This is what you want, right?' and rang up the sale. Denny counted out ninety dollars on the counter. When the drawer slid open the clerk said, 'That will be $98.05.'

'No, it's on sale, see?' Denny pointed to the tag.

'Yes, but then I have to add sales tax, dear.'

'Oh.' Denny's voice grew smaller. 'I forgot about that.' She began pulling dollar bills and quarters out of her wallet. People waiting in line were watching. Her hands had begun to shake. There wasn't going to be enough.

'Denny, let me pay the tax, OK? Really,' she said as the child looked up, 'I want to.' She slid a ten across the counter.

They got their purchase in a big sack and fought their way outside. Beside the car, Denny said, 'Thank you, Aunt Sarah.'

Sarah looked at her niece fondly. 'You're welcome. I have to say, Denny, shopping with you is a real eye-opener and a very great pleasure.'

'Oh, yeah, now that I'm safely broke you say that.'

'Hey ... did I really look that reluctant?'

'I know how much you hate to shop. So thanks again for doing this for me.'

After they belted the box carefully into the back seat so it couldn't fall, Sarah looked at her watch and said, 'I know you're anxious to go home and give Grandma her present, but ... we got that done so fast. Why don't we give ourselves a treat?'

'OK. What?'

'Oh, hot chocolate or ... I wonder, is it legal to eat ice cream this soon after breakfast?'

Denny giggled. 'You're the cop, you tell me.'

'Let's see, have I ever arrested anybody for inappropriate consumption of dairy products? I don't think so. Let's give it a try.'

THREE

Monday morning, Delaney called his crew into conference.

'Jason's right – the dead man's name is Edward Lacey.' He held up a service jacket, put it down and sighed. 'For eighteen years this man worked for the Tucson Police Department.' He slid a tall stack of pages onto his desk.

'Soon as I saw his old photo I recognized him just fine. Back in the day, he and I worked the same shift, two to midnight, for more than a year.' He pushed the yellowing pages around on his desk, remembering. 'We backed each other on many a hinky call, and I can tell you, he was solid as a rock.

'About the time I made detective – let's see, that's almost ten years ago now – I heard Ed got a spot on the training crew, where it seems he always did well and was pleased with the job. But he came back on street patrol, didn't he, three years ago? I wonder why?' He was leafing through the records, asking himself questions. 'He had

47

his first big problem then. A couple of months after he got his old shift back at East Side, he was accused of handling an arrestee too rough. Earned a reprimand and a few days' suspension ... After that no comments on his file till he wrecked his car and got fired, a little over two years ago. How could anybody change that much in only two years? He doesn't even look like the same man.'

'He didn't do it all in two years,' Leo Tobin said. 'That last year on patrol, he was a train wreck.'

'Oh? I guess I just didn't happen to see him. But you usually hear something...'

'The department didn't want to talk about it when they fired him,' Leo said. 'They put the lid on tight, told the media something vague about his health. The incident that led to it was a one-car crash, so there weren't any complainants to be dealt with. But anybody who had to work with him during the second half of his shifts that last year knew he was going down.'

'What, he was using on the job?'

'Sure was. Vodka and weed. And sometimes something else ... I heard meth.'

'Meth ... That's what I figured when I saw him today,' Menendez said. 'You notice the way his mouth was wrecked?'

Sarah tried to remember, but it had been

the bullet hole beneath his chin which had attracted her attention.

'Of course,' Tobin was nodding to himself, remembering, 'he didn't look quite this bad while he was still working ... he used to clean up for roll call and make a pretty decent show, but he had stuff stashed along his route, and by the time he checked out at night he was way up in the clouds.'

'Huh.' Delaney shuffled through the pages, looking. 'His record doesn't reflect any of that till he wrapped his squad car around a light pole, and then people came out of the woodwork, apparently, to say what a bad boy he was. He went off the charts for DUI, it says here, and flunked the narc screen big time.' He pulled off his glasses. Polishing them, he asked the table, 'Anybody know what set him off?'

'His wife left him,' Menendez said.

'OK, but what was the *bad* news?' Jason said, and got his laugh from everybody but Delaney, who just looked impatient.

'Well, before that his uncle got, you know, disgraced...' Cifuentes said.

'Disgraced by what?' Delaney hated gossip, and always got mean and sharp when, as now, it became useful and he had to tolerate it.

'That's right, that Martin guy was his uncle, wasn't he?' Tobin said.

Delaney looked around the desk at his suddenly buzzing detectives and said, 'You are not talking about Frank Martin, are you?'

'Yup.' Tobin always remembered the best stories. 'The beloved do-gooder who got caught with his hand in the till at the Old Pueblo Credit Union, then shot himself in the head. It was in all the local papers. They never found the money, though.'

'That was Ed Lacey's uncle? Why didn't I know that?'

The faces around the table all grew a little half-smile until Leo Tobin said, kindly, 'Boss, you don't schmooze much.' He shrugged in an understanding way. 'It's not a problem.' He nodded at the rest of the crew. 'We all gossip enough to make up for your share.'

What will we do when Leo retires? Sarah wondered. He always knew how to walk the talk back from the place where sparks might fly.

Delaney gave a derisive snort and muttered, 'You got that right.' He peered at the ceiling light for a while as if it might hold answers up there instead of only dead flies. 'That was a strange case, all right. But when's the last time you knew a guy to go off the rails over something that happened to his uncle? Must've been something else

50

going on.'

He closed the jacket. 'Oh, the crime-scene crew picked up all three of Spurlock's bullets off the asphalt, did I tell you that? They all went through Lacey so they're pretty beat up but they think they can ID them. They found one in the street, too, right at the edge of the driveway. Looks like a match for the rimfire casing they picked up earlier beside Lacey's body. If so it's almost certainly from Lacey's Sig Sauer. Except the angle's all wrong – I don't see how Lacey could have been that far off with his shot, but ... the lab's got all four of them now. I asked them for a rush job on the one from the street. No use wasting time on it if it isn't from Lacey's gun. Well, what else? Ollie's still at the autopsy, huh?' He looked at his watch. 'Let's all take an early lunch and then start on what we can do in the meantime. Sarah, you will be following through with IA, of course...'

'Did most of that Saturday,' she said. 'The rest is on hold till the autopsy reports come back.'

'OK, then you've got some time? Hold that good thought, I'll get back to you. Leo, I want you to go back to that bar where the call came from, talk to everybody there, try to find the two guys who called nine-one-one on Saturday. Ray and Jason, you canvass all the buildings around there, both sides of the block, see if you can find anybody who witnessed the shooting.'

'Boss, we've got the video,' Sarah said.

'I know. But juries like eyewitnesses and you never know what's going to end up in court. And Oscar, you go after Lacey's wife – or ex-wife, it sounds like, OK?' There was a funny little frisson around the table – everybody's head up suddenly, the same expression of disbelief on all their faces. Did Delaney really mean to say that to Oscar? Or give him that job? Sarah saw Jason nudge Ray's elbow.

Oscar Cifuentes was famous throughout the department for two things: his prowess with the ladies, and how close he had come to losing his spot on the homicide crew when his first case there had collided with his colorful romantic life.

'Find her,' Delaney said, his preoccupied face innocent as a choirboy's, 'and get her take on the marriage and why they broke up. It won't be the whole truth, of course, no divorce story ever is, but it's a place to start. Well, um, and Sarah, since you're free for now, see if you can find any more of Lacey's family and ask them what they think happened to Ed. Did they see the wreck coming? Can they explain what made a good cop go nuts like this? Anything you

52

can find.'

He looked around. 'That goes for all of you. Look for neighbors, colleagues in clubs, drinking buddies ... Jason, see if you can find out where he was selling his copper wire and the rest of the trash, will you? Keep picking every brain you can find because I smell a bad story coming and I'd like to see us get a handle on it before the TV guys start having fun with it.'

Gathering up papers, he sailed into his office, leaving a momentarily speechless crew behind him.

Oscar Cifuentes walked into the break room as Sarah started on the second half of her sandwich and said, 'Well, Sarah, you brown-bagging again today?'

'Today and forever, probably,' she said, getting up when the kettle whistled, pouring water for tea. 'Will and I bought an old house and we need to completely remodel the kitchen. We hope to get it done before the hot water heater dies.'

'Keeping house is so much fun, isn't it? OK if I join you?' That was a rhetorical question; Oscar Cifuentes had self-confidence enough to be always sure of his welcome, especially with women. He pulled out the gloriously greasy cheeseburger he had obviously just bought from the In-and-Out

up the street and wiped his hands contentedly on a couple of paper napkins. 'I got a
question.'

'Just one? Most people will have more.
Makes everybody kind of paranoid, seeing a
good cop go down the tubes like that.'

'*Was* he such a good cop? All those happy
years I worked in Auto Theft, I never realized how much hot news I was missing. All I
know about Ed Lacey is what I've read in
the paper. Did you know him?'

'About like I knew you in Auto Theft – just
to say hello. But you don't get on the training crew till you've shown some chops.'

'I guess that's right. You know, I didn't
think about it till we were done talking in
there, but then I remembered I know one of
his aunts. Cecelia ... you might want to talk
to her, what do you think? I forget her married name but it's probably changed by now
anyway ... Seems to me she was just getting
divorced when I dated her a few years back.'

'You dated Ed Lacey's aunt?' Sarah
brought the tea back to her place. 'Wasn't
she kind of old for you?'

'No, actually she's a couple years younger
than Ed was ... it's one of those big Mexican
families like you hardly ever see any more.
Vicente García was the papi – he's no longer
with us. His first wife died and after a
couple of years he started all over with a

younger wife. Eddie's mother was one of the older girls in the first family and Cecelia was one of the second bunch.' He shrugged. 'I could probably get on the grapevine and find her.'

'And you'd be glad to do that, to help me jump-start my search for Lacey's family,' Sarah said, watching him thoughtfully over her Swiss cheese on rye, 'in return for which favor, exactly?'

'Hey, hold your fire, I come in peace,' Cifuentes said, hands up, trying for the easy joke. Then, beginning to twitch under her unrelenting stare, he said, 'I just thought maybe you wouldn't mind riding along with me while I interview Ed Lacey's wife.' He studied his fingernails. 'Ex-wife, actually. Angela.'

'Oscar,' Sarah said, 'if you know so much more about this family than the rest of us do, why didn't you speak up in there?'

'Well, see,' he re-crossed his legs and looked out a window, 'the thing is I dated Angela, too, a long, long time ago, before she met Ed. Just a couple of times, but ... the second date I took her out dancing and one thing kind of led to another...'

'As it so often does with you. Well, and?'

'And I guess she kind of thought we had something going on, but I ... didn't. No real chemistry there at all – it was just the drinks and the music. But then she kept calling me, so I just sort of … made myself scarce till she gave up on me.'

'And then along came Ed Lacey and took her mind off you.'

'Well, yes. A little bit later.'

'So what's the problem?' Her smile held a little edge. 'You think she's still hot for you after all these years?'

Looking offended, he shrugged and concentrated on his lunch for a while. Finally, he said, 'Hey, forget I said anything, OK? It was just a thought. But if you don't want to work with me—'

'Oh, come on, I'm just pulling your chain. The truth is I'd be grateful for any info you've got about the family, especially Ed Lacey's ex-wife. She could be the key to the whole thing. But the truth also is, you should have told Delaney if there was a problem about you getting in touch with her—'

'Oh, Sarah, *por favor,* you know better than that. If Delaney hears one whisper about a problem between me and a woman ever again, he'll throw me off this crew. I half suspect he assigned me to Lacey's wife hoping I'd give him an excuse to fire me.'

'I didn't hear you say that.' Sarah wanted to stay out of this fight, if that's what it was going to be. But she did think Cifuentes was trying hard to succeed in his job, and Delaney was being a little judgmental about his personal life. 'So what do you want from me?'

'Well, I thought maybe if I gave you the number you could make the call.'

'Really, is that what you thought? How very surprising. I would never have guessed that was what you were after.' She waited while he got his face arranged in his pleading-puppy look before she said, 'Oh, go get the damn number, Oscar.'

He pulled a small card out of his shirt pocket and handed it over. 'She works at this used clothing store on West Ina.'

'She does? That's funny; I thought I read that she worked in the credit union where the uncle stole the money.'

'Allegedly stole.' Cifuentes shrugged. 'After the investigation she quit her job there and went back to the store where Lacey found her, is how I heard it.'

'He did? What in the world would a good street cop like Ed Lacey be looking for in the used rag shop?'

'Tell you what, Sarah,' Cifuentes said, 'let's find her and ask her.'

Sarah opened her phone. 'I'll drive my car and you buy the coffee and snacks. Deal?'

FOUR

A whiskey-voiced woman said, 'Twice As Nice.' When Sarah asked for Angela Lacey, she said, 'Hang on.' After a click, Sarah listened to dead air for some time. She'd begun to debate hanging up and starting over again when a second click opened a line and a quiet voice said, 'This is Angela.'

Sarah identified herself and her reason for calling, hoping the ex-wife would have read the weekend coverage in *The Star*. Angela had not been on the list of kin to be notified – the only person on that list was Lacey's mother, Luz García-Lacey, who did not answer at the only number they could find for her.

'Yes, I saw the story,' Angela said.

'I'm sorry for your loss,' Sarah said. 'I'm calling to set up a time for an interview. We need to talk to you at your earliest convenience.'

'Oh? You know, Ed and I have been divorced for over a year.'

'Yes, I see you're no longer listed as next of

kin,' Sarah said. 'But we'd still like to ask you some questions.'

'Um, what about?'

'Well ... we think maybe you could help us understand the uh, the manner of his death and the way he left the department.'

'He got fired is why he left,' the woman said.

'So I understand. When could we talk, Ms Lacey?'

'Well ... I already went to lunch and we don't get coffee breaks, so I guess it can't be today.'

'We could meet you after work...'

'No, I'm busy tonight.' She didn't explain – Angela was no chatterbox.

'How about lunch at twelve tomorrow?'

'Um ... I guess I could do that. I get exactly one hour, so it has to be someplace close. There's a McDonald's in this mall, can you put up with that?'

'Of course. How about ... I could order lunch, have it waiting for you, would that help?'

'Well ... yes. I'll take a chicken Caesar salad and a large coke.'

Sarah pushed *end* and listened as Cifuentes wound up the last of several chatty calls. Closing his phone, he told her Cecelia García Lopez was living in a house on Calle Aragon, 'And she can talk to us if we go

59

there right now.'

'You certainly made out better than I did,' Sarah said, getting her gear together. She told him how hard it had been to get an appointment for tomorrow at noon.

'Was she hostile?'

'Not exactly. Just kind of ... disengaged, But you hit pay dirt, huh?'

He chuckled. 'She said, "Get your handsome ass over here, baby, I give you the whole skee-nee." Cecelia's kind of a hoot. You'll see.'

Kind of hot, you mean, Sarah thought when Cecelia answered her doorbell. She posed a full three seconds with her arms spread wide in the open door, making sure they got an eyeful of a voluptuous, vividly made-up woman in her early thirties, wearing a low-cut emerald-green top over jeans that did full justice to her curves.

Sarah had never felt the pull of Oscar's fabled allure, and had a hard time understanding it. He was not as handsome as Ray Menendez, who lived a happy, blameless life with one girlfriend. Oscar was tall and wore his clothes well, but so did many other Hispanic young men in Tucson, without setting off earthquakes of yearning in female breasts all over town. Maybe it was that he really liked women and they responded to that. Whatever it was, Cecelia stood in her doorway clearly ready to prove it worked for her.

Her house was small and old but Oscar complimented her on the artful arrangement of brightly colored pots by the door.

'Oh, honey,' she said, 'I keep my old *casa* up as nice as I can, but ... it's hard, I have to do everything myself. Papi used to help me but ... you know we lost him last year?'

'I was so sorry ... I was there at the funeral but the crowds were so dense I never had a chance to say hello to you. Rightly so, of course; he was a fine man and it was a great loss.'

'Yes ... that's very well said, my friend.' She sighed, tossing back her great mane of hair. 'And this is your partner? Come in, sweetie, this is your house.'

As Sarah took off her coat, Cecelia said, 'Wow, a gun and handcuffs, you're ready for a fight, huh? That's what I should have done – be a cop. I could have used some of those weapons on that pond scum I married. But no, I had to go to beauty school, have the glamour. So now I work at Desert Cuts and listen all day while women have hysterics about hair and nails. Some glamour, huh? Here, sit down, the coffee's ready.'

She poured it, black and aromatic, into handsome white porcelain cups, and gave them hand-embroidered linen napkins, flawlessly ironed. Eddie's aunt was showing her style. Mostly for Oscar, Sarah figured. *Let's just hope she stays friendly after we start asking questions.*

Questions were no problem, it turned out – Cecelia was happy to talk about Ed Lacey, her darling nephew. That sweet boy, she said, who always made everyone happy. But now in the end his life story had tragically begun to echo that of his Uncle Frank.

'It does seem an odd coincidence,' Sarah said. 'Good, useful lives that both ended badly. Did you know Frank well?'

'Of course I knew him. He was a saint, that man, and they adored each other.' She batted her lovely dark eyes at Oscar. 'Always the caretaker, Frank, remember?'

'I remember you always said so.' Oscar was walking some fine line here, trying to be the close friend Cecelia seemed to want him to be, while maintaining his non-involved stance for Sarah.

'Yes, well, we all did. Because when Luz,' she turned to Sarah, 'Eddie's mother? My second-oldest sister? When Morgan Lacey, her no-good Anglo husband disappeared, she took in a still more worthless loser for a boyfriend. And from that time on, Uncle Frank dropped by often, to keep an eye on Eddie, who wasn't even in school yet and was being sorely neglected by his mother.

So Frank often took him to the park or for an ice cream.'

'I'm curious,' Sarah said. 'Frank Martin wasn't Hispanic, was he?'

'No, Frank was married to our oldest sister, Anita. Luz's next older sister, you see? She died in childbirth in the second year of their marriage, and her baby died a few hours later. Terrible – it doesn't happen anymore, thanks to God. But when it happened to them, Frank, of course, was bereft. But our family – you know, we are warm—'

'Everybody knows that,' Oscar said, and got a blazing smile for a reward.

'Yes, well, we held him close, we tried to help. So even though Anita was gone, Frank remained our beloved uncle, always at family celebrations.

'So – this is a few years later I'm talking about, now. Luz's husband was gone, the boyfriend was in the house, and – she is my sister but I have to say it – she was drinking too much with that man.'

'Ah, well,' Oscar had his hands folded like an undertaker, 'nobody's perfect.'

'And some of us are more imperfect than others. So one day when Luz was out of the house, probably making an emergency tequila run because God forbid they might find themselves short on margaritas, the boyfriend decided Eddie was a pest and started beating on him. He got a little carried away and broke the child's nose. Eddie ran crying to his Uncle Frank, blood running down his face – in a panic, he thought he was dying.

'Luckily it was a Saturday and Frank was home from work. He rushed Eddie to the hospital. And the next day when the boy was ready to come home, Frank asked my sister, "Why don't you let him stay with me a while till your life settles down a little?" Something like that, making it seem OK. Just an extended visit.

'But as time passed, he kept making up little stories so it was easy for her to leave him there – she was so busy, he said, her husband was gone and she had to look for a job. Like she ever would. My parents were a little alarmed at first. They kept saying, "Why is Eddie never home?" But when they saw how happy he was at Frank's house, and how well taken care of … I know it's crazy but it just became the way things were. Eddie stayed at Frank's house and Luz came to visit, do the big kissy-kissy and leave.'

'So Frank Martin raised Ed Lacey?'

'Yes. And did all the things fathers do, or used to do when the world was more decent. Attended all the school plays, helped with the homework. You know, Frank was very frugal about his own things, always bought two-year-old cars, kept them till they were eight or nine – he was careful that way. But the best was none too good for Eddie – whatever clothes and gear he needed for games at school, and he went to all the games when Eddie made the football team. That's how they got the scholarship so Eddie could go to college. Got his degree and went straight to the police academy from there, made us all proud.'

'So you were pretty surprised, I suppose,' Sarah said, 'when Frank was accused of stealing money from the credit union?'

'Surprised does not begin to describe it.' Cecelia, ablaze with indignation, was a sight worth watching, Sarah thought – fake fingernails tracing crimson parabolas in the air, her remarkable bosom testing the seams of the emerald jersey. 'We all begged him to fight it. Plainly, they had no proof. His whole character and life up till then made the claims ridiculous, and where was the money? Frank didn't have it in his bank account. They searched all the drawers in his house – in both houses, his and Eddie's. They even went through Eddie's accounts, though he was married by then and had joint accounts with his wife. But Eddie said to go ahead, they wouldn't find anything, and of course they never did.'

'Where do you think it went?'

'I have no idea. Well, I have one idea, but I have no proof either so...' Cecelia paused and looked down, and for a moment Sarah thought she might be about to divulge further, but suddenly her head shot back up, her eyes blazing. 'All I know is, Frank didn't do it. I don't care whose handwriting is on the' – she waved the handwriting away – 'deposits, or whatever they said. Somehow, a giant injustice has been done.'

'But he left a sort of mea culpa when he killed himself, didn't he?'

'A what? Oh, the note. Some silly thing, I forget what it said...'

'I can tell you exactly,' Oscar Cifuentes said.

Sarah looked at him, her face saying, *What?*

Pulling another piece of paper out of that same handy shirt pocket, he began to read. '"I didn't take the money, but I won't put my family through this investigation any longer." And then a postscript: "Eddie, I'm sorry for everything. I've loved you all your life, please try to forgive me."'

When he stopped, both women stared at him, waiting for him to add something more. But there wasn't any more. Cifuentes put the paper back in his pocket and asked Cecelia, 'Why do you think he wrote that?'

'Oscar, *querido mio* – how would I know? It doesn't make any sense. What was he apologizing for? Eddie owed his *life* to Uncle Frank.' She made a fist of her soft, manicured left hand and beat on the sofa's upholstered arm three times. 'I. (Thump.) Don't. (Thump.) Know. (Thump.)'

Tears welled in her eyes.

Sarah asked her for names and addresses of other members of the family. Cecelia wrote out a list, muttering to herself, 'Let's see, Luz, Guillermo – we call him Memo, Chico—' she took a while to remember addresses, and had no phone numbers or email addresses. 'We always just go see each other,' she said.

As they were preparing to leave, putting coats on in the small foyer, Oscar said, 'Are you going to tell us your idea about who got the money? Or must we dig that out of one of your sisters?'

'No and no, Oscar.' She looked deep into his eyes and the temperature in the foyer rose, Sarah thought, about two degrees. 'Dig it out of Chico. Talk to the man of the family, for once. Give yourself a change of pace.'

'Always a pleasure to talk to Francisco,' Oscar said. 'Does he still operate his fish taco stand near the ball field?'

'No, no, darling, he sold that some time

ago. Chico is retired on social security. Retirement is turning out to be Chico's best thing. It suits him like nothing before in his life.'

'Would he be likely to be at home now, at this address?' He was looking at her list.

'I should think so. It's about Happy Hour, isn't it? Not that Chico confines himself to one hour.'

'Looking forward to finding him then,' Oscar said, 'though he's not nearly as charming as his sisters.'

'Get out of here, you rogue.' She gave him a very small push.

'Thanks for the wonderful coffee,' Sarah said, feeling like the schoolmarm in the play. 'And for talking to us. Here's my card – all my numbers, my email. Call any time if you think of anything you want to add.'

'How very kind,' Cecelia said, patting Sarah on the shoulder like a sister.

But it was to Oscar that she tossed the final invitation. 'Don't be a stranger, *primo*.'

'*Primo* means cousin, doesn't it?' Sarah asked him, when they were back outside by the car. 'She doesn't act like your cousin.'

'Oh, we're not, really. Except, you know, we both grew up down here in the south side of town. And people from the old neighborhoods – there's a saying that if you go back far enough, we're all related.'

'But you don't buy into the Old Pueblo stuff much, do you?'

'Nope. I like to swim in the mainstream,' Cifuentes said.

'Except like today, when it works better to be Chicano.'

'Well, sure. We all use what we've got to use, don't we? At Cecelia's house, you were using me, right?'

Sarah studied her shoes. 'I suppose that's true. How did you get hold of Frank's note, by the way?'

'Don't worry, it's not the original.' Oscar winked at her. 'OK, then.' He looked at his watch. 'We've still got an hour before we have to head in. You want to see if Chico's home?'

'Sure. Do you know how to get to that address?'

'It's in South Tucson,' Oscar said. 'Let me drive, it's easier than telling you.'

He was right, so Sarah gave up the wheel, something she rarely did in her departmental car. She always said she wanted to be able to defend any dings it brought back. But mostly her attitude was left over from the beginning of her career, when the men all expressed their hostility to the presence of women investigators by criticizing their driving. Sarah, determined to be treated as an equal, decided she would drive, by God, when it was her turn, and they would ride with her and shut up about it.

'I always thought the nickname for Francisco was Pancho,' Sarah said, as they rolled along.

'It is,' Oscar said. 'So's Chico.'

'So many things I don't understand in this part of town.'

'You should try making the trip in the other direction.'

Oscar made his way quickly through the narrow streets of the mile-square Hispanic municipality encapsulated in the middle of Tucson. Francisco García's house was a small, tidy adobe next to a junkyard – zoning was somewhat casual in South Tucson.

'Aren't we going to knock?' she said as they followed a brick path around the front of the house.

'Let's look in the backyard first.'

The backyard belonged to a whole different world than the front. It looked as if sections of the junkyard next door had tunneled under the fence and settled in here, where they lounged about, waiting to be useful. A long, ramshackle shed along the back fence held at least three old cars they briefly registered, one on blocks, and parts of several others. Piles of worn tires, two benches and an ancient rowboat with no motor filled the rest of the yard – there were paths through the jungles of equipment. Hammers, machetes, shovels and other tools hung from nails on every upright.

It was shady under the tall trees, darker still under the thatched ramada, and too cold, this late December afternoon, to be lying outdoors in a hammock. But the man who lay there had solved the problem by wrapping himself in an electric blanket. His features were hard to see in the gloom, but Sarah got an impression of a big mustache under a shock of white hair. As they watched, he lifted a beer can to his lips and drank the last swallow, sighed happily and pitched the can over his left shoulder toward a trash can. It landed inside with a jolly clink.

Oscar knocked on the wooden upright of the open patio just as the man turned to reach for the handle of the cooler, on the ground by his right side. Its cord, and the one for the blanket, ran together to a power outlet that snaked out from an outlet on the patio. The man had put serious effort into his comforts.

'Whoa,' he said, peering toward the noise. 'Who's there?'

'It's Oscar Cifuentes, Chico.'

'You big bad boy!' He spread his arms. 'Too long since I've seen you, man. How you been?'

'Better than ever, can you believe it?'

Oscar bent for a big *abrazo*. 'And this is my partner, Sarah Burke.'

She held out her hand. The old man covered it with both of his and said, 'My pleasure, Officer. Detective, is it? Well!' He beamed at them both equally. 'Do cops drink beer?'

'We do, but unfortunately we're still working,' Oscar said.

'So late? Well, come back sometime when you're off-duty, huh? Sit, sit.' He waved at chairs and they each pulled one closer as he opened the cooler, rattled ice, and came out with a dripping can of beer. 'Meantime, please pardon me, my thirst won't wait.' He popped the cap, swigged, belched contentedly and lay back.

The two men batted some small talk back and forth, neighborhood news, and then Oscar said, 'Cecelia suggested we should talk to you about Eddie.'

'She did, huh?' He scratched his ear. 'Cecelia is good at deciding what other people should do. You know' – he fished a pack of Marlboros off a small table by the trash can and lit one with a huge flame from a lighter while Sarah held her breath, expecting his mustache to go up in flames – 'when she was not much bigger than a Chihuahua I used to carry her on my shoulders to the bodega and buy her a popsicle. She

72

thought I was wonderful then. Now she wants to tell me what to eat and drink, and can't understand why I won't follow her orders to the letter.'

'I'm sure she has your best interests at heart,' Oscar said.

'Oh, absolutely. Mine and everybody else's.' He puffed a while, drank again and sighed. 'She wants me to dish the dirt on Eddie, so she won't be heard speaking ill of the dead.'

'Is there some dirt on Eddie?'

'Well, he was a ... when he was little, he was kind of a pain in the neck.'

'How so?'

'Anxious and demanding ... always *wanting* something. "Will you give me that, can I have one of those?"' His imitation of a child's voice was very funny strained through his big white mustache. 'His mother didn't really want to be bothered with him, you know ... after her husband left her she was always after boyfriends and Eddie slowed her down. So the kid was angry and ... what's that word they use all the time now? *Needy.* I didn't like him myself, tell you the truth. But after he went to live with Frank, he straightened out.'

'Cecelia said how proud you all were when he joined the department.'

'Oh, sure. And you can ask anybody, he

was a nice man and a damn good cop for years and years. But then...' He studied the ocotillo fence along the street side of his yard for a while. When he turned back to Oscar his face was sad. 'He kind of lost it there at the end, didn't he?'

'Seems like it,' Oscar said. 'It's funny, but I never knew him, really. He was too much older when I was a kid down here, and in the department he was always working someplace I wasn't. What was so nice about him, especially?'

'He was always helping people. Learned that from his uncle, of course. Frank spent years driving for Meals on Wheels, dishing up Thanksgiving dinner for the homeless. *Señor* Do-Good, working his way into Heaven, I used to think. After Eddie grew up, the two of them for years were the go-to boys when anybody needed a timekeeper for a charity bike ride, or somebody to help out at the wounded bird shelter.'

'So what do you think happened to change them?'

'What happened to Eddie, I *think*, is he felt so bad about what happened to Frank he couldn't stand it, so he started using drugs and alcohol to kill the pain, and before long he was a dead man walking. Long before those bullets found him, the Eddie I knew was gone. What happened to Frank, though ... I can't explain that and I don't know anybody who can.'

'Except Cecelia seemed to think she had an idea. I got the impression she had shared her thoughts with you and you didn't disagree.'

He lifted both hands in a helpless gesture. 'What's the use? Might as well stand in front of an avalanche as disagree with Cecelia.'

Sarah and Oscar kept their eyes on him and waited.

He did a funny little flouncing maneuver that Sarah would not have thought possible in a hammock. 'But she's partly right.'

The two detectives waited again while Chico poured the last of his beer down his throat, took one more fierce drag from his cigarette and dropped it sizzling into the can. 'For different reasons we both think the one who got the money was his wife.'

Oscar said, 'Eddie's wife?'

'Yes, of course Eddie's. Frank's wife died years ago, don't you remember that?'

'Yes, yes ... why does Cecelia think Angela's got it?'

'Angela was working in the credit union – she had access. She could have forged Frank's signature on the receipts.'

Sarah said, 'Mr García—'

'Chico. Everybody calls me Chico.'

'OK, Chico. But where's the evidence?

Has Angela taken nice trips, or bought a new car?'

'No.'

'Has she paid off the house?'

'No, apparently not.'

'Then why does she think Angela got the money?'

'Cecelia thinks she's hiding it somewhere. Partly it's just anger. Cecelia says she never fit in, and she always spoiled everything for Eddie. She was jealous of his family – she wanted Eddie all to herself.'

'What did she spoil?'

'Well ... we're a big family, we share birthdays and holidays, help each other out when there's an emergency. Till Angela came along, Eddie and Frank could always be counted on when somebody moved house or had a baby.'

'Or needed a loan?'

'That too. But Angela seemed to resent our closeness – she wanted Eddie to herself. She would always say they were too busy to move the furniture, they couldn't afford potlucks right now, they had no money to spare.'

'I can see why that would hurt. But what has it got to do with the missing money?'

'Cecelia says Angela got Eddie to rescue her from her stupid job in the used clothing store and help her get a job with Frank at the credit union. Then, when the going got rough and Eddie wrecked his car and got fired, she divorced him and kept the house they bought together.'

'I don't see how that shows she got the bank money.'

He suddenly laughed. 'Now that I say it out loud, you're right, it sounds ridiculous. I told you, Cecelia has no proof, just a strong feeling.'

'What do *you* think?'

'About the marriage part, I think nobody understands anybody else's marriage and we should just accept the fact that Eddie was crazy about Angela and quit trying to figure it out.'

'Fair enough. But you have different reasons for suspecting her? Tell me about that.'

'She left the bank soon after Frank killed himself. And she went back to that used clothing store Eddie rescued her from. Do you realize what a steep drop in living standards that caused her? Much harder work, lower salary, no benefits? Why would she do that? Unless she has money we don't know about, she must be very hard up. I think the management at the credit union must have suspected her too, forced her out somehow and refused to give her a reference.'

'But you don't know.'

'No, but you could find out, couldn't you?'

'Yes. Anything else?'

Darkness was falling, the streetlights coming on. In Chico's yard, one tiny bulb burned above his patio entrance, but didn't produce enough light to brighten the space under the ramada. In deep shadow, Chico fished in the cooler and came out with another can. 'I guess if I'm honest,' he said as he wiped it off on his blanket, 'I'd have to admit I want her to be the guilty party because I just don't like her. She can't be trusted.'

'That's refreshingly candid,' Sarah said. 'Any reasons you want to share?'

Chico waved his drink vaguely. 'Have you talked to her yet?'

'Tomorrow.'

He smiled. 'You'll see what I mean,' he said.

FIVE

At the station on Tuesday morning Ollie
Greenaway had everybody's attention – for
a while. He'd attended yesterday's autopsy,
and while the written report was not ready
yet, he felt certain he already knew what
would be in it. Unlike some detectives who
had to keep a stern watch on themselves to
get through an autopsy without hurling,
Ollie got rosy and cheerful at his. He enjoyed the precision of the work the doctors did,
and was always glad to draw that assignment.

'The Animal went through all the proto-
cols but he assured me several times that
he was probably wasting his time,' he told
his teammates. 'He kept saying' – Ollie
drew himself up and looked superior, doing
his best imitation of Dr Greenberg – '"this
body shows exactly the process I predicted
at the crime scene. You see this bullet track
through the spinal cord?"' At the words
'spinal cord' Ollie lapsed into broad carica-
ture. '"You do see, don't you, my poor

ignorant little police person, that this explains the small amount of blood loss?"' Seeing Delaney getting ready to put his foot down, Ollie got serious. 'What the doc is saying is that this guy was almost certainly dead after the first shot. We won't have the written report till all the lab reports are back, and he'll be even more cautious than usual since this is officer-involved. But I don't think Spurlock has anything to fear from the autopsy report. And since there weren't any witnesses, the autopsy settles everything, doesn't it?'

'Unless the neighborhood canvass turned up any watchers – did it?'

'No,' Ray said. 'We had trouble finding anybody who'd even admit to being on that block on Saturday. That area's about due to get torn down and rebuilt, I think – even during the week it's mostly storage space for stuff that's being sold somewhere else. All that's open is the bar where the call originated. Even that looks about ready to close.'

'Except don't hold your breath, because it's looked that way for five years that I know of,' Jason said.

'I wondered that day how that bar could stay in business,' Sarah said. 'It's so dilapidated, and half the buildings around it are padlocked shut.'

'Oh, come on, you know the answer to

that,' Jason said. 'It's your friendly neighbor-hood head shop.'

'And rumor has it,' Ray said, 'that those rascals might also be doing a little trade in copper wire.'

'How about it, Jason?' Delaney said. 'You got any skinny on that yet?'

'Plenty of these rumors like Ray's hearing.' Jason looked condescending; too cool a cat to chase every little rustle in the wall. 'Nobody local's doing time for it yet, way I heard it.'

'This doesn't make sense though,' Delaney said. 'If they're fencing wire why would they want to sic the cops on Ed Lacey?'

'I managed to ask the bartender that question,' Leo said, 'while being, you know, extremely discreet so as not to risk offense.'

'Uh-huh.' Delaney looked amused. He tolerated more irony from Leo than any of the other detectives, Sarah thought. Probably because Leo was quite suave, actually – a canny old cop who could walk through a room full of half-drunk ranting people and come out the other side unscratched with the information he went in after. 'What did the bartender say?'

'Seems to have been a couple of new customers, out-of-towners just driving by looking for a beer and some chips. One of them whipped out a smartphone and called nine-one-one while the bartender and his regulars were busy minding their own business.'

'Bet they hate when that happens.'

'Sure didn't do the bar any good,' he said. 'Emptied the place out in two minutes.'

'OK, Leo, be serious now. That bartender must have been watching this whole thing go down.'

'Maybe you can get him to cop to that, boss, but I couldn't. He swears that soon as the place cleared out he decided to open the storeroom and re-stock the long-necks. Said he heard some funny popping noises while he was in there putting supplies on the two-wheeler, thought somebody must be playing with firecrackers. By the time he got back out by the window transferring beer into the cooler there, he looked outside and saw the lot across the street getting taped off and a row of official vehicles parked at the curb in front.'

'Well,' Delaney said, 'you got his numbers, in case we have to try to get him into court later? Good. How do you think Internal Affairs sees this, Sarah?'

'The way I read him, Jeffries wants to keep his nose clean and his briefcase neat. He's always walking that fine line, one of us but not quite. If we can furnish him with a pat answer, I don't see him going out of his way to cause trouble.'

Back at her desk, she opened her cell and found a text message from Oscar: 'Don't forget we have a lunch date with Angela and we have to have food waiting.' The unwritten subtext was that Oscar wanted to get them both out of the building without Delaney finding out Sarah was helping him with this interview. Feeling like a high-school senior on skip day, she finished a report, grabbed her purse and jacket, and pussy-footed off the floor.

Oscar said he was afraid his presence might cause Angela to stamp off in anger, claiming she had been duped into an encounter that was distasteful to her. Sarah offered to do the interview alone if he thought it was safer, but he said he did not dare to risk lying to Delaney.

'He can see through my head into my brain, I think,' he said.

'Oh, come on. Delaney's shrewd but he doesn't have magical powers. How about this – we can both be there, but I'll do most of the talking. I'll just tell her we're partners and I brought you along to run the recorder and fetch the drinks, OK?'

Cifuentes had to do some deep breathing to agree to that; he had a profound need to be the Alpha Dog. But in the end he decided it was the safest way. They went over the checklist, making sure they had the right food waiting for her, plenty of condiments and extra straws for the big icy drink. They checked their questions again, and Oscar trotted back and forth fetching more salt and pepper and extra napkins. He brought salads and water for himself and Sarah, also, and insisted on paying for everything – keeping busy, being in charge of the food, eased his anxieties.

At 12:08 p.m. he nudged Sarah's elbow and nodded toward the woman coming through the door. Sarah's first thought was, *She must get a price break on the clothes at the store.* She wore a garishly printed smock made of some limp synthetic over too-long black pants of the same fabric. Her hair was mousey but neat, held in a ponytail by a purple scrunchy. She probably carried about the same amount of superfluous flesh as Cecelia Lopez, but arranged differently – the eye did not want to linger on Angela's extras.

She looked surprised when she saw Oscar, but not angry – more like she was trying to remember his name. Sarah said Oscar was her partner today and was going to facilitate the interview by operating the recorder, 'Because I hate taking notes. Do you mind?'

'No, of course not,' Angela said, with a

little shrug that somehow ridiculed both the recorder and Sarah's concern about it.

'I wish I'd known you were going to be here, though,' she said, directly to Oscar. He looked at Sarah in alarm, but Angela went on serenely, 'You left your gloves on my couch the last time I saw you ... Nice driving gloves – leather. I called you a couple of times to remind you to come get them. You never called back so in the end I think I threw them in a drawer and forgot about them. I probably still have them somewhere.'

'How careless of me,' Oscar said. 'I'm sorry.' He didn't offer to come get them, though.

'No problem.' Her stoical expression put the whole thing in the rear-view mirror as she tore into the food.

'Wrestling old clothes all day,' she said, 'is like baling hay. Sure gives you an appetite.' She downed the salty mouthfuls of chicken and greens and sucked up a bucket-sized soft drink while bopping back very short answers to Sarah's first questions. They started with the easy stuff – last name (it was still Lacey), address, home phone and email.

She was refreshingly direct about her marriage to Ed Lacey. It had lasted seven years and was good as long as Eddie was good, she said. But he started drinking after Frank Martin got arrested. When he drank he got unreliable, and when he added marijuana to the mix he became 'just impossible.'

'Impossible how? Did he beat you?'

'Oh, good heavens no, Ed would never do that. No, I mean he became incompetent, he failed at his job. And at home he was – like an empty suit.'

'You're sure it was Martin's arrest that started his drinking?'

'Yes. It was part of his whole effort at denial. He could not accept the truth about his uncle; he was determined to make everybody see that Frank could not have been guilty of stealing the money. Like it was somebody else's fault and his uncle shouldn't be punished. "Look at all the nice things he's done for people over the years," he kept saying. "Where's the gratitude now when he needs it?"'

'But after all, what else could they do? Depositors kept insisting their money was missing, and it happened on Frank's watch. His signature was on the deposit slips that they claimed were short. People were demanding answers and the credit union had to fix blame.'

'You were right there through the whole thing, weren't you? Did the two of you try to figure it out together?'

'Ed was pretty much past the point where he could figure anything out by then. I told him, "Honey, it's sad and all, but you're not going to make it better hitting the bottle the way you're doing." But then when Frank killed himself, Ed just couldn't stand it. "It's not right," he kept saying. "I should have been able to do something."'

'One thing I wondered ... were you aware, while you were living with him, that Frank Martin owned a gun?'

'No. I don't remember that he ever mentioned it.'

'Do you think he bought a gun just to shoot himself?'

'Or borrowed it,' Angela said, with the slightest hint of distain. 'He was like most accountants – always very careful with a dollar.'

'They didn't go target practicing together, Ed and his uncle?'

'No. Never, in my experience. What they always did together was *good works*.' Angela's lip curled a little on the last two words.

'You weren't so crazy about helping people?'

'I just thought they overdid it. Ed had a hard job; I thought he needed some fun and relaxation like he had with me. But Frank would call and off he'd go.' Her eyes narrowed.

'They were close, were they?'

'Oh, well, sure. Frank was the knight in shining armor that *saved* him, so close doesn't even begin to cover it. They were like *this*.' She put her fork down and clenched both hands into one big fist. 'And that was what made him so sure Frank was innocent. "I was right there," he said. "I'd have known if he was stealing money."'

'That does sound reasonable in a way, doesn't it?'

'Except it wasn't true. We were married and living in our own house by the time Frank allegedly started stealing. So ... we saw him, of course, but not every day.'

'Cecelia Lopez told me how Frank took Ed in and raised him, helped him get through school and all.'

'Oh, you talked to Cecelia? Well, then you got the hearts-and-flowers version of the embezzlement, didn't you?'

'What does that mean?'

'Oh, just ... everybody in Ed's family is in deep denial about Uncle Frank and the money. "He couldn't have done it – look at all the good he did all his life."' Angela had a tiny shrug and ironic half-smile that was not quite a sneer but somehow did the same work. 'Helping with the bike race to fight cancer, making the clothing pickups for the homeless, I heard it over and over till I could recite it in my sleep. And it's all true, but it doesn't change the fact that his signature is on the deposits, you know? So what else could they do?'

Something in Angela's manner made her seem twitchy. She clearly wasn't happy talking to them, but Sarah couldn't decide if that was down to shyness or something more suspicious. She remembered Chico's words: *She can't be trusted.* It wasn't easy figuring Angela Lacey out, that's for sure. 'You were working there,' Sarah said. 'Can you explain how he did it?'

'Not entirely,' she said. 'It's a small credit union, he was the comptroller, and some functions he always did himself. He had all of us, his little helpers, out front smiling and taking in the money. And that regular work, the individual and business deposits, nobody ever claimed there was anything wrong with that. Making the deposits for the charities, that part he did himself. Because he was usually at all those events, helping in some capacity, it was only natural to have him take the money and make the deposits. And the stealing was only going on for four years or so – they were pretty sure of that by the end. Till then, I think, he was just as pure as everybody thought he was.'

'Even small banks get audited, though, don't they?' Sarah asked. 'How could he be cooking the books and nobody noticed?'

'That's the thing. He wasn't cooking the credit union's books at all – the money all came out in cash before the deposits were ever made.'

'I think it's amazing he could steal such large amounts for so long. What did they say, somewhere between seventy and eighty thousand dollars?'

'But over four years, maybe more. If you do the math, that turns out to be a small percentage of what the bank was taking in – less than people in this town throw away on bingo every year.'

'I see. You knew Frank well, didn't you?'

'Sure, I told you, we lived with him after we were married.' In her years of questioning suspects, Sarah thought, she had rarely met one whose lifted eyebrow could imply as much distaste as Angela's. 'Yes, we stayed with Frank three years. Till we got enough saved for the down payment on our own house.'

'How'd you all get along?'

'Fine. Frank was easy to be around, is that what you want to know?' She took a long swig of her drink, put it down and regarded Sarah with a demanding stare. 'But it doesn't bring the money back, does it, to know that whenever I cooked, he insisted on doing the dishes?'

'No.' Sarah thought about the unlikely mix in her own household – four mismatched people who didn't really belong together but shared space because each of them needed something the household provided. They were all still being extra polite and careful with each other, eager to please. *Like four people on a honeymoon. But I'd know if one of them was stealing or doing drugs. Wouldn't I? Of course I would.*

'Sarah, you need some more water?' Oscar spoke sharply, reaching for her glass.

'What? Oh, yes, please. Angela, how's your drink, want some more?'

Oscar went off to fetch drinks after an anxious glance. Sarah re-focused and asked Angela, 'You never saw any sign of stress? No clue what Frank might need money for? Was he gambling?'

'Mr Homebody? Hardly. I was as big a sap as everybody else, I guess. I just thought he was a nice old guy. While we lived together he would do anything to make me happy – anything – because he thought it was wonderful that Ed had found a wife. I remember being surprised by how happy he seemed to be when we got married. I believe he thought of it as kind of like a *passing grade*, you know?'

'A passing grade for what?'

'For how well he had done at raising Ed.

Like it proved Ed was all normal and could be happy like anybody else.'

'Why was that a question?'

'I don't know. Maybe because he had been neglected by his mother and kicked around by her boyfriends when he was small. And frankly they were all ... kind of odd, but in different ways. Luz was just this side of a whore, if she missed it at all. Marisol was like a nun, always in church. And Memo was hell-bent on becoming a tycoon – I think he thought if he made enough money he could make them all respectable. I used to look at them sometimes and wonder if they really did all have the same father. But everybody assured me that the first wife had been a saint, and you only had to watch Teresa look at Vicente to see she would never stray. And in spite of all the commotion I was happy, too, till Frank got arrested and Ed went nuts over it.

'After Frank got hauled off to jail Ed began to say, over and over, "I owe him everything. I should be able to help him."

'Then Frank got out on bail, and for a few days Ed was like his old self. He was sure all they had to do was find a good lawyer and beat this thing. But when Frank killed himself and left that note the way he did, without saying a personal goodbye or anything, well, that was the last straw for Ed.

He really never got over it.'

'But you weren't, um, sympathetic?'

'What do you mean?' Angela was instantly on the defensive. 'Of course I was.'

'But you said he was impossible.'

'Well ... sympathy is all very well but facts still have to be faced, you know what I mean? I was sorry for him, and for a few months I waited for him to start getting over it. Then I saw that he wasn't healing – he was going down the tubes instead. So I started asking people, counselors and so on, what I should do. Because anybody could see he was headed for a crack-up. We were starting to have financial problems, too. His drug habit cost big time.

'All the pros said, "You have to confront him. Tell him he's got to get some counseling and snap out of this now or you're done." They said, "He's got a life, he's got you! He's got a good career, it's ridiculous that he's throwing good life after bad. You have to make him stop."' She shook her head. 'Counselors say things like that with great confidence. As if the wife could just ... push a button.'

'But you did make an effort?'

'Yes, of course I did. And Ed tried, for a couple of weeks. He made appointments with the department counselor, and he kept the first two or three. But then he said he couldn't do it any more – talk to a stranger about personal matters – so he didn't go. What none of us realized was that by then he was addicted to meth.'

'Oh.'

'Yeah. The greasy slide to nowhere. I've ... I've done a little investigating of my own since I've been single – a little research in the evenings. It's something to do, you know? Fire up the laptop when *Jeopardy*'s over and it's still not bedtime?' Angela hesitated, as if she were weighing up a dilemma, then looked straight at Sarah. 'The runaway father, Morgan Lacey? He abandoned Luz when Eddie was small, and the family has managed to pretty much forget about him. But he was typical of the men Luz always picked – a lay-about when she married him and a fully-fledged drunk soon after. *His* father was a lifelong alcoholic who died of cirrhosis. Ed had addiction in his DNA all along. It never surfaced before because Frank forbade him to drink. He told him why it was too dangerous for him. Ed was chosen for the training crew partly because he was always so straight-arrow and sober. "Edley Do-Right," they used to call him at the academy.'

'And threatening to leave him didn't help?'

This time the half-smile blossomed into a bitter laugh. 'Talk about your unintended

94

consequences. Ed saw that threat as an escape hatch and jumped right through it. He said, "You're right – you'd be better off without me." He insisted we file for divorce right away.'

'Any problems about who got what?'

'Not one. He didn't care about his own life – why would he give a hoot about a few sticks of cheap furniture?'

Sarah and Oscar, both veterans of divorce wars, raised eyebrows at each other. 'You kept everything?'

'Yes, I did. It was all he had to give me and he was glad to be rid of it by then. He'd been fired from the police force and was making no effort to find another job. I took his name off our joint account and gave him his half. It wasn't much. I told him he could come back any time if he got his head straight and he said, "Right, I'll let you know if that happens." He packed two suit-cases full of clothes and he left.'

'Where did he go?'

'He lived in his uncle's house for a while. But he couldn't pay the taxes so he sold it and I think he rented a trailer. In a mobile home park? Not sure which one – he didn't keep in touch.' She looked around for her purse and came up with it. 'I've got to go.'

'Well, one more question: why did you leave the credit union?'

'Everybody there thought I had something to do with the theft, that I knew where the money went. I went through a couple of grilling sessions with them about it. Then I said, "You know what? I think I've suffered enough over this. I'm not going to do any more of these heart-to-heart talks." They said if I left before they were ready to release me they wouldn't give me a reference. I told them they could stick their recommendation where the sun doesn't shine. Took off my name badge and walked out the door.'

'It must be kind of hard,' Sarah said, observing her closely, 'getting used to the lower pay scale.'

'Well, my present employer is an old friend and likes my work. So I was able to get a couple of bennies. She owns two apartment buildings as well as the store. I clean the public areas on my days off and live in one of the apartments rent-free.'

'You sold your house?'

She shook her head. 'Bad time to sell. But a couple who got foreclosed out of their house is renting mine with an option to buy when we're both ready. I almost break even on the bank payments and taxes. Have to live poor for a few years but I'm building a nest egg.'

'Good for you. What's the other bennie?'

'Half price on as much of our high-class

merchandize as I want.' The little smile came back as she closed her purse with a snap and put the strap over her shoulder. 'I may not be elegant but my clothing bill is rock bottom.'

Sarah said quickly, 'What do you think about the way Ed Lacey died?'

'I think he was looking for a way out of his life and he found one. I'm sorry for the cop who had to shoot him, but for Ed's sake I'm glad it's over.'

'Uh-huh.' Then something made Sarah add, 'If it's over.'

Angela had slid out of the booth and was turning to go. She turned back, gave them a hard look and asked, 'What does that mean?'

'Just that the case isn't closed yet.'

Angela was not intimidated. 'Whatever you people decide to call it, for Ed it's over.' She flipped a quick glance at Oscar and said, 'Thanks for lunch,' in a way that somehow made it seem as if she had said, *thanks for nothing*. She walked away without looking back.

'Well,' Oscar said, as Sarah drove back to the station, 'now you've met Angela. What do you think?'

'She's either shy, or there's something she's not telling us. But if she took the money why is she still here? There's nothing

97

to hold her that I can see.'

'Maybe she isn't quite ready to move it.'

'From where?'

'No idea. She still seems angry.'

'And she's not very good at hiding it. She's certainly straightforward when she does talk, isn't she?'

'And negative, negative. You can see why I wasn't anxious to continue that relationship.'

'Turns out she wasn't trying to either, was she?'

'I think she made that part up,' Oscar said. 'I don't remember losing any gloves.'

'Nice leather ones? I bet they cost a packet.' As she made the turn onto South Stone, she said, 'What I *can't* understand is how you two ever got started.' She was thinking about the contempt on Angela's face when she thanked him for lunch. 'I couldn't see any chemistry there at all.'

'Well ... she was maybe thirty pounds lighter in those days. And the night we went dancing she had on a low-necked dress, and, you know, she did have a very nice rack.'

'God,' Sarah said, parking the Impala, 'I had to ask.'

SIX

Inside the station, walking toward the elevator, Oscar said, 'I'm going to write up my report of Angela's interview right away. Can I get you to check it before I turn it in?'

'Sure,' Sarah said. She left him there and headed for the stairs. These days, her crowded home life often forced her to skip workouts. She was trying to compensate by climbing every set of stairs she encountered.

Ollie Greenaway, walking into the lobby as she reached the bottom step, called out, 'Ah, there goes the Queen of the Risers, climbing again.' Like all her mates in the investigative division, he thought her stair-climbing habits were amusingly retro, something like canning pickles or spinning one's own yarn. 'Hang on, Sarah, I'll walk up with you. We'll tighten up those glutes together, by golly.' He reached her in a few long strides and clattered upstairs with her, chuckling.

'You're in an unusually good mood,' Sarah said. 'You just find a clue or something?'

'Not yet, but maybe any minute now. I just got a message to call Moses Greenberg ASAP.'

'Oh, well, he always wants everything ten minutes ago. Don't tell me he's changing his opinion about the Lacey killing.'

'Beats me. Why do you care?'

'I'd just like to see us get that poor Spurling kid off the hook. Less than a year out of the academy and he has to shoot a guy? Pretty tough.'

'Aw, come on, Sarah, you can't go around feeling sympathy for this bunch of yahoos, you'll wear yourself out. The thing to do is find out what the Spurling kid's worst faults are and keep telling yourself it serves him right.'

Reaching the top step, Sarah stopped for a deep breath. 'You know,' she said, still thinking of what Cifuentes had said about Angela, 'amazingly enough, I believe that's only the second worst thing I've heard in the last ten minutes.'

'You see? What other workplace affords this level of amusement?' Ollie went on to his cubicle, smiling benignly.

Passing Delaney's open door, Sarah saw that Banjo Bailey, the pint-size firearms and toolmarks criminalist from the crime lab on Miracle Mile, was curled in a chair in front of the sergeant's desk. He moonlighted in a bluegrass band and groomed himself to look appropriate in bib overalls and loggers' boots. Evidently he thought the lab could tolerate a few idiosyncrasies but the band needed validation. Right now he was caressing his soul patch and handlebar mustache as he read from a report form, looking like some unlikely cross between Santa's helper and Mephistopheles.

Whatever he was saying appeared to have Delaney's full attention. Hoping to slide on by and let the day's commotion cover her tracks with Cifuentes, Sarah kept her head down and avoided eye contact. Delaney saw her anyway out of a corner of his eye, and waved her inside.

'Hey, Sarah, where you been?' Luckily he was too full of his own fresh news to wait for an answer. 'Come in and listen to this. You are going to like what Banjo's got to say.'

'The three bullets from Spurlock's Glock, no surprises there,' Banjo said, reprising quickly for Sarah. 'They were all pretty beat up from going through the wire thief. But because he was standing when they hit, none of them dug into the asphalt – just laid on top till we picked them up. So I'm going to get pictures good enough to show they're our ammo and they all match.

'The fourth bullet, the one the crime-scene techs dug out of the edge of the street

101

– it was just a fantastic piece of luck the way it landed, right in the middle of a pothole patch that the street crews had just finished. Nice soft tar, mostly. That bullet looks like it was preserved in a bowl of Jello. I don't get to look at much used ammo like this, looka here.' He showed her the picture he'd brought along.

'I mean, it's like the textbook example for lands and grooves. Can you see the right-hand twist?'

'Plain as day,' Sarah said, and passed it to Delaney.

Banjo would have no problem, he said, showing that this bullet came out of the barrel of the Sig-Sauer the suspect had used – 'I guess I'm supposed to say allegedly used, huh?' – to shoot at the cop.

'Well, but you've tested the gun, right? You know it was fired?'

'Yes. The gun that was found at the scene was fired. So I guess we can dispense with the "allegedly" nonsense, huh? But I'm curious ... the Sig's a surprisingly elegant weapon for this bozo, isn't it? Your average wire thief, most of them are losers, just trying to raise a few bucks for their next fix.'

'But this wasn't your average wire thief; this was Ed Lacey.' Delaney reminded Banjo about the shocking two-year-old case, the role-model officer turned suddenly into a hapless screw-up who wrecked his squad car and got fired from the TPD. 'The Sig's a popular weapon amongst expert shooters like Lacey used to be. He probably kept one for his personal use after he left the police.'

Probably the only thing he saved out of all that wreckage, Sarah thought but didn't say. She wasn't going to admit to knowing what she knew about the Angela-keeps-all divorce, unless she had to. If Delaney found out she'd done Cifuentes' interview for him, he'd be pissed. And really, why did he need to know? They'd brought back the info, shouldn't that be good enough?

'An ex-cop, I'll be damned.' Banjo curled his mustache ends, thinking. 'That makes the other thing I wondered about seem even harder to explain.' He curled into a smaller ball and twisted the end of his long braid.

Watching Banjo turning himself into a sofa cushion, Delaney lifted his eyebrows to Sarah, shrugged, turned back to Banjo and said, '*What?*'

'Well, see ... the angle...' He drew them a diagram on a piece of scratch paper. 'All the reports say he fell straight down from where he was shooting, here beside the pickup. But if that's where he fired from, and he's such a crack shot, how come the bullet ends up way out here in the mended pothole?' He drew a dotted line across the driveway to the edge of the street. 'I mean, not even close.'

Delaney did some hemming and scratching and finally stated the obvious. 'He was in a hurry, of course.'

'Not as much as the guy he was shooting at. He had the advantage of knowing what he was going to do.'

'He's right, boss,' Sarah said. 'Spurling thought he was making a routine arrest until his suspect pulled a gun out of a most unlikely place.'

'Yet he still put three bullets in the kill zone,' Banjo said. 'Very impressive. Even granted Spurling's better than average—'

'Which he sure as hell is,' Delaney said.

'But even so, how come the man who used to teach kids like Spurling how to do that can't come even close to that level now?'

Delaney tortured his ear a while longer before he said, 'Meth takes you down fast.'

'Uh-huh,' Banjo said. 'Well, think about it.' He unwound himself and got up. 'I'll add this report to the case file before close of business today.'

'Very good,' Delaney said, and as Banjo walked out, he said, 'Sarah, how are you doing with the background checks? You got enough evidence yet to support a claim of PTSD, or some such reason why Lacey went nuts?'

'I've done several interesting interviews

that all seem to contradict each other in some ways. If it's OK with you, I still know some of the trainers at the academy, and I'd like to run down there and see what they say. It won't take long and I've got time right now.'

'Fine. Go ahead.' Was he cool? Did he watch her curiously as she went out? *Now don't start getting paranoid over this one little thing.* She hurried to her own cubicle, feeling slightly wired. *A few yoga stretches to chill out and I'll be ready to go.*

Her email dinged with a new message. Checking, she found Oscar's account of 'his' interview with Angela. Except for substituting his name for hers at the beginning of most questions, it was accurate, but awkwardly worded in spots and with a couple of mistakes in punctuation. She fixed those places and sent it back.

Two minutes later, he walked in on the last of her stretches and stood by her desk like a good schoolboy waiting for teacher. Sarah unwound and said, 'What?'

Oscar moved her pencil mug nearer the lamp and lined up the stapler precisely with the edge of her desk. 'I saw you in Delaney's office. You haven't told him we did that interview together, have you?'

'No, of course not. Will you leave my desk alone and quit looking guilty? It's not a crime for detectives to co-operate!'

He went away looking worried, but at least he went away. Sarah tucked her fresh notebook into her belt and trotted out of the building, past detectives tapping at keyboards. They still called it 'catching up on paperwork,' although every word of it was out in the ether and with luck would stay there and never cause ink to soil paper.

Sarah had trained at the old academy on West Silverbell, which at that time (before the recent now-busted housing boom) had seemed 'way out in the boonies.' The new school wasn't just around the corner, either; it had co-opted a nice big site on South Wilmot to share with the fire department. Handsomely appointed and proud of its stature as a training facility for smaller towns statewide, it boasted views of two big prisons and the miles of open desert many inmates probably dreamed of escaping to – but electronic surveillance and razor wire had relegated prison escapes to the stuff of dreams and old Elmore Leonard novels.

She had phoned on the way and landed a coffee date with Yuri, one of the driving instructors. He met her in the lobby, grinning all over his little pointed face. His last name was Kuznetzov; his parents were Russian immigrants. His features greatly resembled Vladimir Putin, but because of his cheerful expression and frequent smiles people often spent days after they met him asking themselves, *Who does he remind me of?*

'I've got half an hour till my next class,' he said, leading her to the break room. 'But Charlie's out on the field with the other group. Want to see what a fancy setup we got now?' He led her along a shining hall to a big window. Across a wide pebbled field divided into long lanes by hundreds of orange traffic cones, a school car with two passengers on the front seat was driving fast along a straightaway. While Sarah watched, the driver, who had been one second late starting the sharp turn at the end of the row, had to watch the orange cones flying as he plowed them down.

And then you so want to quit and swear, Sarah remembered. *But the instructor is already yelling, 'No, no, don't slow down! Go right on to the cul-de-sac!'* She watched as the car drove to the other end of the field, where the wide, curved track led along the slope, till it debauched abruptly at the other end onto a flat where two side-by-side lights flashed alternately red and green. The student had half a second to decide which lane to take, and about twice that much to stop the car before he hurled them both over the speed bump.

'Handsomer than when I did it,' Sarah

said, 'but essentially the brake-squealer hasn't changed at all, has it? How has your neck survived all those quick stops for so many years?'

'Ah, well,' Yuri chuckled, leading her back toward the coffee, 'you remember how you all used to call me "The Mule"?'

'I didn't know you knew that.'

'Oh, sure. They still call me that behind my back and I guess they must be onto something – my neck's OK.'

'It's just ... it's so hard at first, it felt like we had to have somebody to blame or we couldn't bear it. Although come to think of it, all the way through, it's just as hard. But you get used to it.'

'Yup. You know that place in the Bible where it says, "Many are called but few are chosen"? I bet those old monks didn't know they were describing a police training academy, did they?'

'That's one of the things you don't get used to: the ones who try so hard and still don't make it. We'd put in those hellish long days and come back to the dorm, and somebody would be kicking the wall and swearing because he just got news he flunked a test the second time. One day it was Annie, the best friend I'd made in the course, packing her bag and trying to hide the fact that she was crying.'

'And then about halfway, it changes, doesn't it?'

'You see yourself surviving where others fail, and you start to think you might be one of the "few who are chosen." I asked my mother once, "Did I change at the academy?" because, you know, so many things felt different. And she said, "Are you kidding? Everything about you changed – even the way you drive a car."'

'Well, I should hope so. That's the whole point, isn't it?'

'Mom says cops drive as if they own the street.'

'Well, they do, in a way. Have to, to do the job.'

'Mmm. You heard about what happened to Ed Lacey?'

Briefly looking as depressed as the President of Russia, Yuri said, 'Damn shame. Everybody's talking about it out here, of course. We're kind of—' He ducked his head in what she remembered was a characteristic gesture. 'It sounds kind of stuck up to say it, I guess, but we think of the training crew as kind of the elite within what's already a special group, you know?'

'Well, you are. We all know that. Did you ever see any signs, while he worked with you, that Ed was overstressed, or ... going to pieces in some way?'

'Absolutely not. That's why there's so much talk – we just can't believe ... He was good at his job. Sure, there's pressure, we need to show good numbers, but ... Ed seemed to enjoy his work; he was proud of what good cops we turn out.'

'Delaney said he was solid as a rock.'

'I agree. I can't even guess at what happened. Well, I better get ready.' He got up. 'Take a look at the firing range on your way out, it's got all the bells and whistles.'

At South Stone, she walked onto the second floor to the rare sound of near-silence, the welcome peacefulness of detectives getting ready to clear their desks. It continued for five more minutes, till Ollie Greenaway walked into the work area and said, 'Boy, have I got news for all of you.'

'Go away,' Leo Tobin said, not looking up, and Jason said, simultaneously, 'I don't want to hear it.'

'What's the matter with you guys? Sarah, get your head out of the computer and listen to this; it shines a whole new light on Lacey's motivation.'

'It does? Let's see if we can find Delaney then – no use saying it all twice.'

'He's in his office,' Ollie said, 'on his phone, as always.'

In the end, the insatiable need to know whatever anybody else knows brought all the detectives trooping along behind Ollie. Delaney looked up from the row of stats he was checking with the state budget director and said, with enviable poise, 'Excuse me, Bernie, I'm afraid the barbarians are at the gate, I'll have to call you back.' He took out his ear buds and said, 'What now, for God's sake?'

'I got a call from our very own Animal,' Ollie said. *'Ranting.* "You left too soon, Oliver," he said, "while your arrogant medical examiner was still busy pre-judging the results of an autopsy." Even for Greenberg, it was an unusual show of temper. You know how he hates to be wrong about anything?'

'Ollie,' Delaney said, 'are you going to tell me a bullet in the throat didn't kill Ed Lacey?'

'No, no, of course that was the immediate cause of death. But at the autopsy, after Greenberg had shown me how the spinal cord was shattered and said that was the cause of death, well, it looked like there was nothing left to do but get all the bits and pieces ready to send for DNA work and toxicology scans and so forth. And I figured I didn't need to watch all that slicing and dicing so I said, "Doc, this is pretty much it, isn't it?" And he said, "Sure, run along – we know what killed Ed Lacey."

'But after I was gone, when he was prepping a sample of liver tissue he saw something he didn't like at all, so he ran it over to an oncologist buddy of his and got the diagnosis back in a couple of hours. Lacey had advanced liver cancer.' Ollie pulled a slip of paper out of his pocket and read, 'Hepatocellular carcinoma, if you're curious. Greenburg says it starts in the cells that filter the bad stuff out of your blood. Which Lacey's liver has had to do quite a bit of, lately.'

'I don't see ... he still died from getting shot though, didn't he?'

'Goes to motivation for suicide, maybe. I asked the doc if Lacey knew.'

'That's a good question,' Sarah said. 'He's been living pretty far off the grid, hasn't he? He may not have seen a doctor in some time.'

'Greenberg says liver cancer's a sneaky bitch, often doesn't show symptoms till it's too late for treatment. But with this degree of involvement, he figures, Lacey would have been in so much pain he'd know *something* was wrong. Question is, did he see a doctor or did he just up the dosage on the meth? Doc said there was no sign of a biopsy, so Ed wouldn't have known anything for sure.'

Sarah and Ollie took pains with the report

they gave the information officer who released the final story to the news media. They made certain Ed Lacey's long and honorable service with the Tucson Police Department would be cited. At the end of his career, they explained, family problems, traumatic stress and a devastating illness combined to create a loss of judgment and a series of reckless behaviors. 'Discharged from the police department two years ago, he was interrupted Saturday morning in the apparent perpetration of a burglary. He initiated an exchange of gunfire, in the course of which he was killed.'

'We wrapped it up in euphemisms and buried it in a puzzling news story,' she told her family that night. 'And we hope it stays buried, because the only person who knows the whole truth is dead.'

Delaney had insisted they were not to suggest 'suicide by cop,' which they all thought this was.

'You can't prove it,' he said, 'and it's a rude phrase nobody wants to hear.'

They murmured it to each other, though, and Sarah said it aloud in private to Jeffries. He agreed, and had a quiet conversation with the County Attorney to supplement his written report.

Spurling went back to work on schedule. The letter absolving him of blame would follow weeks later.

The crew at 270 South Stone, pleased with the quick resolution of a troubling case, went back to their ever-burgeoning backlog, while Sarah tried to put lingering, unanswered questions to the back of her mind.

Two weeks later, on a bright Tuesday morning when Angela Lacey failed to show up on time at the used clothing store, her employer phoned her at home. Getting no answer, she called the manager of her apartments and told her to go up and check number 214. When the manager called back in hysterics, the employer called 911.

The EMT crew from the Mountain Vista Fire District wasted no time trying to revive Angela Lacey. Their leader called the ME's office. By 9:30 a.m., Delaney had his whole crew on the site.

SEVEN

The smell of death was still faint in the cheap little apartment on Prince Road. Angela Lacey had not been hanging in that closet very long, Sarah judged.

It seemed grotesque and uncivilized that she was still hanging there now. The blunt-speaking divorcee with whom Sarah had lunched two weeks ago was depersonalized, an object hanging in a closet, packed tight into a small space filled with nearly worn-out clothes. Sarah even recognized the smock she was wearing. But now, Sarah was surprised to see, her light brown hair had lost its scrunchy. Angela had treated herself to a neat Dutch-bob haircut, the ends turned under just below her ears. What a shame that now her face was distorted and swollen, hardly resembling the one Sarah remembered.

'I left her just as we found her,' the leader of the EMT team had told the dispatcher. 'I figured the ME would want to see her just as she was.'

And the doctor was in the bedroom closet, sharing uncomfortably close quarters with his victim and the photographer.

'OK, I've seen her just as she is, time to move along. Meg, you got enough pictures? Good, let's get her down from there. I can't do anything more in here.' He pushed his way out, batting aside clinging garments that snapped with static electricity. They'd sent the new guy, a tall, freckled Scot named Stuart Cameron. He was annoyed, Sarah thought, about being cooped up in such a small, dark space between a corpse and a wardrobe – so undignified, and it spooked him a little. But he could hardly protest because the EMT team had followed the book.

The clatter coming up from below proved to be his van drivers, heaving a gurney up the narrow stairway. In the tiny foyer they unfolded its legs and maneuvered it through the cramped kitchen and across the living/ dining room, setting chairs and a small table out of their way as they came. At the door of the bedroom they stopped and leaned in, eyeballing the even smaller spaces around the bed.

'Yeah, all right, it will not fit in here,' Cameron said. 'We'll have to carry her out. Come in here, both of you.' The two men sidled in reluctantly as the photographer ducked out. With three men packed around a body and surrounded by clothes, the closet became a suffocating squeeze box. Cameron's nice, quiet voice, muffled by fabric and taking on an edge of irritation, said, 'I don't know, this is a good, heavy nylon line and that's a helluva knot. Damon, you got a knife?'

'No,' Damon said. 'Ain't you the knife man?'

'No way I'm using a good scalpel on this,' Cameron said. 'Find something.'

'Here are scissors,' Sarah said, passing a pair in from the desk space in the kitchen counter.

Leo Tobin signed in just then with the officer at the door. He ducked under the tape and came in to stand behind her, watching – she felt his breath on her neck.

They heard the doctor say, 'I don't think they are sharp enough to cut ... Mike, can you lift up a little on your side?' A good deal of grunting and breathless swearing followed and then, 'OK, I think I'm getting it now, have you both got a good grip? Because here she comes—' There was a clatter as many clothes hangers crashed to the floor and then the three of them staggered out under their burden, trailing blouses and belts on their shoulders. None too gently, they laid Angela Lacey's dead body on the gurney.

Delaney and three more detectives, plus two crime-scene specialists, had come up the stairs during the struggle. Clustered uneasily in the kitchen, they stood by the stove, wanting to come in and start work, but not sure where to put their feet.

The doctor and his two helpers leaned above the victim, breathing hard. 'No, leave the noose where it is till we get her back to the lab,' the doctor said. 'Where's that body bag now?'

Delaney said, 'Well! Looks like we're going to have to organize a quick viewing for detectives and then let the doctor get on his way, huh? So, Ollie and Sarah, have you...?' The detectives all began filing around the gurney, like caring relatives at a wake.

Angela Lacey had bruises on her neck, noticeable though not as bad as Sarah would have expected. Her eyes were open and the petechiae of strangulation were easy to see on her eyelids and lips. She had voided her bladder and bowels, of course, but again, the smell was surprisingly mild.

Delaney came last in line. He asked and answered a few quick questions with the doctor, who seemed intrigued to see so much quick reaction by so many detectives and lab personnel to what to his eyes looked like the death of a totally unimportant person. Cameron was new in town and had never read a word of the Frank Martin story. Delaney promised to send him some background and warned he would be asking Cameron's superior for results asap.

Cameron shrugged and said, 'I'm the new kid on the block. Contact my boss – whatever he says to do, I'll do.'

They made even more of a racket getting down the stairs than they had coming up. All the tenants watched Angela Lacey's body leave the building – she was probably getting more attention today, Sarah thought, than she had ever had from any of them while she lived here.

Leo went around opening the meager blinds, trying to get as much sunshine as possible through the small windows. Delaney assigned them each a portion of the apartment to search, and went off to talk to the building manager about the decedent's car. While he was gone the detectives walked, peered, stooped and scrutinized. But in truth there was very little to see. Angela had kept a meager minimum of household items here. And her employer had not sacrificed much when she gave her this scruffy little apartment.

The one item Sarah could see that seemed to place her somewhere in the mainstream was a small laptop, battered and old, center-ed on the gateleg table in the tiny foyer. It was plugged into the wall outlet behind the table, and lit up when she tapped the space-bar.

'Heaven's sake,' she said. 'This building has wifi?'

'Most of these old apartment buildings in town have it,' Leo said. 'It's cheaper than redecorating and it holds the tenants. Most of the people in this building are probably looking for another job.'

'I don't get it,' Ollie said. 'Why would she live in a squat like this when she owned a house?'

'She rented the house,' Oscar said, not looking at Sarah, 'to start a nest egg for her old age.'

Sarah could see them all avoiding each other's eyes, hoping nobody said any more about *that*. It embarrassed them all, some-how, to think of somebody living this poorly on purpose, in pursuit of a goal so easily lost as the future.

The fingerprints tech was busy, busy – prints everywhere, she said. The closet where Angela had been hanging had a set of built-in drawers and Jason spent a long time shining a flashlight beam into each one and taking out the liner paper, looking under-neath. His total yield was two shirt buttons and a tiny safety pin.

The whole apartment had an impersonal air, Sarah thought, as if it might have been occupied part-time by someone whose real life was somewhere else. She found one item that seemed to be a keepsake, in a drawer of the nightstand by the bed. It was a faded snapshot, black and white, in a cheap metallic frame, nested carefully in a pile of underwear. A woman who somewhat resembled Angela, and a young man in a US Army private's uniform faced the camera, smiling, with their hands clasped. She was wearing a hat with a small veil, and had a flower pinned to the lapel of her suit.

Sarah showed it to the other detectives.

'That's one of the first camo uniforms,' Leo said. 'My mom had one of those packed away. She said it was Dad's, from when he fought in Vietnam. She let me wear it once in a school play. Talk about oily, that fabric.'

Probably Angela's grandparents, then, looking pleased with themselves, optimistic about what the future held. Maybe their wedding picture, Sarah decided. But why would Angela keep it in a drawer, instead of out where she could see it?

Holding it by its edges in gloved hands, she took it to the scene techs to be photographed and tested for fingerprints, then signed out for it. She thought about it while she continued the search, wondering, did

121

Angela keep that small, cheap picture near her because it was her best family picture? Or her only one?

The picture merged with her earlier impression about a real life somewhere else, causing Sarah to stand still with her head cocked like a beagle on a scent. Ollie noticed her standing that way and said, 'What?'

'This can't be all there is,' she said.

'Of what?'

'Of, you know, *stuff*. Think about it, they were married for seven years, moved out of Frank's house into their own after three. You move into a house, you start getting stuff – pots and pans, blankets and towels. Furniture. Ed moved out of that house, but she stayed there till a few months ago. Where's all the stuff?'

The other detectives, bored with searching empty grids, had gathered around this conversation and began to comment.

'Maybe she rented the house furnished?' Ollie said. 'Easy enough to find out.' He made a note.

'And held a yard sale,' Jason said. Yard sales were a reliable Saturday feature in his churning, up-and-downwardly-mobile neighborhood.

'Maybe, but you never sell it all,' Leo, the faithful husband and father, had endured many moves. 'Dishes, pictures, books –

those things you move.'

They all looked around at the bare walls and sparse furniture. 'You're right,' Ray said. Bombarded with wedding gifts, he was newly sensitized to housewares. 'Geez, not even a good mixing bowl in this kitchen. Looks like she did all her cooking in these two pans.'

'What you can't use at the moment,' Leo said, 'you store.'

Delaney, coming back in with the spare keys to the apartment and to Angela's car, heard them speculating and said, 'Let's talk to that building manager some more.'

She was round, tan and hard-surfaced, like a nut. Her brown hair was wound around her head in braids, and she wore a blue denim apron with several pockets. 'She's got one trunk in the basement, come to think of it,' the woman said. She picked a key off a pegboard wall and opened a door that connected the building's office to her living quarters. Sarah could see a pair of men's legs on the footrest of a tan plastic recliner.

'Herb,' the woman shouted, above a TV game show on high, 'show these officers to the storage room of number two hundred and fourteen, please.' A hand reached across the feet and took the key that dangled from her fingers. Another hand, out of sight, snuffed the noise and lowered the footrest. With a grunt, the man stood up. In the doorway, whiskery and disheveled, he muttered, 'This way.' He didn't speak again as they followed him out the doorway and across the graveled dooryard to Angela's building.

In a suffocating storeroom, he helped them find the crude metal rectangle with Angela's nametag on it. It was about four feet wide and six feet long, with seams welded on the outside. The hasp lock was held by a padlock. And the key? The man shrugged. When Ollie went back to the office, the woman said, 'She sure never gave it to me.'

The next thing they noticed was that the trunk was too heavy to lift. They called for an assist from the operator of their tow service, who brought the truck with the cowcatcher. Four men heaved it up from the basement and onto the scoop, which ferried it back to the station.

The detectives went back to Angela's apartment to search for the key – not very hopefully.

'Hell,' Ollie said, 'we already looked at every hair and bug in this place.'

'Twice,' Jason said, rubbing his neck, which was sore from his long search of closet drawers.

Ten minutes into the fruitless search for the key, Delaney came back to check on progress. 'Never mind the key,' he said. 'We'll just cut the hasp.'

'But I just thought of something,' Sarah said. 'It's probably in her purse.'

'All right,' Delaney said. 'Where's her purse?'

All the detectives grew guilty looks as they realized that in two hours of searching this small space, they had never asked that question.

'Maybe she left it at that store where she works,' Jason said.

'Nah,' Sarah said, shaking her head. 'If she did, she'd go back for it. She was here, so her purse should be here.' She looked around at doubting faces. 'Trust me, guys. A woman would not go ten minutes without having her purse. It's got all her stuff. Driver's license, credit cards, makeup...'

'OK, OK, I agree,' Delaney said. 'Just for the hell of it, though, let's call that store and ask.' He looked around. 'Who's got the number?'

'Um. I've got it, come to think of it ... in my notes from...' She went back through pages in her notebook till she found it. Then she stood with her smartphone in her hand, looking pained. 'I don't remember what her purse looked like.'

'I do,' Oscar said. He looked around at the astonished faces of the other male detectives. 'I told you,' he reminded Sarah, 'that my sister owns a women's clothing boutique. I help her there sometimes, so I notice purses. You're right, women care a lot about them – they take forever to decide which one to buy. Angela's purse was old but not shoddy like the rest of her outfit. It was a leather Coach bag – cowhide, not cheap – from back when they made quality purses that lasted forever. Had several compartments—'

'I remember now. With neat brass toggles. A place for everything.'

'Yes. Magenta. With a shoulder strap.'

Sarah dialed the store while the rest of the detectives worked to contain their amusement. Jason, in fact, had lost it when Oscar said 'magenta,' and stood with his back turned, shaking.

The store owner, who said her name was Marjorie Springer, answered with her customary rasp. 'We keep all our purses and junk in one bin,' she said, 'Hang on a minute.' In a minute she came back on the phone to assure Sarah that Angela's purse was not there.

'Are you sure? It's a Coach...'

'I remember her purse very well, Detective. The day that it showed up in the store,

126

Angela and my other helper just about came to blows over it.'

'Would you happen to remember if she was carrying it when she left work Monday evening?'

'No. But I'm sure she was. Angela was well organized; she didn't forget things.'

'You know, I really need to ask you several more questions. Could I come and see you at the store?'

'Too many interruptions here. Why don't I come to you?' She knew where the head-quarters building was, she said, 'but now that I've lost my one reliable helper, I can't get away from here during store hours. Give me a couple of days to get somebody in here I can trust. I'll call you, OK?'

'Fine.' To be safe, she wrote down the woman's name and numbers. She punched *end*, looking thoughtful. 'Imagine that. Somebody who actually *wants* to talk to me.'

'Be careful,' Leo said. 'She must be selling tickets to something.'

Back at the station, Delaney sent out a Need to Locate order on Angela's purse, putting Oscar on the phone for the description. He agreed they need not go back to the bare apartment, and went looking for some-body to break open the trunk. The detectives went back to their desks and returned phone calls till Delaney called Leo and said,

'OK, come and see. I recruited a kid from the support staff to make a list for us.'

They all trooped down to the evidence room, where Delaney waited with a legal tablet and a white board. His recruit was pretzeled behind the board, tightening screws and muttering to the legs, which kept threatening to collapse. As the detectives deployed around the board, the recruit dropped his wrench, swore, dropped to the floor and crawled after it as it slid across the tiles.

Leo bent to look under the board and said, 'Genius Geek! Good to see you. Look what we got here,' he told the other detectives. 'This quirky smart-ass finds information that's invisible to the rest of us.' At Sarah's urging, he'd partnered skeptically with the teenaged temp on an earlier case, and been surprised by how fast the noisy kid could pull information out of a computer.

He turned to Sarah now and said, as if the boy he'd just called Genius Geek were not in the room, 'I can never remember, is his name Scott Tracy or—'

'Tracy Scott,' Sarah said. She felt a proprietary interest in the bright temp she had rescued last year from exile behind the file cabinets. Unable to keep from annoying his supervisor, who liked his speed and skill on computers but couldn't abide his noise, he was frequently sequestered in a remote corner of the support staff room. Sarah had learned to enjoy his outlandishness because she greatly valued his skill and speed.

She bent over the pocked face and super-thick glasses peering up from the floor. 'Glad to see you, Tracy,' she said. 'You haven't been around much lately.'

'Dear lady!' Tracy said. Dust bunnies and hairs cascaded from him as he rose and bowed from the waist. 'I had to get serious about college applications for a while. Now that I've compromised my soul and mort-gaged my future to at least a dozen bloated exploiters of team sports, I can work for justice while I wait to get rejected.'

'Oh, nonsense, they'll all want you! And I think you're just what we need right now. Because in the foyer of her apartment we found what we believe to be the decedent's laptop computer. We did bring it over, didn't we?'

'Yes, I've got it,' Delaney said.

'Reckon I can probably suss out what-all's inside it if'n ya like, ma'am.'

'Ah, you've been reading the southern novelists again.'

'There you go, detecting as usual. Soon as I get this evil instrument set up,' he said, tackling the wobbly legs again, 'I am yours to command.'

'Here, let me do that,' Delaney said. He grabbed the wrench away from Tracy and straightened the legs with two expert motions. 'Here's a marker, Tracy. You remember how to write?'

Tracy looked down at it, sniffing. 'We're going back to whiteboards and markers? Why not stone tablets and a stylus?'

'Shut up and listen. Make three columns, label them ITEM, SENT TO, and RETURNED. Got that? We'll start with the computer – one laptop, Dell. Ollie, you're doing the search for Angela's background, you take it. Now, Tracy, write 'laptop' in the first column and 'Ollie' in the second.'

Tracy watched the transfer of the laptop with glistening eyes. Sarah caught his eye and made a hand motion, *wait*.

Ollie said, 'What if it doesn't have anything I need?'

'That's what the third column's for. Listen to this, everybody: you get done looking at anything signed out to you, bring it to me and we put it in the column marked, Returned.'

'And we put the item back in the trunk?'

'Yes.'

'You're keeping the list?'

'Better believe it. Next? Four nested stainless steel pans—'

Jason said, 'This isn't all going to be useful

130

stuff, is it? For us.'

'No, but we better look at all of it once before we decide. So take the pans, Jason. What's next?'

They each acquired a stack of goods they would be responsible for inspecting and entering in the case record. Eventually, Delaney claimed, all items would get signed back to Returned and put back in the metal trunk. Sarah got a collegiate dictionary, four sweaters in a plastic bag, a stack of six white porcelain soup bowls, two pillow covers featuring needlework in shades of lavender and rose, and a quilted tea cozy.

Handling the things Angela Lacey had carefully stored away – to wait for what? – seemed rude, like a violation of her privacy. At the same time, Sarah began to feel the satisfaction a successful search always brought. This was the nearest she had come, in all the Martin/Lacey investigations, to a sense of what had been killed. Whatever the cause, it had sometimes seemed as if these three people had public lives but no private ones.

But looking at some of the things Angela had considered worth keeping, Sarah began revising her opinions of Ed Lacey's wife. The woman she'd met at lunch had seemed cold, contemptuous and edgy. This one showed evidence of caring and warmth.

Angela Lacey had never had much money or social status in the time they were examining, but these items suggested an attempt to live well, hold things of lasting value and to give and take small comforts. For Angela, during the few years when her marriage with Ed Lacey thrived, it appeared that life had been a pleasure. Even when it ended, she had made a careful effort to preserve the best of it. Would such a person embezzle money from a bank and pin the blame on someone so dear to her loving husband? Sarah felt another strong suspicion fade.

EIGHT

Ray Menendez drew the autopsy assignment and spent most of Wednesday at East District Street. Delaney called all the rest of his crew into his office first thing to kick-start the Angela Lacey investigation.

'A couple of reporters turned me every way but loose last night,' he said, 'trying to get me to say what killed Angela Lacey. I told them, "She died of suffocation." They said, "But was it self-inflicted?" and I said, "We don't know yet. You're just gonna have to report that no conclusions have been reached." They carried on like I owed them an answer.'

'My wise old gut says this is one too many suicides in the same family in so short a time,' Tobin said. 'But of course my wise old gut has been wrong before, once or twice.'

'I don't think it is this time,' Sarah said.

'Me neither,' Jason said. When they all looked at him, he ducked his shining scalp and mumbled, 'For what it's worth.' But then Ollie and Oscar said together, 'I agree.'

133

'It seems to me,' Sarah said, 'that we ought to go back and re-open the investigation into all three deaths. Take another look at Frank's alleged theft of the money and that crazy message he left. Every one of these deaths is bizarre in some way. And all in one family – it feels now as if they form a series, doesn't it? Like they're each part of the same story.'

'Maybe,' Delaney said. 'I don't know. Remember, when Ed Lacey pulled his wire-pulling stunt and got shot we were speculating over why he went so bad so fast, and somebody mentioned that his uncle got disgraced. So I asked you all, "When's the last time you knew a guy to go off the rails over something that happened to his uncle?" And as I remember it, none of you said a word.' He looked around. 'So what's changed that makes you think different now?'

'We found out he wasn't just any uncle,' Oscar said. 'He was the man who rescued Ed Lacey from his mother's house, where the boyfriend was beating him up. And besides raising his nephew, he did all these volunteer things for the whole community. Everybody loved him because he drove for Meals on Wheels and helped with Bike Safety Day...'

'Stop before you make me cry,' Delaney said. 'How do you know this?'

'Angela told us,' Sarah said.

Oscar said quickly, with a little head-shake at Sarah, 'And other members of his family – Cecelia and Chico – both said everybody loved him.'

'And I went back and checked some old records yesterday,' Sarah said. 'The newspaper was indeed full of it at the time Frank got arrested. People tweeted and called in from all over town to talk about his good deeds. "He helped with the Kiwanis car wash, he found shelters for homeless vets," they said, "you've made a mistake." They wanted the bad bank examiners to stop persecuting Frank and go find the person who took the money. You don't remember any of this?'

'I usually just read the headlines,' Delaney said. 'I get all the drama I require right here, most days.'

'Ah. But surely you do remember that the bank examiners never found the money, and neither did we. If Frank Martin hadn't killed himself, convicting him would have been difficult, if not impossible. Because if he ever had the money he must have buried it under a bush somewhere, in coffee cans. It isn't in anything he owned, or in any account those hard-working examiners were ever able to find.'

'I know, I remember that part. But why'd

he off himself if he wasn't guilty?'

'That's what everybody in town wants to know,' Jason said.

'He left a note worthy of the Delphic Oracle,' Leo said.

'I forget – what did it say?'

'I have a copy,' Oscar said, 'if you want to...' He stopped when every eye in the room turned toward him.

'What does it say?' Delaney asked him.

Keeping his poise under scrutiny, Cifuentes pulled that same slip of paper out of his shirt pocket (Sarah thinking, *It can't be the same pocket, he's changed shirts two dozen times since we talked to Cecelia*). In a voice as expressionless as if he was reading a grocery list, he read again that tragic and puzzling message: "I didn't take the money, but I won't put my family through this investigation any longer." And then the postscript: "Eddie, I'm sorry for everything. I've loved you all your life, please try to forgive me."

Delaney said, 'You carry the damn thing around with you?'

Oscar shook his head a stoical inch each way and said, 'I thought we might be discussing it today.'

'What do you think he was sorry about?'

'Taking the money, I guess.'

'But he says he didn't do that.'

'Well then, I guess I have no idea, do I?'

Delaney scanned around the circle. 'Where is it, by the way? The actual note?'

'I don't know that, either. Does anybody?' They all shook their heads. 'Must be in the case files, I guess.'

Delaney swiveled his chair sideways and faced the wall above his console, where a number of plain black frames held pictures of his children winning awards at school. He was not admiring his family, though, Sarah saw. His eyes were closed and his lips were moving, but no sound came out.

All his detectives waited, watching the clear plastic clock on his desk scroll through thirty seconds. When he turned back he said, 'I'm not sure you're right that this death is connected to the other two. But it seems to make sense out of a confusing string of events, so let's run with it for now and see if we can prove it right or wrong. Here's what I want you all to do. Everybody ready? Leo, you're a good searcher, find everything that was printed in the local papers about the embezzlement case at the time it was discovered. Make one copy and bring it to me.'

'I can certainly do that,' Leo said.

'I know you can or I wouldn't have asked you. Editorial comments can wait, folks – we don't have all day to fuck around here.' Detectives began stealing furtive glances at each other. Delaney seldom had recourse to obscenity, unless he was pressured or angry.

'Oscar,' he swiveled his fierce blue gaze toward Cifuentes, whose face turned to polished granite as he stared back. 'You seem to have a knack for remembering details, so let's put it to work. Pull out the case files for both Frank Martin and Ed Lacey. Read them all the way through, including the autopsy reports. Keep on reading them until I tell you to stop. I want you to be totally conversant with everything that's in them, so that if I ask you a question, you can answer it. I want you to do this all by yourself. Is that clear?'

Oscar glanced quickly at Sarah, his mouth a grim line, and said, 'Yes.'

'Jason, put fresh batteries in your pocket recorder, go back to that bar on Flowing Wells where the two men phoned in about the wire stripper. Hang out there for a couple of hours drinking plain soda and striking up conversations with everybody who comes in – but not about the shooting, understand? Talk about the weather and the band you heard Saturday night and the Cats' chances in the playoffs – any old shit to get in everybody's face, make sure they've seen your Glock and your badge and are changing the plan they came in with. About the third time you empty the place, the bartender will start trying to find out what you want. Keep smiling till he asks. Then tell him we need to know exactly what he saw during that shooting. And how well did he know Ed Lacey, for how long, how much of what did he sell him and what did he buy from him? Tell him we're Homicide, we don't give shit about what he's buying and selling, unless he fails to tell us exactly how much he knows about Ed Lacey. You know the drill – if he helps us we forget his name and address; if he doesn't his whole operation is toast.'

Jason, who had been nodding steadily for some time, said only, 'Gotcha.'

'Good. Ollie, here's the keys to Angela Lacey's car. Use her license and registration to find every record that exists, state, county and city, for her since the day she was born. Family, schools, work history, medical records, what she owned and what she drove, if there's anything left who gets it? Any questions?'

'What was her last name before she was married?'

'No idea. Look it up. OK, that's it. Let's get at it. Sarah, you stay where you are, please.' He got up and ushered them all out, closed his door and came back to his desk. Sarah, marooned among empty chairs, watched him carefully. *If I only hadn't said,*

'Angela told us.'

'You're the best detective I've got, in some ways,' Delaney said without preamble. Sarah swallowed, waiting for the *but*. 'You don't gag at autopsies, or fold in a fight; you listen well at interviews and you've got good instincts about what people don't want to talk about. I've known for some time you want my job and I like that too – it means you'll work your tail off to keep your place in line.' He sat back and gave her the pop-eyed stare he usually saved for suspects. 'So what the holy shit were you thinking when you helped Oscar two-step his way around the job I gave him to do?'

'It was just a fair trade to save time, boss.' It sounded pretty credible when you said it that way, she thought, forgetting how she had ridiculed Oscar when he first offered the swap. 'He knew some of Ed Lacey's family members and he offered to help me find them if I helped him with Angela.' Watching his implacable stare she ventured, 'What's so bad about detectives helping each other sometimes?'

'Nothing, when I know about it. Why did he need help with Angela?'

'Well ... I don't know, exactly...'

'Uh-huh, you don't want to talk about that, do you? I can do it too, Sarah, that's just shit-sniffing 101, we all learn that. You

140

knew when I gave him the order – I saw you all looking at each other – that it was some kind of a test.'

'What kind, though? I mean ... isn't he entitled to a personal life?'

'Oh, bullshit!' He hit the desk and she flinched. 'Oscar Cifuentes has a crotch problem – he's sniffing around one all the time. Maybe it was just a colorful hobby while he stayed in Auto Theft, but if he can't stop being an alley cat he's got no future in Homicide. Think about the decisions you have to make all day about people. Homicide is serious business, you can't have your brains between your legs on this job. Oscar has to grow up if he wants to work here.'

He leaned back and scrutinized his ceiling for a few seconds, then put his elbows on his desk and said, 'And so do you. You still want to sit over here on this side of the desk?'

'Yes,' she said. 'You know I do.' Her face said, *Not enough to beg for it.*

'Well, if you keep your nose clean you're not the only candidate, but you're definitely in the running. The way to wrap it up tight is not to help other members of the crew find a way around my orders so you can all snicker at the boss.'

'I never meant to—'

'Maybe not, but that's the way it came out. Getting along with colleagues is very nice,

Sarah, but following orders is also a proven road to success. So now...' He sat back again. 'That's enough of that. Except to tell you I don't ever want to have this conversation with you again, understand?'

'Yes.'

'OK. How much digging up of old stuff do you think we need to do? Ed Lacey's family on both sides for three generations?'

'Well, no, but ... I'd like to talk to Angela's present employer, and everybody in Ed's mother's family. His father took off early, never played any part.'

'OK, mother's family ... big family?'

'Huge, but some are dead ... I've got a list of the ones who live here. I can find them.'

'What's your take on them so far?'

'All different, but ... Cecelia, the younger sister? She says they're warm, but ... they all seem a bit secretive to me, as if they're hiding something. Or guilty of something? Or afraid of someone? I can't figure it out.'

'Oh? Big warm family but the kid's raised by his uncle – how come?'

'Why don't I find them all and then tell you?'

'Yes,' Sergeant Delaney said, turning away as his phone rang, 'why don't you do that?'

Luz García-Lacey said she had never been tempted to add any more hyphenated names

142

after Lacey. 'Boyfriends only. One husband was definitely enough,' she said. She looked like Cecelia for a moment, when her eyes flashed. Then she settled comfortably back into her wrinkles and wattles and sighed.

'But like every other woman in my family I always wanted a man around. Could not *stand* to live alone. And I liked the lively ones,' she said. 'The ones who wanted to go out nights, dance and play games. Each one brightened my life for a while, and when they grew tiresome I put them out. Boyfriends...' Lying on her chaise in the shade, comfortable now in assisted living, she laughed and waved her hands in a gesture that said, *What can you do?* 'After a while they get like yesterday's fish.'

'But your son,' Sarah said. 'They didn't brighten his life as much, hmmm?'

'He was jealous,' Luz tossed her head, defensive. 'He liked having me to himself and each time when I found a new man he resented the attention I gave him. Adolpho, the one who beat him up? That was an outrage, of course, and we broke up over it, but in a way I understood – when Eddie got anxious he could be an awful pest.'

'So your son went to live with your brother-in-law.'

'By now I'm sure you have heard from the whole family what a careless mother I was.

143

It's true; I was never cut out for the part. But it made Frank very happy to care for Eddie, and my boy thrived there, so where's the harm?'

'Everybody tells me about Frank's good deeds,' Sarah said. 'Why did he want to help everybody, do you know? Was he very religious?'

'No, not really. He went to church when we all did, as a way of celebrating holidays. No, I think it started when Anita died. My poor sister suffered very much in the last two days of her life. She could not give birth to the child, and the pain...' Luz closed her eyes and shook her head. All the Garcías had a knack for story-telling, Sarah thought, and were particularly good at the silent pause that conveyed, *Words cannot express*. '...and then the baby died too, after they finally had the good sense to cut it out of her body, and to see it, just born and already exhausted ... I think Frank suffered from survivor's guilt after that. He was trying to do enough good to wipe out the evil in the world.' A sad little chuckle. 'Good luck with that, amigo.'

'Why do you think he stole the money?'

'He didn't. I knew that man as well as I know myself, and I tell you, Frank could not have done that. It was not in his nature.'

'But his signatures—'

'I don't know how that was arranged. Some clever, evil person ... I know nothing about accounting so I cannot help with details. But look at how he lived, always so careful – he even carried his own lunch from home, like a schoolboy, in a dinner pail, with a thermos for coffee. So no, he was not taking money from the charities. I don't know who did; I can only assure you that there is an explanation and if you look hard enough you will find it.'

'That's what we're doing – looking hard at everything. And talking to everybody in the family ... Which reminds me, your brother Guillermo lives in this facility too, doesn't he?'

'He does, but there is no use trying to talk to poor Memo any more. His mind is totally gone.'

'Ah. I'm sorry to hear it.'

'Yes, so are we all. It's quite surprising, too, that he should be the one who loses his marbles. While I sit here, as Cecelia says, still thinking sinful thoughts as nimbly as ever. Cecelia, perhaps you have noticed, is the family judge. It's a tough job but she feels uniquely qualified to do it. Memo was the family entrepreneur, the one who was clever and organized. He made plenty of money and had only one child. So we could usually tap him for a loan, which I think it's safe to say none of us has ever repaid.'

'So your family was blessed with two help-ers?'

'Yes. Unfortunately Memo's help always came with good advice which was so hard to listen to that we put off going to him until we were truly desperate.'

'But Frank didn't give good advice?'

'Or any other kind. That dear, sweet man. He would come to my door and say, "What can I do to help?"'

'What kind of help did he give you?'

'Everything from hauling away the broken furniture from the latest fight to re-stocking my empty food shelves – he did that one time when the brute I threw out stole all the money out of my purse before he left.'

'So who else from your family is around to talk to?' Sarah consulted her list. 'Eduardo?'

'He is deceased.'

'Marisol?'

'Gone to her reward also. Mimi married a man from Nicaragua and lives down there now. So except for Chico and me, only the younger family is left in Tucson; the second wife, Teresa's children – Cecelia, Pilar and Joey. Cecelia you have met, no? Pilar is the perfect example of the Catholic housewife and mother – a slave to her husband and four children. She wants only to serve them and the Lord. A pillar of the Altar Society.'

Luz shook her head sadly. 'Otherwise she appears quite sane. You have her address there?' She looked at the list. 'Yes, that is correct.'

'And Joey? Nobody's mentioned him to me before – does he live in Tucson?'

'Usually. He is the baby of the family. His mother named him José, but as soon as he was able to watch movies he said, "This is the USA, so call me Joey." He wanted to be like the tough guys in the movies. I don't know how tough he is, but he does get in his share of trouble.'

'Where can I find him?'

'Ah. Well. Occasionally he sublets a single-wide in one of the seedier RV parks. Or house-sits for people out of town. Sometimes with their knowledge, sometimes not. No fixed address, I think is how he says it. Except when he's in jail, when he is, of course, fixed.'

'Oh? Besides trespassing, which laws does he usually break?'

'Whatever's paying best at the moment. Some weed, some gun sales. A little social security fraud, which we all thought was too wicked, so Memo made him stop. Now that Memo's off his back he may have started that up again – he likes non-violent low-risk crimes that yield easy money to skilled victimizers. Joey shares that instinct for profit that Memo had. They get it from our father, who was always quite successful even though he was undocumented. The difference between his sons is that Memo made his money as a legitimate merchant and Joey's income is entirely ... how do they say it? Off the grid?'

'If I assure him I have no interest in his income streams, will he talk to me, do you think?'

'Oh, I should think so. Usually the problem with Joey is to get him to stop talking before he has a bloody nose.'

'And this address here is ... Oh, I see, that is Cecelia's house, isn't it? Does he sometimes live in her house?'

'No, God no, over her dead body.'

'But she what, takes his messages?'

'I guess. Mail, anyway.'

'Are they close?'

'Much closer than she would like, but ... he's her baby brother and although she often threatens, she never quite cuts him off. She complains to me, "He's such a leech," but then the next time I look they are giggling in the corner.'

'He doesn't try to take advantage of you?'

'He used to try, till I developed a strategy. Every time he came to my house, before I even let him sit down, I asked him to do some little task. "Fix the hinge on my gate, will you?" I would say, or "Take that pile of trash to the dump." He doesn't want to do any favors – he only came for the free lunch. So I would nag him and he would say he's too busy right now but he will do it tomorrow. That ensured that he would not come back any time soon.' She laughed, pleased with herself.

'As for finding him now ... you know that section of Speedway where most of the antique shops are? Well, in one of the bars along that stretch you will usually find Joey, sometime between noon and midnight. Where he survives the rest of the day, I would say is anybody's guess.' Luz's eyes were suddenly bright above her sagging cheeks. 'Why do you want to talk to Joey, anyway? Are you thinking he knows something about Angela's death?'

'We have to investigate everything,' Sarah said, looking at her notes to avoid Luz's hawk-like stare.

'Yes, well ... not that you care about my opinion...'

'On the contrary, I think your opinions are very interesting.'

'Oh? All right then, here is one for you. I will be very surprised if you prove that Angela killed herself. She was a truly steady person – never particularly joyous, but I have never seen her depressed either, much less suicidal. Cecelia and Chico always said, "My God, whatever possessed Eddie to marry such a dull girl?" But I think her quietness was what Eddie liked about her. He had been surrounded by García women all his life – so much drama and screaming. We get it from our mother, a hysteric if ever there was one. You know what I think you should be asking?' She laid a claw-like finger alongside her nose and thought a minute. 'What did Angela see in Eddie? Because, you know, he was my own son and I loved him, but it was obvious that she was the brighter of the two.'

Sarah was surprised. 'If she was so intelligent why did he find her working in a used clothing store? And what was he doing in that store, by the way?'

'Well, you know, that's another family story that's not quite accurate. I mean, it's true she was making her living selling used clothes. But they met at one of those do-gooder events that Frank was always dragging Eddie to. Poor Eddie, I don't think he ever did anything for fun, as an adult, until he found Angela. She gave him a life at last, and he loved her for it.'

'But why didn't she have a better job?'

'I have often wondered. All I can say is there must have been a story there but she did not choose to share it with me. But then, you know, I was the mother who let Eddie go, so ... Angela never talked to me much about anything.'

Sarah looked at her list. 'Well, of the two I haven't talked to yet, Pilar and Joey ... sounds like Pilar will be the easiest to find.'

'Yes, she will. Not forthcoming, I'm afraid, but reliably there at that same address.'

'Your relationship is not warm?'

Luz chuckled. 'Our relationship would curdle milk. Pilar disapproves of me.'

'And if I find Joey, will he have anything to say about Angela? Did they get along?'

'I doubt if they ever met. Joey does not usually show up at family parties. People might want some of their things returned. Joey is not a credit to the family, we all agree to that. He was the youngest of ten children and I think Papi was getting too tired by then to dust him off. That's what Papi called it when the boys needed a touch of the belt.'

She held up her glass. Sarah got up and poured water into it and Luz took a long drink, sighed, and put it down. She was getting tired, Sarah saw, so she asked quickly, 'Can you think of anyone who had a reason to want Angela out of the way?'

'Oh, well, Detective, speculation is always amusing, but you know, from where I sit now...' she waved a languid hand, '...I don't see much.'

After you just showed me you see everything from here. Surprised to find herself feeling friendly toward this shrewd woman whose life seemed to have been one long folly, she smiled into the ruined old face and thanked her. 'You've been very helpful. I hope I haven't taken too much of your time.'

Luz wiggled her fingers dismissively. 'I have nothing else to do. Which, believe me, is not as bad a situation as everybody seems to think.'

Pilar's married name was Campion. She lived in a tidy tract house in Marana, with a vest-pocket pool shaded by desert willows. Her eyes were dark and beautiful like Cecelia's, but her glossy black hair was cut short and her body had been to the gym. Lithe in jeans and an untucked shirt, she led Sarah to a pair of facing couches in a dim, cool living room. A couple of middle-school girls in braids, doing homework in the study, smiled politely.

'My high-school boys have practice today,' Pilar said. 'Basketball and soccer – they both made the team they wanted this year. So we have some time to talk before the house gets noisy. Soon as you finish that,' she told the two little girls, closing the study door, 'you can watch your game show.' A flat-screen TV beckoned from the console –

Pilar's house was old-school American Dream.

'Good. I won't take too much of your time,' Sarah said. 'First, let me say I'm sorry for all your losses. Your family has had one calamity after another, hasn't it?'

'What? Oh, you mean Ed and Frank? Well, I think some members of the family took those things pretty hard. But we ... my husband and I ... are quite occupied with our own family...'

'I suppose. Four children, is it? Plenty to do.'

'Yes. And we both have mothers to look after now too, so ... we try to get together with the clan for big events like weddings and funerals but, otherwise, we pretty much go our own way.'

'Oh ... your mother is ... forgive me, I guess because everybody spoke of your father's old age and death ... but your mother is still with you?'

'Yes, actually Mom is still in her early sixties. A little younger than Luz and Chico – and in good health, fortunately. But because she was always a homemaker and left decisions to my father, she has had a hard time establishing an independent life. So we try to help her with that.'

'I see. Was she as fond of Frank Martin as all the rest of you?'

'Well ... she felt sorry for him when his wife died, I suppose. I was a child then, I don't remember much about that time.' Pilar seemed cool about many things the other Garcías were passionate about. In this volatile family her manner was surprisingly circumspect. Sarah had come into her house expecting a nun-like woman with modestly downcast eyes who strung rosaries around pictures of a crucified Savior. But everything about Pilar's surroundings and demeanor bespoke a modern woman cherry-picking her influences to suit herself. The pictures on the piano included one of Pilar radiant in a white wedding dress and veil, on the arm of a grinning young man who looked decidedly mainstream Anglo.

Also, she was the first García to mention being in touch with her mother, the second wife. *Let's add that name and address to our collection, shall we?* 'I need to talk to your mother, Pilar. May I have her address and phone number, please?' she asked in a rhetorical way, not expecting opposition, and stood with her ballpoint poised above her notebook. When Pilar didn't answer she looked up. Cool had turned to cold; Pilar was hostile now.

'I'm not going to let my family get dragged into this,' she said.

'This is a homicide investigation, Pilar.'

Sarah kept her voice gentle, the kindly teacher explaining police work. 'Your family has experienced three violent deaths in three years. You're in it because you're part of that family. I'm not dragging you anywhere.'

'No, and you're not going to. I come from a large immigrant family with a lot of emotional baggage. Screaming and crying, cousins from Mazatlan turning up in the middle of the night with worn-out sandals falling off their feet. I left all that behind when I married Jim and it's going to stay behind. I'm never going back to that old barrio point of view.'

'I'm not asking you to. All I need is a few minutes of conversation – just touching base, really. As soon as I get the answers I need, I'll be gone.'

'All right.' Pilar folded her arms across her chest. 'What's first?'

'Your mother's name, address and phone number.'

Pilar faced Sarah for a few seconds with her stubborn face set in a refusal stare. Then she seemed to reflect that Sarah probably had the clout to get whatever she needed. Sarah watched her eyes change as she came to a reasonable conclusion, shrugged and reeled off the numbers for a house nearby.

'Good. Thank you. Now, did you know Ed Lacey's wife very well?'

'Oh ... Angela? No. Let me think ... I know I first met her the day they got married. After that ... maybe once or twice at big family gatherings.'

'Did you like her?'

'I didn't have much feeling about her one way or the other. She wasn't ... outgoing. But Eddie seemed happy and I was glad for him.'

'Do you have an opinion about the manner of her death? Did she seem a likely suicide, to you?'

'I really have no ideas about that at all.'

'Do you agree with your sisters that Frank Martin was not the sort of person who would have stolen money from the credit union?'

'I haven't talked to them about it.'

'But do you agree?'

'I hardly knew the man. I have no way of knowing what he would do.'

This is going no place. 'Luz didn't seem to know if your brother Joey has an address,' Sarah said. 'Do you have an address, or ... any way to find him when you want him?'

'No.' Pilar's cold face grew an expression of amused contempt. 'Why on earth would I want to find Joey?'

I should have guessed that would be her answer. Time to thank her and get out of here.

Still, it wasn't all a waste of gas, she decided as she drove away. She had a new name and address and she knew Pilar was not, as Cecelia would say, warm. It wasn't only Luz she disapproved of – Pilar had turned her back on her entire family.

In fact, the big, warm García family that Cecelia had described seemed to be morphing more and more into a loose collection of outliers. So where to go next?

Before she could decide, her phone rang. Delaney said, 'All hands back to the station. Ray's back with autopsy results.'

Cheerful by nature, Ray Menendez was practically incandescent this winter. He was getting married in a couple of months, and two large and loving Tucson families were showering parties and presents on the happy couple. Raimundo's smile, Jason had recently remarked, was going to break his jaw one of these days if he didn't dial it back.

And Angela Lacey's autopsy had done nothing to dim his enthusiasm for police work.

'Man, you know,' he beamed at the crew, 'it's really something to watch an expert like Cameron examine a body. He proceeds with such confidence – like he's reading *signs*.'

'All right,' Delaney said, trying to be patient with Ray's enthusiasm. 'Tell us what the signs told him today, please.'

'Wow, a whole lot of confusing stuff.' Ray had made his notes on an iPad. It was small and light, so he could hold it in his left hand, scroll with his right, and still use a pen to jot additional questions on paper. Pressing the *start* key now, he said, 'I don't think I've ever heard the word "ambiguous" used so often.' Seeing Delaney start to puff up and turn pink, he said, 'OK, I'll give it to you just the way I got it from the doc.

'Clear signs of suffocation – face and neck puffy and dark red, petechiae numerous and fully developed. Wooden stool found tipped in doorway of closet indicates that subject stood on it to fasten the knot, then kicked it away. But not conclusive because stool could have been placed by anyone. Evidence of hanging ambiguous – subject was found suspended, but marks of strangulation – he's not happy about the *hanging groove*, he went on and on about it. The hanging groove should be more pronounced, he says, with such a strong, slender rope as the one this victim was hanging on.

'Also, the hyoid bone was not broken, which it often is by a hanging. Often but not always, he says we should remember. Especially with a short drop like the one she had in the closet. So ... it appears possible the body was suspended after death – possible,

158

but not certain.

'On the other hand, the knot used to fasten the noose around the clothes pole is huge and clumsy, wrapped many times, the way an amateur or excited person would do it – consistent with self-inflicted death by hanging. And the edge of the hanging groove, at one point, was slightly puckered in the direction of slippage the cord would have taken when the weight of the body settled on it. He was proud of himself for noticing that, but to be honest I wasn't sure I could see it.

'Lividity evidence is not consistent – some blood settled in back and rear parts of arms, but also some lividity in soles of the feet.

'Two puncture marks on upper left shoulder appear to match the footprint of the taser used by the Tucson Police Department. He was very unhappy that I hadn't worn a taser, so he could match up the marks. I reminded him that's for street patrolmen and he called Dispatch and got them to send a car. It was Byron, and you should have seen his face when . . . He wasn't wearing his taser, he had to go back out to his car to get it. OK' – as Delaney shuffled his feet impatiently – 'yes, the marks matched. "Appeared to match" is how the doc said it – there was nothing he wasn't prepared to question by then. Burn marks in those puncture wounds, by the way, indicate the jolt may have been sent more than once. Unless the puncture wounds were made by two hypodermic needles, in which case the burning might be due to whatever was injected. He's having that tissue tested.

'There's a bruise at the base of the skull, indicating something soft but strong may have been pressed there for a minute or two while the victim was still alive.'

'Like what?'

'Like a fist, maybe? Or a large knot of some kind. The doc is sending out beaucoup samples of blood and tissue, of course,' Ray said, 'and he won't reach any conclusions till they're back. But for now, what he says is, "Don't bet the farm on suicide. But don't make up your mind to reject it, either."'

'Jesus,' Delaney said, 'I could have said that much without an autopsy.'

'I kind of thought you might feel that way, so I asked him if he couldn't give us a nudge in either direction. He got sort of offended and said, "I'm not going to tell you I know something before I know it."'

NINE

Four-thirty ... too late to go looking for Joey, Sarah decided. She walked around to Ollie's desk and found him with Angela's laptop, laughing quietly with his hand on his mouse.

Sarah asked him, 'Finding any good stuff?'

'Yeah, great old stuff. Did you ever get this dog email?' He showed her a long message with pictures of dogs looking guiltily up at the camera. 'The captions are priceless!'

'You're looking at dog videos? Have you lost your mind? You're supposed to be looking for emails from Frank!'

Ollie looked sheepish, the way everybody does when they're caught wasting time in the intellectual swamp of the internet. 'I went looking for Ed's email messages and I got distracted for a minute. So shoot me.'

'OK,' Sarah said, pretending patience. 'Play FBI profiler for me and tell me all about Angela as a computer user.'

'She's just like my Aunt Kate – barely a computer user at all. It's an old installation of Windows XP. The logon screen asks for a password but you can just hit Enter and it lets you in – she never bothered to set up a password. The machine has Microsoft Office on it but I can't see that she ever created a document or saved a spreadsheet. Press the Outlook Express icon on the desktop and her inbox opens up. Almost every email she ever got is in that inbox, including the original Welcome to Outlook message. Nothing in the trash but some particularly nasty spam messages from random Russians. She read every joke email she ever got, but hardly ever forwarded one. Most of the junk email came from that clothing store owner she worked for. She had a very small circle of email correspondents.'

'What about email from Frank? Or Ed?'

'None from Frank at all. A few replies from Ed, including one suggesting very politely that she not forward junk email to him at work. *I'll see it when I get home, honey*, he said. Amazingly sweet, for a Red Man.'

'So, Ed did have an email account of his own?'

'Yeah, somewhere. But he didn't use this laptop for it that I can see. If he had, there'd be a folder with his name on it under Documents and Settings. The only folders here are the ones that come with the machine and Angela's. You need me to show you or you want to believe me on that?'

Sarah held up her hands and said, 'Hey, it's not a question of believing. You know more about this stuff than I thought. How come?'

'Most families have one person who is the designated technical support person. In my family, that's me. Kids, wife, grandma, Aunt Kate – I spend a lot of time figuring out where things have gone to on the box.'

'I do that too for my family, but I think in another year or two I'll be asking Denny for help instead of the other way around. So ... anything else you can tell me about Angela from what you see there?'

'Her email usage started to peter out right after Frank's death – and ended about when her marriage was breaking up. Probably got to the point where she couldn't stand to turn on the laptop and just let it sit on that table.'

'I don't understand; what's painful about turning on a computer?'

Ollie clicked the mouse a couple of times and rotated the laptop. 'Check out her desktop background.'

Sarah stared at the full-screen picture of Angela and Ed, radiant and laughing, cutting their wedding cake on what may have been the happiest day of their lives. When she nodded, Ollie pulled the screen back around to face him again.

Having placated and praised, Sarah went back to her strong suit – persistence. 'I still would like to have Genius Geek take a look at the machine before we put it back in that trunk. I've seen him find stuff that just wasn't there for us mere mortals.'

'Aw, come on. What's a kid with zits going to find that I haven't?'

'Plenty, I bet. Ask Leo.'

'Go away, Sarah.' He put on his don't-mess-with-me look.

'Trust me,' she said. 'Go on, ask him.'

For a few seconds, Ollie looked as if he might be getting seriously annoyed – she saw, now, how proud he was of his keyboard skills. She was counting on their history – some speed bumps they'd shared during their years as street cops, and the fund of trust it built up. And before long she saw him get up and walk, grumbling, two cubicles east, where he said, to Leo Tobin's wide rumpled back, 'Sarah says you think this Genius Geek kid is the real deal on a computer search.'

'Uh-huh.' Leo kept his eyes on his screen and went on tapping keys.

'You think he might find something in this machine even if I can't?'

'Almost certainly.'

'Well, what's that silly kid got that—'

Losing patience with the ongoing interruption, Leo leaped out of his chair, scattering paper clips and memo pads over a wide area, and yelled, 'What the fuck's the matter with you? Can't you take yes for an answer?'

Startled, Ollie jumped back. Unfortunately, Sarah had followed close behind him. He barely missed crushing her instep, but trod heavily on her right small toe.

Leo blinked as Sarah jumped out from behind Ollie, yelling in pain. She kicked off her shoe and cradled her right foot in both hands. Standing on one leg like a stork, she groaned, 'Oh, it's all my fault.'

'What is?'

'I'm the one who insisted he come over here. Ow. I should have checked to see if you were busy. Oh, hell, this hurts.'

Leo said, 'What's the matter with your foot?'

'Ollie stepped on it.'

'Did I?' Ollie said. 'I'm sorry.' He didn't sound sorry – just absent-minded. He was staring open-mouthed at Leo's screen. 'Leo, what are you looking at?'

'What does it look like? It's a perp walk, the unnecessary spectacle beloved of two-bit lawmen everywhere. Two policemen are leading Frank Martin out of the credit union in handcuffs, as if that poor little weenie there was any kind of a threat to anybody. Look at him. Wouldn't it make you barf?'

Sarah was already looking, but not at poor, cringing Frank Martin. And Ollie was seeing the same thing she was, evidently. Behind a desk, to the right of Frank Martin and his clinging lawmen, an attractive female observer registered shock.

Cifuentes walked up and looked at the screen and then around at the others, saying, 'Why are you all looking at Angela Lacey?'

'Can you believe that's only three years ago? She looks so...' Her hair was golden – OK, maybe with a little help from a bottle. Her eyes were bright blue. *She's maybe a couple of pounds overweight and, sure enough, she did have a very nice* ... the screen blurred; Sarah realized she was weeping. The pain in her foot had melded with the infinite pathos of lost time, and for one panicky moment she felt as if she might stand on one foot in this busy building and cry them a river.

But the other detectives had heard the commotion and crowded around. Ray looked over and said, 'Oh, you found the ugly perp-walk picture.'

Jason walked all the way into Leo's workspace, animated and smiling, and said, 'Leo, what's up, baby, you find something so ugly it made Sarah cry?'

Delaney heard the commotion and came out of his office, looked at the odd grouping and said, 'Sarah, why are you crying?'

'Oh ... I hurt my foot.'

'Well, let's get it tended to. Guys, are you going to let her stand there all day holding her foot? Give her a hand, will you?' With Ollie and Oscar boosting her on either side, Sarah hopped into the good light in front of Delaney's office and sat down in a straight chair.

Holding the shoe Ollie had handed him, Delaney bent over her foot, which looked undamaged in its pristine nylon sock. He said, 'It looks OK, but you need the city doc? Shall I get somebody to drive you?'

'Boss, no – listen. It's just a bruise – my foot's OK.' She nodded toward Tobin's work station. 'It was that picture on Leo's computer that made me cry.'

Delaney walked over, read the caption under the picture, and shook his head, puzzled. He came back saying, 'I don't get it. What's so sad about a stupid perp walk?'

'Frank Martin had worked there for over twenty years.'

'So?'

Sarah blinked a couple of times. 'I guess it just struck me how fast even very substantial people can sometimes lose everything.'

'Well, Jesus, you been a cop half your life

and you just noticed that?' He looked at his watch. 'Time to go home. Here's your shoe – can you make it to your car, Sarah? Sure? Better soak that foot tonight.'

On Bentley Street, Sarah gimped into the kitchen and said, 'Something smells wonderful here.'

'Scalloped potatoes and ham,' Denny said, 'sliced into a casserole by your very own personal niece.'

'And cooked by your personal mother in this sweet little device,' Aggie said, pulling the dish out of the toaster oven on the counter. 'See how easy?'

Sarah winked at Denny, who was beaming with satisfaction. Aggie looked up from spooning food onto plates and said, 'Why are you limping?'

'Dumbest cop move of the year,' Sarah said. 'I let myself get stepped on by a cow-footed detective.'

'Better soak it after we eat.'

Sarah seriously intended to do that, but fell asleep after dinner watching the news. She woke with a start when her mother poked her, and stumbled off to bed.

Dietz wasn't home from work yet when she woke in the gray dawn, feeling her right foot throb. Pulling it out from under the covers carefully, she saw that it was swollen, especially the bulbous fifth toe, and now sported rainbow hues.

'My pinkie is purple with a blue and yellow surround,' she told Delaney when he answered his cell at home. 'It's sore as hell – I can't stand on it.'

'OK, this is what we pay work comp for – go to the city doc and get something done about it.'

'I will. And depending on what that turns out to be, I'll try to make it in around noon.'

'Get the foot fixed first, then decide.'

She took along a magazine and a short novel, and almost finished both during the alternating pain and boredom of the long morning. She waited for a doctor, then for an X-ray technician, then for the development of X-rays.

'Well, you're lucky,' the doctor said, 'your toe's not broken. It is dislocated, though. I can put it back right here in the office, but' – he patted her shoulder – 'I better put some happy juice in there before I do that, or you might punch my lights out before I finish.'

She had another nice read while a couple of shots deadened the area. Then she watched with wonder as the doctor put a toe joint she now couldn't feel back where it belonged. Downing the Ibuprofen he swore would not render her unsafe to drive, she watched him wrap a light bandage around the whole set of toes and tape it in place. Beginning to feel like a movie monster, she replaced the thick white sock and ugly sandal that were now the only footwear her right foot would tolerate, and clumped out of the building into worsening weather. *I live in a land of perpetual sunshine, so of course I have to mangle my foot during the only cold snap we have all winter.*

It didn't hurt any more, though, so as soon as she got used to walking unevenly and ignoring the odd sound effect of one clicking suede flat and one rubber-tired monster sandal, she decided she was good to go back to work.

It was a little awkward driving the car with a right foot she couldn't feel, but she relied on exterior clues like the speedometer and made it back to South Stone without killing any bystanders. Her balance was somewhat precarious; she cursed the heavy outside doors at South Stone and waddled like a beginning toddler on the highly waxed floors inside. She watched the elevator doors close as she approached, not daring to try a last-minute jump. Waiting for the car to come back, she whispered, 'Patience, patience,' knowing it would never be her area of talent. She normally took the stairs.

Ollie saw her getting off on the second floor and said, 'Sarah, you're actually riding the ... Oh!' He looked at her big right foot in the sandal. 'God, buddy, I really busted you up, huh? Jesus, I'm sorry. Can I help you some way?'

'It's not broken. I'll be out of this lash-up in a couple of days. Just ... would you mind bringing me a glass of water? No, wait – can you find me a pitcher? With ice cubes. I'm dehydrated all the way to my ankles.' He brought it, tinkling, and she drank one whole glass before she said, 'Thank you,' and poured a second glass. He was still standing there, wanting to do something. 'How are you doing with that computer?'

'Genius Geek has it. I told him I was looking for whatever he could find that looked like what you need to run a life, and he carried it away with glad little cries.' He quit looking sorry as his good news bubbled to the surface. 'Then I went ahead with a routine search on Angela's driver's license and found when she changed it from her maiden name. Which was Goodman, by the way. Then it was Upshaw, for a couple of years, before it was Lacey. As soon as I had all that, I started finding school records and library cards, work records and apartment rentals – all that jazz. You know what? She first worked for that store more than fourteen years ago, and this is the second time she's gone back to work there since then.'

'I don't know what to make of that.'

'I don't either. Just saying ... it seems to be some kind of a home base.'

'If I can get that manager to talk to me, maybe we'll find out.'

Phone messages and emails were stacked up as if she'd been away from her desk a week. Prioritizing, her eye almost passed over 'Marjorie Springer.' Then she saw the subject line – Angela Lacey – and opened the message. 'Got a helper starting today. Might be able to get away by tomorrow,' it said. 'Call me.'

She replied, 'Out tomorrow. Will call Monday,' and dialed the number for Teresa, the second wife of Vicente García, whom she had begun to think of as 'the little woman.' She had not been able to form a mental picture of the mother of two daughters as different as Pilar and Cecelia, but had an impression of Vicente, the duster-off of sons, as a dominating patriarch.

A woman answered, her musical voice retaining just a suggestion of antecedents south of the border. She listened while Sarah explained her job and reason for calling. Then she said she would be willing to come to the station someday soon, 'when my daughter has time to give me a ride.'

'How can you live in Marana without a car?'

172

'Oh, I have one, but ... you know that I'm a recent widow? Well, in the confusion of this first year, so many things to consider, I let my driver's license lapse, and I haven't got around to getting it renewed. It's ridiculous, I know ... but right now I can't drive.'

Sarah said, 'Oh, well, Mrs García, I would be happy to come to your house.'

'Oh? Well ... perhaps that would be all right.' Her voice said she had grave doubts.

'I got your address from your daughter, Pilar, and I could be there within the hour,' Sarah said. 'I'll show you my credentials so you'll know you're totally safe with me, OK?' She hoped her tone indicated that they both knew this was a joke. When the silence continued on the other end of the line, she added, 'Or if you prefer I could send a patrolman in uniform, in a black-and-white patrol car with a light bar on top, so you'll know you're totally safe on the journey, and he can bring you downtown. He'll bring you right up to my office and take you home again after we've finished talking.'

The more I talk, the more I sound like a crazed rapist's evil henchwoman.

Teresa could not quite buy the deal over the phone from a stranger. She said, 'Maybe tomorrow my daughter can bring me.' Rather than try to explain that four ten-hour

173

shifts meant she would never work Friday except in an emergency, Sarah said, 'Tell you what. I'll call your daughter Pilar and explain that I've talked to you and you seemed to need reassurance. Then she can call you and tell you it's all right. Will that work for you?'

Assured that it would, Sarah called Pilar, who delivered a blistering tirade forbidding Sarah to 'pester' her widowed mother. Sarah listened for two minutes before she delivered an ultimatum: 'If you want to bring her in yourself and wait while we talk, feel free. But if it's easier to have me out there on the pavement, call your mother now, because I need to talk to her today.'

That worked, and soon Sarah was back on I-10, driving northwest to Marana again. The sky was now the color of pewter, the forecast was for possible rain with snow at higher elevations. *Promises, promises*, Sarah thought, though the radio voice hadn't actually promised her anything but more of this cold wind.

Teresa's house was in a development closer to the town center than Pilar's, surrounded by houses exactly like it, distinguished from each other only by the size of the attached garage and the color of the front door. You would not want to get lost out here at night without a GPS, Sarah

174

decided.

The woman who opened the door was as round and bosomy as you'd expect Cecelia's mother to be, but quiet and self-contained like Pilar. Her salt-and-pepper hairdo hung at a neatly brushed midpoint between Cecelia's Big Hair and Pilar's short wedge; her shirt was pristine white like a schoolgirl's and her shoes were polished and discreet.

Sarah explained her own odd choice of footwear without ever quite admitting she had simply let herself get stepped on. Then with the suggestion of a 'broken foot' hanging in the air, she went after the red meat: how well had Teresa known Frank Martin and Ed Lacey?

'At first, hardly at all,' she said. 'It was a large family and there was a lot to get used to. I was younger than all but two of Vicente's children when we married, and at first the older ones didn't take me very seriously ... I believe they thought if they ignored me I would soon go away.'

'How did your husband find you?'

'We found each other – quite by chance. I was keeping house for my father on his ranch near Patagonia after my mother died. Our house was damaged in a storm and Vicente came to bid on the repairs.'

'He was a builder?'

'Amongst other things. My husband was

self-taught at most of the trades he prac-
ticed, but he was very intelligent and strong,
so he always had work.'

'How old was he then, when you met?'

'Forty-eight. I was twenty-two. I know, it
sounds extreme. I should explain that he
was a vigorous man' – she blushed and looked at her hands – 'and I was somewhat
mature for my age since my mother died
when I was fifteen and I had been helping
run the ranch and raise the other children
since then.'

*But today you couldn't decide by yourself to
get in a police car and come downtown. What
happened to you?*

'Vicente got the job, and since he was
repairing the spaces where I worked, we
began to talk. He moved a cupboard to
make my work space more efficient. I asked
him for a cutting board I had always wanted
and he built it. There was a strong attraction
between us from the start, but because he
was so much older he felt it was unsuitable
and didn't make ... what my children call
"the moves." So on the last day, as he was
preparing the bill at the kitchen table, I sat
down beside him and said, "I think we need
to talk."

'My heart nearly failed me when I said
that, but he turned to me right away and
said, "Your father may try to kill me but I

think so too." After that it was all settled very quickly. My father wasn't surprised at all. He said, "I wondered what was holding you back."

'I was never sorry; I had a wonderful marriage. But the last years – he died a year ago at Thanksgiving – well, at the end he was very dependent. He didn't want me out of his sight for long, and he had to be in charge of everything. I checked every little thing with him first, and I got out of the habit of making my own decisions. I'm trying to regain that skill now.

'But to get back to your question ... I never paid much attention to Frank Martin and Ed Lacey. I couldn't understand the relationship. Luz's son lived with an uncle who wasn't even related by blood? Why? Anyway, I had my hands full – Vicente had seven children. The youngest two, Eduardo and Marisol, still lived at home. For a while, those two tried to turn me into their slave. And the ones who had started independent lives still came home whenever they chose, took anything they wanted and stayed as long as they pleased. It was some time before I felt like the mistress of that house.'

'Where was your house?'

'In the barrio in Tucson that was torn down before the convention center was built. We had a big old house, not modern and convenient like this one, but comfortable, with a garden and fruit trees. And then I got pregnant right away. When Pilar was born, I said, "This household needs sorting out." And Vicente said, "Tell me what's wrong, and I'll fix it." That was when the really good years began. For me, that is – some of the children didn't see it quite the same way. Luz and Guillermo were particularly outraged at the idea that they couldn't come into my house and help themselves to whatever they wanted there. Since their mother's death they had had the run of the place, under the pretext of helping out. Luz would say, "I've come to weed the garden," and go home with whatever was ripe.' Remembering, she shook her head ruefully.

Sarah used her momentary silence to get back to what she wanted to know. 'Everybody else in the family seems to be sure Frank Martin would never steal. Do you have an opinion about the embezzlement?'

'I'm afraid not. To me he was always completely mysterious.'

'How so?'

'All those favors he did for people, and yet he didn't really have *friends*. He would do the good works, then roll up his apron or put his tools in the box and go home. If there was a meal afterward, he hardly ever stayed for that.'

'And Ed? Did you know him better?'

'Not in the early years. I thought it was terrible that he lived with Frank.'

'Really? All the other Garcías have said how much they loved each other.'

'Maybe so. But what a life, being this quiet, creepy kid who followed his uncle around to all the charities and then went home. After he got into games, made some teams and then got on the police force, he had a more normal life. When he married Angela, though, that's when he blossomed.'

'Yet when his uncle killed himself, it seems he fell apart.'

'Yes ... I'm not a psychiatrist, so I guess my opinion about that is not worth much.'

'Oh, so far I think your opinions are right on the money.' Sarah smiled encouragement, waited, and finally said, 'You think maybe Frank was a little ... too possessive?'

'To put it politely, yes. After Ed grew up and had that great career with the police force, I used to look at him and wonder how he had managed to escape that smothering embrace. But when he went to hell I realized he had not made it all the way out after all.'

Sarah sighed. 'I'm raising my niece because my sister became addicted to drugs and other foolishness. It seems to me that parenthood is very humbling.'

'Indeed – the perfect word. I used to say to Vicente, "Why didn't I try something easy, like hiking the Arizona Trail in bare feet?" And he said, "Imagine how I feel, Dovey. I raised seven children before I met you. I swear I treated them all the same, and I've no idea why are they all so different."'

'He called you Dovey?'

She nodded, smiling. 'He said I reminded him of a little brown Inca dove, the one with spots on the sides and the gentle call.' She sighed, remembering. 'The grand thing about marrying an older man is that in his eyes I was always young and beautiful. I miss that, of course. I went from young and beautiful to old and useless overnight.'

'Oh, I don't think you should consign yourself to the dustbin quite yet. May I ask – do you have any idea why Angela would kill herself? I mean, I know Ed just died, but—'

'But he was her ex-husband, wasn't he? And she could not have grieved over his death any more than I did when Vicente died, but I never thought of killing myself. I didn't know Angela well, but honestly I can't imagine her hanging herself in a closet. I think she must have surprised a burglar in that apartment ... it's not a very nice neighborhood, you know.'

'I guess not. Burglars don't usually stay

long enough to make nooses, though, do they?'

'Perhaps not. You know more about burglars than I do.'

'Next question: your daughters are indeed very different. Do Pilar and Cecelia get along?'

'They pull together sometimes when they want to win a point against the older siblings. By themselves, they fight like sharks.'

'And with their brother?'

'Pilar will have nothing to do with Joey. Cecelia seems to find him amusing, off and on.' She sighed. 'I suppose you've heard that Joey is the family bad boy. My fault, I guess. He was adorable when he was small and I could never say no to him and make it stick. Vicente was equally hopeless, just putty in his hands.'

'The youngest in such a large family, I suppose...'

'Yes. They get so much love when they're small ... maybe it gives them unrealistic expectations. He has always believed that everything should come to him easily – he's never worked hard for anything.'

'Does he still come home? Would I find him sometimes in your house?'

'No, now that he's not so pretty and often smells bad, I find I can resist him. He's an impossible house guest – he can reduce a

181

nice clean room to a pile of trash faster than anyone I've ever seen. Anyway, he won't be visiting anybody for a while, because as of yesterday afternoon he's back in the Pima County Jail.'

'Oh?' Sarah picked up her pen. 'Has he been arraigned yet?'

'Yes. You know, they do it right there in the jail now, on an electronic hook-up. Very sophisticated.' She made a face. 'Thanks to my son I know a lot about how Pima County Jail works.'

'What's the charge?'

'Several charges this time – and rather severe, I'm afraid. Criminal trespass and home invasion ... he inadvertently broke an expensive dish so they are charging him with, I don't know, is it willful destruction? And several other property crimes. Then he tried to run, so there's one about resisting arrest. This is his third arrest in three years and he drew Judge Mary Kahler, who is determined, they say, to teach recidivists a lesson.'

'What was he trying to do?'

'Somehow he became convinced there was no one home at a certain house in El Encanto. But the owner was right there, in his studio, painting. When he glanced out and saw a poorly dressed stranger breaking the lock on his back door he went into a bathroom with his cell phone and called the police. Joey walked out with an armload of electronic gadgets and met the patrolmen who were waiting for him.'

'Do you know the name of the arresting officer?'

'I suppose they told me but I forgot. Joey always makes light of what he calls his "brushes with the law." And you know, till about three years ago, that's all it was – some loitering, and once he got in a fight. He never could seem to keep a job, so he got in the kind of trouble young men find when they're idle. But lately ... he's done more serious property crimes. We hired lawyers before, got his sentence suspended the first time and shortened the second. But this time I think the judge is determined to show him the law is no joke. She set the bail very high.'

'Are you going to bail him out anyway?'

'Well ... not right away. He expects me to, of course. But I think we would all be best served if he sat still in there for a while.'

'Then you will?'

'I don't know. They have all the evidence they need to convict him, so I think he will serve some serious time over this. And I'm thinking, why spend a lot of money for a few days on the outside? In the end he has to go back and face the music anyway, so he might as well get used to it.'

'That's very sensible. Does all the family agree?'

'Yes. I told my other children, and Luz and Chico too, not to put up the money. They said, "Don't worry." So if you want to interview Joey,' Teresa's smile was sadder than tears, 'I have made it easy for you.'

'I'm so very sorry you had to make that hard decision.'

'It wasn't all bad,' Teresa said with a new note in her voice. 'Pilar was thrilled when she heard that I had decided on my own to refuse him. She said, "You see, it's like riding a bicycle – it will come back to you."'

'Well, hey, a silver lining.'

'About time, too. Sitting here talking to you has made me think back to what a strong and brave person I used to be. I'm going to take a refresher course in driving now. Why have I been putting it off? Maybe if I get my driver's license back I can stop being such a ... what's that word my grandchildren use? A weenie.'

'Good luck with that. Will you do me a favor, Teresa?'

'If I can. What?'

'If you do decide to put up bail for Joey, will you let me know?' Seeing Teresa hesitate, she decided to lock it in. 'Three other people are dead. Till we know where the credit union money is, he might be best off in there where he's safe.'

'Oh,' Teresa said, round-eyed with shock. 'I never thought ... Yes, of course. I'll keep you advised.'

Rolling along I-10 on her way back into the city, Sarah put on her Bluetooth and called her friend, Greta Wahl, a guard at Pima County Adult Detention. She verified that José García was in pre-sentencing detention there. He had been brought in shortly after five the afternoon before, been fingerprinted and strip-searched, and was far enough along in his initial processing to have a visitor.

'You might be the only one he gets, actually,' she said. 'You know, while they're in Admitting they can have all the phone calls they want, and this little crybaby called his mama and every one of his relatives, I think. And one by one they've all turned him down. Looks like he's used up his bonus points with his family.'

'If I get down there in the next hour, can I talk to him in an interview room?'

'Sure. You don't even have to reserve a time today. We're experiencing a lull in criminal activity.'

'Well, aren't we lucky?'

'Except for the ever-present threat of lay-

185

offs, yes.'

Traffic was rolling peacefully along I-10, ten miles over the speed limit with just the occasional speeder bombing through, keeping everybody's heart rate elevated. With a little time to spare, Sarah called Records and got the name of Joey's arresting officer. It was Artie Mendoza, whom she knew well. He was on patrol now, she learned, as she watched her exit coming up. She turned right at Silverlake Road and drove toward the tall flagpole that fronted the jail.

The big brick and glass building sprawled across its site – plenty of parking on both sides of the flagpole, neat sets of metal picnic tables and benches set into the pavers in front. It was not a venue anyone would choose for al-fresco dining, but the benches afford some comfort during the soul-sucking waits that families of law-breakers often have to endure.

Inside the lobby she stowed her Glock and taser in a locker, showed her badge to the officer who sat at the desk under the sign for professionals and signed for a visitor's room.

A family group stood in front of the sign that said, 'Public Visitation,' the adults showing photo ID, then waiting, awkward and self-conscious, while the officer there checked for wants and warrants. The pro-

186

cess was quiet and discreet, like a large doctor's office. The visit they'd come for would take place over a TV-and-telephone hookup, the family in one of the booths that rose in tiers behind the desk, the prisoner in a similar booth deep in the interior of the jail. It was cold comfort, Sarah always thought, telephone talk with a TV picture. But having no physical contact removed the need to search the visitors, or monitor the visit, so it speeded everything up and made more visits possible.

In fact, if you had to go to jail, she reflected, looking around at the shining floors and tidy booth space, Pima County was the place to go. A state-of-the-art holding facility with constant podular supervision, Pima kept the peace and maintained the quiet. No trash on the floor, no fights, no shouting. Sarah privately suspected the constant supervision might make her loony in a week, but it probably beat worrying about getting shanked in the shower.

Since Joey's rap sheet indicated a predilection for non-violent crimes, he would be chained for the trip to the visitation room but could be released inside the room if she so chose. She did, and the officer who unlocked the door said, 'Yeah, so far all he's showed us is a smart mouth, but remember where the buzzer is, Detective. These guys

187

can turn on you in a blink.'

I know, I know.

While she waited at the end of the aisle, by the turn where the stairs went up to the booths, she dialed Artie Mendoza. When he answered from his car and said he had time to talk, she asked him for details about the crime.

'He thought he was breaking into an empty house,' Artie said. 'He's been pulling that trick, you know, of lining up stones on the walk in front of a house where the owner's going to stumble over them or kick them away when he comes out to get the paper or whatever. If nobody moves the stones for a couple of days our burglar figures he's good to go in.

'The homeowner told me later, "I guess I should have noticed those stones out there, but I'm an artist, and when I'm working on a picture I get kind of spacey and vague." So ol' Joey García went in and loaded up some goodies, but the homeowner heard him. He used his head, too – he called nine-one-one and stayed in the john with the door locked till me and my backup had the culprit in chains.'

'So,' Sarah said, 'this one's going to be easy to prove.'

'Absolutely no problem.'

'And here he comes now. Good to talk to

you, Artie.'

The guard who brought Joey was quiet but careful, his face a mask of no emotion whatever. Joey was looking around, smiling a little, looking bright and relaxed. *Been here, done this,* seemed to be the message he was trying to send.

It's hard to look ominous in an orange jumpsuit. But even allowing for that, Sarah didn't think Joey García looked dangerous. Cocky and arrogant, and a little bit ... hyper, maybe? He might be coming down from some habitual drug use. If that was the case he was in trouble: Pima County would offer minimal help with withdrawal symptoms if they got very bad, but essentially it was cold turkey in here.

He was on the short side, with dark hair that curled low over his eyes. He'd had all his jewelry confiscated, of course, but she could see piercings for earrings in both ears and his arms carried colorful tattoos. She sensed some extra tension about him, too – an infantile need for attention. He brought an air of impending disruption into the room with him, like a wet dog getting ready to shake.

Always before an interview, a part of her brain replayed a few sentences from the course she took during her first year in Investigations. *Interrogation 101: it's always your game. Never let them maneuver you into playing their game.* She took a deep breath, envisioned dappled shade along Sonoita Creek. *You have all the power. Use it wisely.*

She liked to go in quietly and give the prisoner a few seconds to get used to her physical presence. Small, neat and harmless was how she figured they read her, and she wanted them to see her that way and relax a little before she talked. She sat down and opened her notebook, waited five seconds, and said, 'José García, good afternoon.'

'Call me Joey,' he said. 'Everybody does.' And it was all there, in the voice – the hubris, aggression and self-satisfaction. She might be Ms Kick-Ass Law, in charge of the doors and the locks, but he was in charge of his name and his image, which he clearly viewed as being supremely important.

'Your legal name is José, though, isn't it?'

'Who cares? Everybody that knows me calls me Joey. You come to get me out?'

'No, that's not what I do. Actually, I'm not here to talk about your case at all.'

He opened his hands in a gesture of futility and said, 'What're we doin' then?'

'Three people related to you have met violent deaths in three years, so I'm interviewing everybody in your family. You're just about last on my list. I went looking for you, and I found you in here.' *Not the whole truth,*

190

but close enough.

He frowned, squinted and shook his head. 'Listen, my family's got nothing to do with this, understand? I just got into a little misunderstanding with this wimpy little artist fella at his house on Claravista. And then the cop he called to the scene simply wouldn't listen to reason. Soon as my lawyer gets here we'll get this all straightened out and I'll be outta here.' He made a child's bye-bye wave.

'I don't think it's going to be quite that easy this time, José. You're charged with criminal trespass, willful destruction of property...'

'Will you stop calling me José? Ain't none of them charges going to matter one bit when my family gets here with the cash. That's all this system is, see? A big scam to take money away from people.'

'OK. But while you wait for that to happen, let's talk about your family. Were you surprised when Frank Martin got accused of stealing money from the credit union, or did you know about that all along?'

'Shee-it, lady, you gonna ask me how long I been beating my girlfriend, too? I ain't some peasant lettuce-picker, you know. I grew up right here in Tucson, speak English and everything.'

'I understand that, José. You knew Ed

191

Lacey for a long time, too, didn't you? All your life, I guess. Do you have any idea what happened to him? Why would he go off half-cocked like that and shoot at a cop?'

'No idea,' Joey said, 'except maybe he finally came to his senses and realized cops are a bunch of overbearing assholes, so he decided to get rid of one or two.'

'Ah.' She closed her notebook. 'Looks like you're not quite ready to have this conversation, José. I think it'll have to wait until you've enjoyed Pima County hospitality a while longer.'

'Better not wait very long, lady. Soon as my bail money gets here I'm history.'

'Better not count on that any time soon, José. Your mother told me she wasn't going to pay your bail, and she's made sure nobody in the family will bring you any money, either.'

'That so? I think I know my family quite a bit better than you do.' He made a good show of indifference but she saw a drop of sweat form beneath each eye. 'Anyway, they ain't the only friends I got.'

'Well, good luck with that. But if nobody shows up with cash you'll have to ask for a court-appointed lawyer, since you decided to plead not guilty – isn't that going to be a stretch, given that they caught you coming out of the back door with the goods? But since that's what you're going for, somebody should warn you that they're very busy, those pro-bono lawyers. There's always a waiting list.'

'You having fun telling stories over there?'

'Some. You might sit here for two or three weeks before your attorney gets around to seeing you, and then there's another long wait for a court date to defend yourself before a jury. Well, at least you're in here out of the weather, hmmm? The food's not great but they won't let you starve.'

'Is there an offer coming along behind this long sad story?'

'Not exactly an offer. More like a suggestion.'

'Oh, hey, a suggestion, that's exciting. Let's hear it.'

'Well, if you were very helpful and forthcoming, and told me everything you know about Frank Martin and Ed Lacey, I could certainly report that to the court. I might even be able to get that court date moved up a little. And it never hurts to have some friends around when the time comes to go before the jury.'

'What a fine speech. I got a suggestion too. Tell the police chief if he wants to get answers so bad he should send a juicier woman down here to visit me. I'd be friendlier to one who ain't a crip and got legs she's able to show off in a nice short skirt. Think you can remember that suggestion all the way back to the station, or are you already getting senile too, Ms Old Dyke Police Lady?'

Sarah stood up and picked up her notebook. 'Good luck with that attitude, Joey. You get ready to help yourself out a little, give us a call. Maybe if we're not too busy we might make time for you, but don't count on it.'

Sometimes they folded when they saw she was really going to leave. But this must have been the first time everybody in the family had refused to help him, and Joey was getting close to choking on his rage, so he was going to have to learn this lesson the hard way. She went out and told the officer at the desk the prisoner was ready to go back to his cell. Then she completed her uneven hike across the lobby, thump-click, thump-click.

She did have to admire the quick way Joey had noticed her mismatched feet below her neat gray slacks, and saved that detail till he wanted to taunt her. *Let's make a note*: *he may be very foolish but he's not stupid.*

The clouds were darker than before and it was breezing up. The 'possible rain' forecast was looking better every minute. In fact, was that a sprinkle? A few grudging drops darkened the asphalt as she thump-clicked her way to the car.

And her mangled toe joint was responding to the abrupt drop in air pressure by hurting enough to send little twinges through the pain meds. She got into the driver's seat, drank the rest of the water left in the bottle she'd brought along and looked at her watch. Quarter to five. She dug out her cell phone and dialed.

'Leo,' she said when he answered the phone, 'I'm just leaving Pima County. I can't make it back in time to do anything useful. Check me out, will you?'

'Sure, kid. Why wouldn't I be glad to risk my retirement by involving myself in corruption for a colleague as swell as you?'

'That's the spirit. If you get written up I'll speak at your defense.'

'Go away, Sarah.'

She drove home alternately wincing at the pain in her foot and crowing approval as the sprinkle grew into a steady rain. That was one thing about living in Tucson: sometimes just watching rainwater sluice down your windshield could put a fresh gloss on a hard-fought day.

TEN

Funny how fast you establish a routine, Sarah thought Friday morning, as she opened the door to Tia Louisa's housekeeping crew.

Sarah and her mother had agreed, when they moved in together, to pool money for a cleaning service, since Sarah's time off was always conditional and Aggie's stroke had bought her the Home Free pass from heavy housework. They'd established Friday as their day to take care of the house, so while the crew cleaned, Will caught a nap after his all-night shift, and Sarah dealt with the blizzard of laundry that cleaning created. Aggie, meanwhile, perched in a quiet spot, usually the patio, and made the week's lists of needed supplies. After Will got up, the crew would clean the master bedroom last and then vacuum their way down the hall and out of the house.

This week Aggie said, 'Why don't you let the laundry wait a few days? No use carrying sheets around on your sore foot.' But

196

Sarah, after a few experimental steps, found that her toe joint seemed to be settling back into its accustomed groove and she could walk a few steps pretty comfortably now on two matching sandals. She set a stool by the folding table, kept the machines whirring and got the cleaning crew to ferry linens back and forth while she washed and folded.

Brain-dead labor needing little mental effort, her mind grew restless and soon wandered off on its own. When Tia Louisa brought the second load of sheets and took away the first stacks of folded towels, Sarah asked her to fetch a tablet and ballpoint from the drawer in the kitchen. Soon she had an almost perfect split going: the lizard brain to fold sheets and towels, the sentient portions to ponder the questions that had begun to cluster around Frank Martin's suicide.

She emerged from this perfect circle once to find herself staring at the control panel on the washer while Tia Louisa asked her, looking a little worried, 'Whatsa matter? You forget how to run the machine?'

Sarah explained that she had been thinking about something else. Louisa nodded, plainly suspecting that her employer had gone a little lame in more than her foot. But when Sarah limped back to the table and added another note on the bottom line of her growing list, she was wearing a small, satisfied smile.

By Monday morning, Sarah's foot had given up the Northern Lights display and settled back to all-over ocher. It was still tender to the touch, though, so none of her shoes would work. Snow had fallen in downtown Tucson Saturday night and quickly melted Sunday morning, but the wind off the mountain had fangs and claws. She put on a pair of her thickest wool hiking socks and the Big Ugly Sandals, and stumped off to work.

She had an idea she wanted to peddle to her fellow detectives, and had made up her mind not to waste any more time thinking about her stupid foot. So as soon as she'd checked her email and answered the essentials, she sought out Cifuentes first in the clustered workstations. He was already bivouacked in his cubicle, almost buried in paper, and raised a cautionary hand as she entered.

'Careful, careful! Don't make a breeze.' He laid staplers, scotch tape and scissors across any mounds not already secured. 'There. I'm reading case histories, remember? If I tip over a pile and lose my place I'll kill myself.'

'How's it going?'

'Autopsy reports are filled with long, technical words. Leo loaned me this.' He held up a dictionary of medical terms.

'Yeah, I have one too. It helps, but I think they add new words every few months.'

'*Exactamente*. Thank God for Google. What do you need?'

'Have you ever found any mention in all those records of the original of Frank Martin's farewell note?' He blinked at her. 'The one you copied and frequently carry in your shirt pocket so you can read it to your admiring teammates. Where's that?'

'The one Frank wrote? I told you – I never had that.'

'What did you copy?'

'Um ... I'm trying to think. Wasn't it in all the newspaper stories when he shot himself?'

'I don't know, that's why I'm asking ... never mind. No, God, don't get up, you'll start an avalanche. I'll ask Leo.'

She walked around the connecting half-wall to his desk, where he was already looking up over half-glasses, saying, 'Ask Leo what?' He was pretty well walled in by stacks of paper himself. All the top pieces were warm, copies he had just made of newspaper stories from the months after Frank Martin's death.

'Have you found any mention yet of Frank Martin's suicide note?'

'Mention, are you kidding? It's quoted verbatim in about a dozen places. All the reporters got their rocks off repeating it. Talk about juicy – right out of Edgar Allen Poe.'

'Well, do any of them say where it was? Who found it?'

'Uhh ... let's see, do they?' He loosened his tie, stuck a judicious forefinger in a stack, read a sentence and thumbed down through a few pages. 'Here we go ... "The note he left ..." That's no help.' He tried another stack. 'Here's from the day he was charged. 'The message he sent his nephew, Tucson police sergeant—' He looked up. 'Ed made Sergeant?'

'While he was a trainer, sure. He lost his rank after the first reprimand.'

'Ah, yeah. OK, the message he sent blah blah, and then the quote again, "I didn't take the money but I won't" blah blah. Doesn't say how it was sent. Or where.' He squinted at her. 'Who cares? You do, obviously, but why?' His squint turned into a scowl. 'You're looking all games-afootish, Sherlock. What's the— Oh.' His forehead smoothed out, and he made a small motion in his chair, like nesting. 'All of a sudden I think I see why.'

'Yeah. We've been looking for a letter, on paper, in Frank Martin's handwriting—'

'So we could all nod wisely and say, "Well, it's right here in his handwriting, and it proves he felt so guilty he offed himself—"'

'But if the message was an email...' They stared at each other, breathing shallowly, thinking about the possibilities. *Anyone can send an email.* Finally Sarah said, 'This can't be the first time anybody ever brought up the question, can it? Remind me ... how long ago did he shoot himself?'

'Uh ... in March, it'll be three years.'

'I was just coming aboard in Homicide. Newly escaped from Auto Theft.'

He gave her his avuncular smile. 'You mean you didn't love all those meaningful conversations about VINs? For shame.' He thought. 'I was here. Dietz was here then, wasn't he?'

'For a few months, before he transferred to Narcotics. Yes. Oscar was still in Auto Theft, Jason was out on Patrol. Ray followed me on board, from Child Abuse. Who's that leave? Ollie. He came in three months after me.'

'So it's you and me – well, and Delaney.'

'And I don't remember us ever talking about the note. Why not?'

Leo raised his eyebrows and shrugged as high as he dared with so much paper around. 'Well, you know, it wasn't our case, at first. And "at first" lasted a long time – the embezzlement thing simmered along for most of the winter in fraud division, while the bank inspectors came in and pawed through records for weeks. Finally they arrested Frank Martin, of all people.'

'That's exactly how we all said it, wasn't it? Like that was his full name, Frank Martin Of All People.'

'Yes. The media people had fun with quotes like that for a week or so. Meantime, Martin was out on bail but also out of a job ... what happened next?'

'I'm trying to remember,' Sarah said. 'Seems to me we had some big case we were working on, multiple shootings...'

'That's right! That miserable drug war that erupted between the, what did we call them?'

'The Snakes and the Worms. God, talk about police arrogance.'

'No, it wasn't,' Leo said. 'We didn't feel we were superior to them. We felt they were inferior to everybody else on earth.'

'I guess that's right. How did they get those names, though?'

'One side was a gang called the South Side Serpents. Mostly cousins, and they had those disgusting tattoos, snakes crawling all over them, remember? The other side was just a bunch of street thugs that aspired to be as rotten as the Serpents, so we ended up calling them the Worms, and pretty soon the Serpents became Snakes because it was easier to say.'

'And even if they were mostly kids they were all full-blown outlaws, weren't they?'

'Every molecule of every person on both sides,' Leo pronounced solemnly, 'deserved heartfelt contempt, right down to their hair follicles and toenails.'

'Remember the baby-killer? He said, "Sure I killed his baby – he took my dope."'

'My phone kept ringing,' Leo remembered. 'Friends and neighbors saying, "We'll all be murdered in our beds if you don't lock every one of these animals up, yadda yadda, what's the world coming to ..." like it was my job to know *that*.'

'So when the quiet little comptroller killed himself after skimming a load of cash, it didn't make much of an impression, did it? On us, I mean. We all said, ho hum, what else is new? We had bigger fish to fry.'

'Yeah, teenage drug lords – sexy stuff.' Leo looked thoughtful. 'Still, though, Martin's wasn't a natural death, so there *was* an autopsy and somebody *was* assigned to that. Who?' He looked at his stacks. 'I haven't come to that part of the story. Stick your head around there and ask Oscar who attended that autopsy.'

Oscar said, without looking up, 'Funny name, Eisenstaat. You need the spelling?'

'No,' Sarah said. 'I knew him.'

'I heard him,' Leo said when she turned back. He shook his head, looking tired. 'Shit. If Harry got the case we'll probably never know how the note got delivered.'

They sat quiet a moment, remembering the frustration of that last year with Eisenstaat. Sarah had heard the acronym LOP, for Live On Payday, before she came to Homicide, but had learned its full implications working around Eisenstaat, while he did as close as possible to nothing, in that last year before he retired.

'We better be a little careful how we talk about this with Delaney,' Leo said. 'Harry was a major embarrassment for him.'

'Oh? I didn't know ... In what way?'

'He should have got him out of the department a year before he went. But Delaney came in as the fresh boss, and Harry was the classic passive-aggressive obstructionist; he used his long tenure to fake Delaney out of putting his foot down, at first. Then, after a few months, it was so close to Harry's retirement that it seemed awkward to make him change jobs so Delaney let it go. But it taught him a lesson; he's been a real hard-ass about not accepting anything but best efforts ever since. I think that's why he's so hard on...' his voice dropped and he inclined his head toward Oscar's workspace, '...you know who over there.'

Damn. I wish I'd known that.

A few minutes later, Delaney walked out of his office and into the cluster of desks where his detectives were rolling up sleeves and peering at computer screens. 'I've got a meeting at nine that's probably going to take the whole damn morning,' he said, 'and maybe suck up the whole rest of the week. So before it starts, let's have a quick huddle in my office.'

They all pulled chairs around his desk, settled their piles of notes and looked at him with impatient faces that said, *Yeah, what?* The second floor of 270 South Stone, on Monday morning, was no place to stand on ceremony.

'OK,' Delaney said, 'who's got any results?'

'Let me go first,' Jason said. 'I'll be quick.'

'Go,' Delaney said.

'It worked just the way you said it would,' Jason said, flashing his evil-wolf smile. 'Except I didn't have to take three turns at being a meathead. After the first bunch of merry-makers cleared out of the bar, the bartender came over to my table, gave me a friendly smile and said his name was Dewey.

I said how glad I was to know him and he said, "I feel the same way, and maybe if you tell me right now what you want, I might not call my goon squad to break your face.'"

'Why didn't you call for backup?'

'Didn't have to. I started to tell him who I was and what I wanted, but he pointed to my pocket recorder. Soon as I turned it off, he said, "I'll tell you what I know but I can't go on the record. And I won't testify. The boys I work for would kill me before I ever got to court." So he did.'

'Fair enough,' Delaney said. 'What's his story?'

'Damn near nothing. He did watch the whole thing as it happened, of course. I mean, second-floor window across the street? All he lacked was a Sky box and champagne. He told me the guy took so long getting his little piece of wire, he figured him for a decoy. Thought maybe a bunch of vets were playing a game they'd learned in Iraq, going to stream out of one of these empty buildings and blow away however many cops showed up. But no, the thief just tried to do the job by himself and got capped.

'Then I grilled ol' Dewey about the buying and selling, said all those bad-cop things you told me to say. He just laughed at me and said, "You kidding? This ain't no amateur hour you walked into here, Officer, no offense. We're not going to get caught dealing with two-bit punks like that bozo, can't even shoot straight enough to get his man when he had the jump on him." He said, "I never saw that screw-up before that day, and I hope you'll do me a favor and never ask me to talk about him again."'

'You believe him?'

'Absolutely. The guy was scared, but not of me. I think the next time we look at that place it's gonna be locked up and empty.'

'All right.' Delaney looked around, nodding. 'That pretty much confirms what we have been thinking about the Ed Lacey shooting, doesn't it? Very nice police work there, Jason.'

'Thanks,' Jason said. 'Please consider me your go-to guy for bar-hopping jobs from now on.'

'Don't spoil it, now,' Delaney said. 'Anybody else have any cute stories? If not let's back up to the first suicide. Frank Martin was living alone at the time, wasn't he?'

'Yes,' Leo said. 'Ed and Angela were in their own house by then.'

'And there was no girlfriend? Never a woman in his life after his wife died?'

'No mention of one, that I found. And I found a lot.' Leo held up his floppy stack of newspaper copies. 'His nephew lived with him from young boyhood on, and he seems to have devoted himself to that. Well, and all those favors he did for people – there's a lot in all these reports about that.'

'Uh-huh.' Delaney brooded briefly. 'Kind of makes you wish you had a psychologist on call, doesn't it?' He looked around the circle of Monday morning faces, all of them taut with the desire to come up with something – anything. 'I mean, a man's been married several years, his wife dies in childbirth and he, what, stays faithful to her memory forever after?'

'Sounds pretty Victorian, when you put it like that,' Leo said.

'Doesn't it? I haven't had time to review any of those newspaper reports, so remind me, he put up his own bail?'

'Yes.'

'And he stayed in his own house, I suppose, waiting for a court date?'

'Yes. He made a date to talk to an attorney, but he didn't show up for the appointment. When the lawyer inquired, a patrolman went to his house and found him missing. His car was gone too, so Dispatch put out a Need to Locate, and a couple of hours later the car was found parked in the lot in front of the Sears store in the Tucson Mall. Frank was in it, sitting behind the wheel. He'd been dead for at least a couple

208

of hours, the ME said. But you know how those estimates go. "Between two and ten hours" was his actual estimate.'

'What killed him? Oscar?'

'One shot in the ear.' Oscar, anxious to show his mastery of the files, didn't even glance at his notes.

'Which ear?'

'The left one. The gun was between his legs on the seat, and his left hand was resting near it, on top of his left thigh.'

'Make and model of the weapon?'

'A .22 caliber Smith & Wesson pistol. The 22A Sport Series, semi-auto, four-inch barrel. Equipped with a ten-round magazine, holds .22 caliber long rifle rimfire cartridges. Had eight rounds left in the magazine, one in the chamber. When tested, it showed residue from recent firing.'

'Was he left-handed?'

'Yes, he was.'

'One bullet recovered from the body?'

'Yes. A .22 caliber slug was found lodged against his skull just above his right eye. It showed lands and grooves consistent with having been fired by the gun on the seat.'

'So all the forensics lined up just right?'

'Yes, they did.'

'It looked like a suicide, and all the evidence supported that conclusion?'

'Yes.'

'And the empty casing was found in the car?'

'By his left foot, yes.'

'It's funny I remember so little about it. Who'd we send from here to that autopsy?'

For the first time, Cifuentes consulted his notes. He read off the name, 'Harold C. Eisenstaat,' with a little hesitation about the pronunciation of the last syllable. Sarah saw Delaney's mouth clamp down in a grim line.

'Any chance we got lucky and found a record of purchase of the weapon, from an authorized dealer?'

'Not in anything I read,' Leo said.

'I didn't find anything on it either,' Oscar said.

Sarah said, 'We touched on it in our interview with Angela, remember?' and looked at Oscar intently. She had read through her notes again over the weekend.

'Oh, ah, yes, that's right,' Oscar said. 'We asked her if she knew Frank Martin had a gun and she said no. And she couldn't remember him ever talking about guns with Ed – he wasn't a hobby shooter or anything like that. So Sarah asked her...' Having abandoned his pretense of having done the whole interview himself, Oscar's face was wrinkled fiercely in the effort to remember. 'Sarah said, "Do you think he bought a gun just to shoot himself?" And she said, let me think, it was something sardonic...'

'She said, "Or borrowed it," Sarah said. 'She claimed that Frank was "like most accountants, always very careful with a dollar."'

'Anybody else suggest Frank was a miser? Sarah?'

'Not a miser. Cecelia mentioned that he was very frugal, always bought two-year-old cars and kept them for eight or nine years. Oh, and Luz said something about carrying his own lunch from home. But they said it in a praising way, as though it was kind of quaint.'

'And everybody in the family stressed his generosity to Ed,' Oscar said.

'Isn't it wonderful how the truth keeps changing shape? Was there a will? Who got what?'

'Frank left his house to Ed,' Leo said. 'The rest of his estate was divided among the surviving Garcías. Not much – no big piles of money, for sure.'

'Did Ed leave a will?'

'He died intestate, but it didn't really matter – he left almost nothing. He'd sold Frank's house and used the money to support himself and his drug habit.'

'So we've got one suicide disguised as a burglary shootout, and one declared suicide we're beginning to have doubts about. What about the third one? Any strong opinions about Angela?'

'Marjorie Springer sounds like she might have some,' Sarah said, 'but I haven't had a chance to interview her yet.'

'Who?'

'Angela's employer and her landlady. Oh, and Luz – Ed Lacey's mother – said she didn't believe Angela was suicidal.'

'OK. Who stands to gain by her death?'

'She left behind a recently-made will in favor of Marjorie,' Ollie said. 'But besides her house, which was mortgaged for just about current market value, she had only a small savings account, her trunk and her car. Anybody find anything of value in the items from the trunk?'

All around the desk, detectives shook their heads. 'Evidence of good taste,' Leo said, 'but not much value.'

'Angela mentioned that she'd been doing "a little research in the evenings,"' Sarah said. 'That's how she learned that Ed's father and grandfather were both addicted to drugs and alcohol.'

'So?'

'So what if we think about it the other way around? What if she found something? Maybe we should quit looking for what somebody stood to gain, and think about what somebody has to lose?'

'Hey, now,' Jason said, and Delaney turned his pop-eyed stare on her – in fact, everybody in the room was looking at Sarah now.

'Just a thought.' She made a fending-off gesture. 'I don't, you know, *know anything*.'

'I like the thought, though,' Delaney said. 'Let's pursue it. What might somebody have to lose? Let's make a list.'

'The truth about something,' Jason said.

'Well, of course. But what?'

'Where the gun came from,' Ray said.

'That's good.' Delaney started a list.

'The money,' Leo said. 'Nobody's ever found the money. Maybe somebody's getting ready to use it.'

'That's even better,' Delaney said. 'Gold star, that one.'

'Who has a taser handy?' Ollie said.

'Anybody who wants one,' Delaney said. 'This is Arizona. Easy to buy a taser similar to the ones we use.'

'What Frank Martin was so sorry about?' Oscar said.

Delaney looked at him, surprised. Oscar hardly ever volunteered anything in meetings. Delaney said, 'What? Say that again.'

'In the farewell letter he left, right at the end, he says...' Oscar had that same slip of paper out of that breast pocket again – he really was carrying it around with him, 'At the end he says, "Eddie, I'm sorry for everything. I've loved you all your life – please try to forgive me."'

'Isn't he apologizing for stealing the money?'

'Why would he need to apologize to Ed for that? It was the credit union that got hurt. And the depositors. Ed didn't lose anything.'

'And while we're on the subject of the message,' Sarah said, and turned to Leo, 'let's ask him about our idea.'

'Go ahead,' Leo said.

Delaney said, 'What now?'

'Well, you know, we've never found the letter.'

'I know. I thought we'd find it in the trunk, but no, huh?'

They all shook their heads.

'So over the weekend I started to think, what if it wasn't a letter? And this morning I asked Leo, any chance it was an email?'

'Sarah, surely that must have been settled three years ago.'

'Well, see,' Leo carefully scrutinized the corner of the desk, 'we thought maybe Eisenstaat might not have, you know, *thought to check*.'

'Uh-huh,' Delaney said. 'That does sound entirely possible, doesn't it?'

'So I was just going to ask you, shall we

ask Tracy to look for it on the laptop, as long as he's going through it anyway—'

Delaney looked at Ollie. 'You gave the laptop to Tracy? The one I signed out to you?'

Ollie said, 'Oops. I'm afraid I did. Was I supposed to make a note on the whiteboard or something?'

Delaney, looking ready to eat glass, said, 'Might have been a good idea, don't you think? So the system would work the way I set it up and we'd all know where everything is?' He collected himself and said, 'Sarah, will you find out if Tracy's here? And get him over here if he's in the building.'

Sarah stepped outside and around the corner to the support staff bullpen where the head stenographer sat talking on two phones and pulling notes out of a pile to hand to an aide. When she got to something resembling a pause, Sarah said, 'Elsie, is Tracy working this morning?'

'Can't you tell by the quiet that he isn't?'

'Oh dear. Back in school, huh? I thought Christmas vacation...'

'No, he was on the schedule but he called in sick. Woke up with a cough, could be flu or valley fever. I told him not to come near us till he'd seen a doctor.' Elsie frowned. 'You really want the little nutcase?'

'I need to ask him a question, yes.'

215

'Well, here, I'll give you his home phone.' Elsie kept neat records; she found it right away. 'Be careful, if he coughs he'll break your eardrum.'

Tracy wasn't coughing when he answered the phone, but he wasn't home, either.

'I'm waiting at the clinic where I go to get my allergies tested. I told the Dragon Lady I get this allergy every year – something pollinates after a winter rain. But she's sure I've turned into Typhoid Mary so I can't come back to work until I get a slip from my doctor. I offered to take the laptop home and finish the job I was doing for you and Leo, but Our Lady of Perpetual Dread was sure that would be a hanging offense, so—'

'No, Tracy, she's right. I'm very glad you didn't do that. But did you work on it on Friday?'

'No. The Dragon Lady came up with some emergency data entry for me to do.'

'Well, soon as you get back will you go to Oscar or Leo or me – whoever's handy when you get here – and ask for a copy of the Frank Martin note ... you got that? ... Martin, yes. And see if you can find any trace of it on the laptop.'

'It's an email? And you think it was sent from the laptop?'

'Hmm, no, I think it came in, not out. Can you do that?'

'Dear lady, surely by now you've noticed that Genius Geek rarely fails?'

'And the laptop – where is it?'

'Back in the trunk. Isn't that what you wanted?'

'Ah, GG, sometimes you're good and other times you're just outstanding.'

'Thanks. I do like it when people notice.'

She went back and told Delaney, 'The laptop's back in the trunk and Tracy's going to look for the message when he gets back. He's ill today.'

'I've got a meeting in ten minutes. He's going to find it if it's there?'

'Yes.'

'Good. Let's try a quick re-boot, here. In the first death, the big question that remains is, where's the money? Leo, make that your problem. Start from the premise that you're Frank and you just took the money. Now answer the obvious questions. Why? You lived all these years without that money – why do you need it now? Then, how? I'm going to give you this card from the forensic accountants we used on the Barrie case. Get them to explain to you exactly how he stole it. Finally, where? He had to put it some-where.'

'Damn funny the bank examiners couldn't find it,' Leo said.

'Well, right. But it was cash money. Money

217

takes up space and is heavy – if he took it, where did he put it? And in that connection, Jason?'

'Mmm?'

'I want you to find out who got Frank's car. Did the family sell it or keep it? Be very nice if they still have it, hmm? You see where I'm going with this?'

'No.'

'The money went somewhere. If it was actual green money, it probably didn't travel away in a backpack being carried by a hiker, do you think?'

'Ah. So Frank's car...' Jason patted his shaved head, his habit when he was deep in thought. 'Where is it, though?'

Leo said, 'Frank's house went to Ed, and everything else to the rest of the family. It's hard to say who got what.'

Delaney said, 'You'll just have to ask. Ray, go after Frank's suicide weapon. Dig into that case file – Oscar can help you. Find out how much we learned about the weapon and what we did with it. Talk to Banjo, see how far he went with it. Check all the usual databases – well, you know. Get me something on that gun. I'm very disappointed we know so little.

'Ollie, I want you to go back to Angela's autopsy. Ambiguous just won't cut it. I want more information about that bruise on the back of the head.

'Oscar, I want you to canvass the people in that building and in the neighborhood, find anybody who was familiar with her movements, anything they noticed different about the last day or week. Anything she said that might indicate she was afraid or suspicious.'

Sarah said, 'Why did she get her hair cut?'

'What?' Looking at his watch, getting ready to leave, Delaney appeared to be dumbfounded by the question.

'I noticed it when we found her and then forgot. There's so much to ... But why would she get a fresh haircut if she was thinking of killing herself?'

'God, I don't ... Add it to the list, I guess. Are you getting anything useful from the family members?'

'Kind of, but they're not all saying the same things ... except when it comes to Frank being a do-gooder. That's unanimous.'

'Oscar made an interesting observation about that farewell letter. What was Frank so sorry about? I think you should print a copy of your own and go talk to everybody you can find who knew Frank well enough to have an opinion. Why would he feel he needed to apologize to Ed? See if you can find anybody who ever asked Ed about it and what he said.'

Sarah said, 'Also, I need to talk to the employer, Marjorie Springer, about Angela – I can do that today.'

'Fine. Ask her about the haircut – did they talk about it? Women talk about hair, don't they?'

'Sometimes. And soon I'd like to bring Joey in here and get him on the record.'

'Oh? Isn't he just a petty thief? What do you expect to get from him?'

'I'd like to find out what he was going after when he got caught. And I wish you could see one of his sudden bursts of anger. His family keeps saying he only does non-violent crimes, and they all treat it like it's just a phase he'll grow out of, almost a joke. But I think he's way past pranks – to me he seems about ready to explode.'

'Well ... when we get to it, you can ask and I'll watch. But right now I've got all these meetings I can't get out of.'

'I know. It's not a problem,' Sarah said. 'We've got enough digging ahead of us to keep us busy for weeks.'

'This is the homicide department, remember?' Delaney said. 'We don't get weeks.'

'I know. We're digging as fast as we can.'

ELEVEN

Waiting for Marjorie Springer in the lobby, Sarah went over her list of questions again. Angela had worked for this employer three times at least – what was that all about? She seemed to be able to hold better jobs, and her descriptions of working conditions in the used rag business sounded pretty grim. But something about this person, or the business she ran, seemed to keep pulling her back.

Marjorie had sounded cordial enough on the phone. In case she was not forthcoming, Sarah wondered where the pressure points were – licenses and taxes – was she up to date with her taxes? *I should have looked it up.* She hated the ham-handed end of interrogation, but sometimes, if you had to ... *I should know more about this woman.* At the last minute she added one last question, sideways along the margin of the page, about the evening investigations Angela had mentioned once. Something about Lacey DNA, but had she found something more?

Knowing only her voice, Sarah had expected the wrinkled face of a heavy smoker, with perhaps a drinker's rueful expression as well. But Marjorie strode into the lobby at 270 South Stone looking sturdy and fit. Sarah was waiting for her, led her to the elevator and rode up with her guest.

From the lack of frown lines, Sarah guessed that Marjorie was usually cheerful too, but today she looked pretty serious. Her voice, she explained, was due to an industrial hazard she couldn't fix: hustling old clothes raises a lot of lint.

'Over the years I've developed an allergy. I sound a little better when I remember to take my pills. Thanks for talking to me, anyway,' she said. 'Some people get scared off because I sound like a thug.'

'Oh, you sound a lot better than most of the people I talk to,' Sarah said. 'And if you tell me everything you know about Angela Lacey I won't care how you sound while you say it.'

'Believe me, I'll be happy to do that. I feel so bad about Angela – if there's any way I can help you find her killer, I'm grateful for the chance.'

'Uh ... you know, Marjorie, so far we haven't proved it wasn't suicide.'

'Oh? Well, I suppose you have to do that for the lawyers, don't you? But you don't

222

need to bother for me.'

'Oh? You know something about that day that I don't?'

'No, but I know Angela. If she was the kind to give up on life, she's had plenty of reasons to do it before now. But she never did because she wasn't a quitter. She came from tough, strong people who'd been through hell in Europe and survived to get to America, and that's what she was, too – a survivor.'

'You've known her a long time?'

'All her life.'

'Oh, is that so? Excuse me, in that case I have a colleague here who I think ought to meet you. He's been searching for details about her life ... he'll be so glad to hear what you have to say.'

She called Ollie, who came in smiling all over his amiable freckled face, pulling his own chair. He introduced himself, at the top of his benign cop game. In two minutes he had established himself as a Friend of Marjorie.

'We sure appreciate your coming in here to tell us Angela's story,' he said. 'You're really a lifelong friend? Was the long life here in Tucson?'

'For Angela and me, yes. Our grandparents all came from Poland. After they met at the Polish church in Milwaukee they became good friends.'

'Your names don't sound...'

'They changed them – nobody could pronounce their names and they had trouble getting jobs, so Zboynevicz turned into Springer and Golbiewski got to be Goodman.'

'Did you know your grandparents?'

'They were around when I was little. I was the daughter of their oldest son, the first grandchild. I was a little princess for the first couple of years, till the others started coming along. Angela was twelve years younger. She was only two years old when her parents left her with her grandparents one Friday night, just to go to the movies, and got killed in a car accident on the way home. Both of them wiped out in one careless minute.'

Preparing for this interview, Sarah had thought about the picture she'd found in Angela's apartment, nested in underwear in a drawer. She had checked it out of Evidence, and showed it to Marjorie now, asking, 'Are these Angela's grandparents?'

'Oh, for heaven's sake, yes, that's Anna and Boris. How'd you get this?'

'It was in the drawer in her bedroom.'

'Imagine her keeping that funny old picture. Boris was so proud that he got accepted in the Army. He never got sent to

Vietnam, though, just served in a support group at Fort Huachuca. They were still living in Milwaukee when he went in the Army, but when he got out he talked Anna into moving out here to Arizona. Said he liked the desert and he knew he could get a job in a copper mine. After they got settled they persuaded my grandparents to come for a visit, and I guess they liked it too. By the time I can remember much, we all lived here in Tucson.

'Anna and Boris were a lot older than that – a whole generation had grown up by the time they got stuck with Angela. Not that they ever said it like that. They loved her and did the best they could with raising her. But they were pretty old-country, you know. Anna never learned much English so Boris spoke Polish to her at home and that's all Angela spoke till she went to school. She had to work hard in school to catch up, and some kids made fun of her accent.'

'I thought I heard something ... just on a few words,' Sarah said.

'Yes. She got rid of most of it – we all did. She was an A student in high school and won a small scholarship to Pima College. She worked in a Kmart and later in a restaurant to support herself while she studied. I was married by then, had two babies. Angela would come to see me and say, "I'm glad you're happy, but I want to get some more schooling and have a career."

'She was only a few courses from her associates' degree when she went on a date with a boy she met at school. He said he was taking her to a movie, but instead he parked the car in an empty lot and raped her. Afterwards he said, "You know very well you led me on, so don't try to complain."

'My husband and I were opening this store at that time – we were crazy busy. So I didn't notice that I hadn't seen her for some time. When I did I knew right away that something had happened. She looked ... like somebody had turned her lights out. I said, "Tell me what's wrong." She didn't want to tell me, but she did, too, you know what I mean? Needed to tell somebody in the worst way.

'The way she looked, I thought she must be pregnant and having morning sickness, but she said no, she'd just lost her appetite. She had been raised very strictly by elderly Catholics, and this rotten boy had treated her with contempt and transferred his guilt to her. She couldn't handle it – her self-respect was gone.

'It was the craziest day and night! I had to talk and talk to her, to get her to see it wasn't her fault. She was too distracted to study, so she'd flunked the course she was taking, and that didn't help. She helped me feed the kids and put them to bed and then we talked almost all night. My husband got outraged, kept saying, "You need your sleep." He was used to having all my attention ... that's another story.'

Ollie smiled cordially and said, 'Husbands are hell, aren't they?'

'Can be, yes. I'm single now and I miss him sometimes. But I've got the store so I don't have much time to pine – enough said about that.' She waved away husbands and pining with a motion like shooing flies. 'Angela dropped out of school for a while and came to work for me in the store.'

'I noticed,' Ollie said. 'She's worked for you three times, right?'

'Yes, every time her life's gone to hell she's come back to me for a while. Something about heaving used clothing around, doing that uncomplicated job, seemed to help her get her head straight. When she was healed up enough, she'd get a better job and try again to build a decent life.'

'What brought her back the second time? That was about eight years ago, wasn't it?'

'Or nine. Yes. She was married for a short time in between, to a real-estate salesman. Moved to Phoenix. There was a housing boom, remember?'

'Very well,' Ollie said. 'I was flipping

houses and making a killing for a while. Then the bubble burst and I gave the last one back to the bank. Lost almost everything I'd made.'

'Then you did better than most. I bet you'll think harder the next time somebody offers to help you get rich quick.'

Ollie raised his hand as if testifying and said, 'My wife has promised to kill me if I even think about it.'

'Good for her. Angela's husband was flipping houses too, in between all those easy sales. When the market went south, he consoled himself with booze. And when he got drunk enough, he took his disappointment out on her. The second time he beat her black and blue, she came back to me and my store. I was single by then and I always had an opening. Still do. I can't pay enough to keep anybody happy.'

'So the second time,' Ollie said. 'We're getting closer to when she met Ed Lacey, right? How did that happen?'

'She started volunteering at the food bank in town. I said, "Jeez, Angie, that's no place to go to cheer up." But she said, "I don't feel like such a failure when I'm helping somebody out." I was always trying to make her see she wasn't the one doing the failing. But she came to feel she had a fatal flaw that made her susceptible to exploiters.'

Well, she did go dancing with Oscar Cifuentes and end up on the couch with his gloves.

'But then she began to notice this other volunteer,' Marjorie said. 'He came with his uncle the first time, but then came several times by himself. Once he stopped by to check on something, while he was on patrol, in uniform. The next day at the store she said, "It was the most amazing thing, I could hardly believe my eyes!" I asked her, "What's so amazing about somebody being a cop?" and she said, "Oh, I always think of them as very tough guys. But you should see how he treats the needy people. I think he's the kindest, gentlest man I've ever met."

'I said, "Angela, be careful," because she was looking, you know, all misty. But then he asked her out, and after the very first date it was obvious that there was no use telling either one of them to slow down. Ed Lacey was even mistier than she was – he was over the moon.'

'So you met him before they were married?'

'Oh, yes. He came in the store to ask ... some little detail – just an excuse to see her, I thought. You know how people get?' Ollie and Sarah both nodded, smiling inanely. 'Yeah, right. Love.' Marjorie shook her head. 'We never really learn, do we? And I must admit, he did look nice in that uniform.'

Marjorie rested her chin in her hand and thought a minute.

'For several years after they married, I thought luck had finally landed in the right place. Those two people just seemed to suit each other right down to the ground. Even though they lived with his uncle at first, which seemed like a great way to kill any romance, you only had to look at them to see they were happy.'

'I wondered about that,' Sarah said. 'Cops may not get rich, but they make a living. Why couldn't Ed and Angela afford a place of their own?'

'Well, Angela didn't have any money because she'd been working for me!' Marjorie shook her head and laughed. 'Poverty City, that's my address. To make my rent and have anything left, I have to squeeze everybody else. And it turned out Ed didn't have anything saved because that big, warm family that was always boasting about how kind they had all been to Frank Martin and little Eddie – turned out they were very good at getting the charity to run the other way. Angela told me, "Every time we get a little ahead, one of them has a crisis and Ed and Frank run to the rescue. I have to get it stopped."

'And to my surprise she actually did it.

Angela the victim turned into Angela the Rottweiler on behalf of Ed Lacey. The next time Cecelia's hot water heater went on the fritz, Angela said, "Sorry, we don't have a nickel to spare this month."

'She put her foot down about Joey's habit of stopping by to raid the refrigerator, too. When she found him sitting in her kitchen with a double-decker sandwich and a beer, she pushed him out the door, took the plate away and made him give her the key he'd begged off Ed. Can you imagine, he actually had a key to her house. He'd been spending time there, eating and watching TV. She'd been wondering about missing food and stains on the couch. She told Joey, "I catch you in my house again I'll have you picked up for home invasion, and with your record you'll spend a good long time in jail."

'He ran and cried to Cecelia, who called Chico. Chico called Ed and said, "Eddie, now, remember whose boy you are; after all, we all raised you, not just Frank." Angela called him back and said, "He's my boy now, get off his back." She stood firm against the whole clan. And although Ed wavered at first, in the end he supported her, because for the first time ever he had a life of his own and he loved it.'

'What went wrong?' Ollie asked her. 'Was it Frank's arrest?'

'Yes. Ed felt so *obligated* to fix it. He kept saying, "He rescued me when I was little, now I gotta help him, I owe it." He did what he could, hired an attorney, talked to everybody who would listen. But then Frank killed himself. He might as well have shot Ed first – it might have been better for everybody if he had. But no, he shot himself and left that stupid note.'

'Ah, yes, the note,' Sarah said. 'Where is it, do you know?'

'You mean you don't have it?'

'No, we can't find it. Did Angela keep a stash of anything at the store? Or at your house?'

'I live above the store. No, Angela never left anything with me. I think she had a trunk in storage somewhere.'

'We have that, but there's no note. No correspondence of any kind, by the way. Didn't Angela have any family?'

'Cousins back in Poland, but they don't read or write English, and I think by now Angela probably had lost most of her Polish. I know I have. I think that was part of why she and Ed were so close – each of them was all the other had.'

'Except Uncle Frank.'

'Yes. But Frank was so ... I don't know ... odd.'

'In what way?'

Marjorie shrugged, turned her hands over in a helpless gesture and sighed. Finally she said, 'I didn't know him well, so maybe I missed something. But what I knew ... He was shy, I guess. Almost ... furtive. Like a little scared rabbit. Angela said she believed Frank, after his wife and baby died, felt too guilty to have anything in his life but work until he adopted Ed. In a sense, she said, they saved each other.'

'But you know,' Ollie said, 'Ed Lacey was a successful police officer for many years. And not to boast or anything, but you don't keep a job in law enforcement by being a wuss.'

'I know. Angela knew it too, and she was so proud to be married to a man who could be as gentle as Ed was at the food bank, and yet be tough enough to be a patrolman in Tucson. She said he was living proof that if you were willing to work hard enough you could make yourself into the person you wanted to be.'

'Wow,' Ollie said. 'Wouldn't I like to get praise like that from my wife.'

'Maybe you do and you just don't listen,' Marjorie said, and got one of Ollie's trademark ironic smiles in reply. 'When Ed passed all his tests to teach at the academy, she was *so happy* for him. They both saw it as the validation of what he had achieved.'

'I guess I didn't see any of that when we talked,' Sarah said. 'She seemed kind of ... detached and cold.'

'She was walking wounded when you saw her. She had really been sure that this time she had something so solid nothing could wreck it. And then something did.'

'She must have been very angry.'

'She was furious at the credit union, yes. Not at Ed. She said what happened to him with the alcohol and drugs was mostly owing to his extreme naiveté. He'd never tried drugs or drinking or gone around with the boys who did. And being a policeman, he thought he was pretty sophisticated. Well, he was – about other people's faults. But he didn't realize how vulnerable *he* was. By the time he knew, he was hooked.'

'So in substance,' Sarah said, 'you still don't think she killed herself.'

'I feel very certain she didn't. She was grieving for Ed, of course. But defending him the way she had earlier had given her a new sense of what she could become. As soon as she healed up a little and figured out her next moves, I was looking for her to get a better job and build her life back, stronger than ever.'

'Was her new haircut a first step, do you think?'

'Maybe. She really surprised me – just

showed up one day with a fresh do and when I told her it looked great she said it was all part of the plan.' Marjorie put her two hands together in a supplication pose. 'It's a rotten shame that someone robbed her of the rest of that plan. Please tell me you'll find the terrible person who did it.'

'We intend to try very hard,' Sarah said.

'It's what we do,' Ollie said.

'Then blessings on you,' Marjorie said, and Ollie gave her his best Alfred E. Neuman gap-toothed smile. The two of them traded cards and she got up, getting ready to leave. Sarah, watching them smile and shake hands, reflected gloomily that interesting conversation and new friendships were all very well, but this one hadn't moved them much closer to the answers she was after. But as Marjorie turned to say goodbye she remembered the question she'd written crosswise on the side of her list, and said, 'One more thing.'

'Yes?'

'Did Angela ever mention anything to you about doing research, looking up things about Ed's family, anything like that?'

'Oh ... yes, I meant to tell you about that. She found his father and grandfather – she tell you that?'

'Yes.'

'Well, a couple of months ago she saw an

235

item in the paper that got her all excited. She brought me the clipping to show me. Something about a burglary in which several guns were stolen, and the homeowner told a reporter, "I guess I should have noticed those stones lined up in my driveway. But I'm making all the gowns for my daughter's wedding; it's a big job and I've been so fixated on it that I sort of blurred out everything else."'

Stones. My God.

'Angela said she bet that was Joey's work. She remembered while she was still married she was out with Ed one day when he said he needed to stop at Chico's house for a minute – something he needed to ask him. She stayed in the car while he went in and talked to Chico, and Joey was there outside the house, in the back-yard with one of his friends. Not knowing she was sitting there at the curb, a few feet away, he was boasting about how much money he'd just made selling handguns. The other man asked him, "How much did you pay for them?" and Joey kind of hummed a certain way and they both laughed. But the friend said, "Joey, be careful, man, you get caught stealing guns you'll go away a long time." And the way Angela remembered it, Joey told his friend he was never going to get caught on a home invasion because he had this trick he did with river stones, the kind everybody's got in the yard. He said he lined up four or five on the front sidewalk of houses he thought looked empty, and if nobody moved them out of the way after a couple of days he knew for sure the occupant was away from home.

'I told her, "Angela, you better leave the investigating to the cops. Nobody's found the money yet, so there could be a killer out there."' Marjorie turned on Sarah the tough, measuring look she normally used for gently used blouses. 'You think maybe she found something?'

'Maybe. This is just me, now, don't quote me. Wouldn't she tell you if she did?'

'Probably. Unless she thought it was too dangerous for me to know.'

For the hell of it, and because she had seen Marjorie's name on Delaney's list of suspects, she took her car information. Marjorie's Chevrolet was eight years old and she'd owned it for six. She gave Sarah all her information willingly, saying she was glad to see them checking everything.

'Don't give up,' Marjorie said.

'Never fear,' Sarah said. 'We're just getting started,'

Sarah's mood brightened considerably when she learned that prescription medicine had worked its promised magic – if two long, frustrating days could be described as magical. Tracy Scott had stopped coughing and been allowed to return to work. He came in carrying a note on his doctor's prescription pad, like a grade-schooler's note from his mother.

In his usual spot behind the file cabinet, she found him tapping away on the laptop, which was now properly signed out to him. He looked up briefly and said, 'Be patient. It's a jungle in here.'

Sarah said, 'If you succeed in finding it you'll have a whole department calling you a miracle worker. The rest of us, the harder we work on this case, the deeper we dig the hole.'

Tracy said, 'I can commiserate or be brilliant – which do you want?'

'Never mind,' she said coldly. 'If you want me, you can come and find me.'

But Ray found her first. He was striding off the elevator with a smile that lit the whole second floor. 'I got the skinny on the gun, kid,' he said. 'Let's go find all the guys.'

Jason and Oscar were off the floor, but the others clustered around him, hot for good news, or at least a break in the routine.

'Banjo did his job, back then, when the suicide investigation was going on. Harry just neglected to add it to the report. What ailed that guy, anyway?'

'Short-timer sickness,' Leo said. 'What about the gun?'

'Banjo sent the number to the manufacturer, got back the report. The 22A Sport Series Smith & Wesson was sold to a dealer in Cincinnati. It was purchased there, during a summer vacation trip, by Tucson citizen Lincoln C. Barnhardt. He went to see his dear old mother and bought the pistol while he was there, because, he says, it's a well-known fact that these bigger cities farther east have better buys. Yessir. The best weapons at the lowest prices. How's that for generalizing freely?'

'Come on, Ray, he brought the .22 home and then what?'

'His house was burgled that November. He had quite a nice little collection of firearms in a locked case. Case was shattered and the guns were gone.'

'Banjo did the search that ID'd the weapon?'

'Yes. Had all the information right there in his files, but Harry never put it in the case file.'

'OK,' Leo said. 'So now all we need to do is answer the big question. What the devil was Frank Martin doing with a stolen gun?'

'Maybe he never did anything with it,' Sarah said. 'Maybe that was somebody else.'

'I know you want to believe that,' Leo said,

'but let's stick with what we can prove today. Where did Jason go?'

'He was fussing about how to find out who got Frank's car, and I suggested he ask Chico. He's friendlier than Cecelia or Pilar, and he would surely remember the negotiations.'

'Which must have been a pip,' Leo said.

'Aren't you glad you weren't there? And since Oscar had about decided to talk to Chico about the famous farewell note, they went off together to Chico's house. Listen, Leo, I need to tell you what I just heard from Marjorie Springer.'

'Which of course I want to hear. May I just answer my phone first?'

'Of course. When did a mere detective ever take precedence over a telephone?' She walked toward her workspace, deciding to type up the interview with Marjorie while the facts were fresh. Not that it was probably as important as it had seemed when she first heard it, she thought, unloading her gear. The more she thought about it, every little lock-picking sap in town probably used the river stone trick sooner or later. Besides, her own phone was ringing.

'Detective,' the bells in Teresa García's voice seemed a little muted today, 'I hope I have not called at a bad time?'

'Not at all,' Sarah said, stifling the little

240

buzz in her brain saying *not now*, *not now*. 'You must call me whenever you have something to say.'

'Well ... I have just spoken to my daughter, Cecelia, and' – she cleared her throat, an anxious sound – 'she has spoken to Joey, I guess, by phone, and she urged me to consider that he is suffering very much in that jail.'

'Believe me, Teresa, he may be discontented but he's not suffering. He's in one of the safest places he's ever been in, well fed and cared for.'

'I know. And I told her what you said, that he is safer there till you find the money. But she said, "They've had three years to find the money and they haven't done it. Joey can't sit in jail till they do." She is determined to mobilize the family, to pool our resources and get Joey out of jail so we can ... um ... plan his defense.'

'Has she hired a lawyer?'

'No. She wants me to do that. She keeps insisting it isn't right that we've turned our backs on one of our own. She asked me, "If it was you in there, how would you feel if nobody came to help you?"'

'But you're not robbing houses, are you?'

'No. She can't seem to see the difference. I know this isn't your problem, but I'm so distressed I felt I had to talk to you.'

'You were quite right too. Teresa, all I can say is that I believe we're close and I hope you can persuade Cecelia to be patient a little longer.'

And I'm going to see if I can get the bail set higher.

She had just put down the phone when Leo's voice boomed along the aisle, 'Sarah Burke over there someplace?'

She poked her head out yelling, 'What?'

'Come back, Jason's got something.'

He was messing with phone buttons, transferring a cell phone call to his landline and then activating the speaker phone. 'Now,' he said as she walked in, 'say it again so Sarah can hear.'

Jason's voice sounded tinny through the old speakers. 'Oscar and I are in Chico's yard. We asked Chico who got Frank's car, and Chico says Joey got it.'

Sarah leaned toward the phone and said, 'Jason, does Chico know where the vehicle is now?'

'You're not gonna believe this,' Jason said and broke up. Laughing so hard he became unintelligible, he choked out, 'He keeps it—' and dissolved into whoops of laughter that turned into coughing.

'Jason, stop, I can't understand you,' Leo yelled, gritting his teeth.

'Wait—' Leo and Sarah stared impatiently

242

at the ceiling, while sounds of coughing and then strangled choking crackled out of the phone. After what felt like a long minute Jason came back on, quiet and sober, saying, 'I'm sorry, but it struck me funny so I laughed ... and I guess I caused a dust storm in this yard. Hoo. Not gonna do *that* again.'

'OK. What was funny?'

'We're all standing around the station with worried frowns saying, "Where in the world is Frank Martin's old auto?" and all the time the damn car's right here in Chico's yard.'

'What? Are you sure? An eleven-year-old Toyota Camry with automatic shift, just over fifty thousand miles?'

'Chico knows the car – he says this is it. Got more miles on it now. It's in this row of cribs he's got along the back of the yard – the ones we saw when we visited.'

'Hang on a minute, Jason.' Sarah turned to Leo. 'I want to talk to Chico about this, Leo. You want to come along?'

'I can't – I'm waiting for a call from those big-shot forensic accountants. What are you looking to learn from Chico?'

'Wait...' Sarah put up her hand like a traffic cop. She turned to the phone and told Jason, 'Hold everything, will you? I'm coming over there right now.'

They rang off and she told Leo, 'It just seems ... very unlikely. They were all so down on him, nobody with a kind word to say for him. So why give him the car? I want to hear how that happened. And now the family's talking about bailing him out. *And* I'm thinking about the tire print that robbery division took from the yard of that home invasion last winter. Joey's in jail because he got caught in a home invasion – doesn't that give me enough probable cause to impound that car?'

'At least three burglaries on his record, and he's got no fixed address? Sure it does.'

'Good. So I'll get that going while I'm looking at the vehicle. And while I do that will you call Judge Mary Kahler and ask her if she'll raise Joey's bail?'

'OK.' He looked up over his half-glasses. 'You do remember I'm tasked with finding the money?'

'How could I forget when my jaw hurts so much?'

'Quit gritting your teeth then. There aren't any lives at stake today.'

'Are you sure? This family seems to be very ... unpredictable.'

'You know some families that aren't?'

Sarah made good time to the south end of town, telling herself there was no use being an overworked detective with heavy responsibilities if you couldn't push the speed limits around once in a while.

TWELVE

An hour later, she was helping Oscar and Jason, plus Chico and the driver's helper, do sweaty manual labor in Chico's gloriously messy yard. They were all pulling spare parts and old tires out of the way so the driver from West Valley Towing could back his enormous vehicle far enough inside to hook up to the Camry.

'It was either this or tear down the shed,' Jason said. 'And Chico just about shit purple when the driver suggested that.' He jumped to help Oscar move a radiator caked with dust, wheezing into the gauze mask he'd dug out of his first-aid kit. He held his end at arm's length, his pecs stretching the seams of his shirt. Ever since his initial coughing fit he had been preoccupied by the amount of dust that had settled on Chico's junkyard.

'I'm destroying my lungs in this place,' he said. 'I can feel my future in law enforcement getting shorter every minute.'

The tow truck inched backward a few

inches, knocked over a wheelbarrow and stopped. The detectives jumped to help, setting the wheelbarrow aside in a pile that included a rocking chair with no seat, two piles of glass bricks and a ladder.

'What are you ever going to do with all this stuff?' Jason asked Chico, who was trotting from one pile to another, trying to save his priceless junk from destruction.

'Listen, this is all good stuff from yard sales. Fix it up a little and I can sell these things. You'd be surprised.'

When the two vehicles were finally hooked together, Sarah signed the charge slip and took the vehicle voucher the driver gave her, while Jason dug the records out of the glove compartment and copied the maintenance stickers out of the driver's-side doorway.

'Well, there it goes,' Chico said a few minutes later, as the tow truck snaked its hazardous way back to the street with the Toyota following. 'You ever see such a wreck? The interior looks like one of those TV shots of towns after tornadoes.'

'It's not as much of a wreck as it appears, though,' Oscar said. 'I took a look under the hood while we were waiting for the tow. That motor looks clean as a whistle, ready to go another fifty thousand easy, and the dipstick comes up with nice fresh oil. Got almost new tires on it too.'

'Is Joey always this hard on his car?' Oscar said.

'Beats anything I've ever seen,' Chico said. 'He always gets the interior looking like a pigsty. Everybody says, "Oh, he's wrecked another one." Yet he can keep one running almost forever. That car you see there had fifty-five thousand miles on it when he got it, and looked as good as new. It's only a little over ninety thousand now, and it looks like it's been through a war.' Chico groped his way back to his hammock. 'Oh, my,' he said as he settled, 'that's better. Do you think you could slide my cooler over this way a little, Oscar? Good boy.' He fished a beer out of the ice, held it up in mute invitation, and popped the top with a sigh as they all refused.

'Memo predicted this when Joey begged for the car. Three years ago, Memo was still talking – isn't that sad, that disease with the strange name?'

'Alzheimer's,' Oscar said.

'Yeah, that. No matter how many times I hear it I can't remember it.' He laughed. 'Actually that's funny, isn't it?' He giggled behind his cigarette smoke. 'Can't remember how to say Alzheimer's, haha.' All the detectives began rolling their eyes up, shaking their heads, while they waited for Chico to get over himself.

'Memo didn't always make sense, toward the end of his talking days, but he sure called it that time. He said Joey will just wreck it the way he did the one his mother got for him before. Kept saying, "This is a nice Toyota Camry, seven or eight years old but those cars are very well built. And Frank was always very careful with his vehicles."' Chico sighed. 'Memo always had a keen eye for value, you know. He was a great loss to us.'

'How come you all gave in though?' Sarah asked him. 'If you were all so sure Joey would trash the car?'

'Well, Cecelia said, "You all have good cars now – do you really want to drive around in that seedy old Camry that Frank was sitting in when he killed himself?" Nobody had thought of it that way; we all said, "No, of course not." But Luz said, "We could sell it and split the money." And Cecelia said, "Sure, the market's going to be brisk for an eight-year-old Toyota with blood on the seats. Who wants to be the seller?" So in the end everybody voted to let Joey have it, although it turned out the little screw-up didn't even have a current driver's license. Cecelia had to take him to the sheriff's office to renew his license. She even paid the fee.'

'Is she usually so generous?'

'Not with anybody else, but sometimes she does favors for Joey. Then she tries to boss him around, which by now she should know is hopeless. He is slippery as an eel, that boy.'

'But then why did you let him keep it in your yard?'

Chico's face curled around his mustache in a rictus of conflict. 'I didn't want to! But he doesn't really *live* anywhere. Cecelia kept saying, "He has no place else to put it, and you have room in your yard. Where's your family solidarity?" I told you, she loves to tell everybody what's right. I said, "Why don't you try a little solidarity at your place?" But she said, "My tiny yard? I don't have an inch anywhere."

'And to tell the truth it hasn't been as much trouble as I expected. Joey's cash flow is very uneven, so often he goes two or three weeks without using the car at all. But when he does take it out, man, sometimes he really puts some miles on it. He comes back and it looks like him and the car both been running on fumes. Then, every two or three months, he takes it to the shop to get it tuned up. Real regular – not like him at all.'

'Where does he take it?'

'Oh, he's found some cheap-o place down below Valencia, an indy who charges much less than the dealers' places. Probably does not have all his papers in order, truth be known. But somehow he keeps the old crate running.'

'Where does Joey go on these long journeys?'

'He never wants to tell me that. Maybe you tough detectives will sweat it out of him, there in that big scary prison, huh?'

'We don't do that anymore,' Jason said. 'Lawmen got laws now too.'

'Sure, sure,' Chico said, winking. 'Regular ladies' aid society these days, I understand.'

Oscar stayed in Chico's yard to talk about the farewell message some more. Sarah and Jason went back to the station to tell Leo about the worn-out Toyota Camry with four almost new tires that they had just sent to the city impound lot.

'Alert detectives are beginning to wonder,' Leo said, 'what complex and difficult journeys are undertaken by the nogoodnik who can't even do home invasions without getting caught?'

'Yeah. This nogoodnik who has some magical way with rolling stock that enables him to wear out automobile bodies completely in only forty thousand miles, yet keep the power train almost like new,' Sarah said. 'Jason and I were talking about that on the way back.'

'Oh?'

'Yes. We find the concept of inconsistent automotive wear highly suspect.'

'That sounds like bullshit language to cover a shaky theory.'

'Well, you know,' Jason said, 'while we have the vehicle sequestered I *could* slide a tracker up under the chassis where it would be very hard to spot, and when Joey gets out of the slammer we could maybe find out where he goes.'

'Jason Peete,' Leo said, 'you are a good man, and one after my own heart. But that idea is hellishly hard to get a judge to sign off on. You don't ask you don't get, though, so go ahead, try it.'

'But then we got a different idea,' Sarah said. 'We thought that maybe while Joey's all snug and quiet in Pima County, a pair of enterprising detectives like Jason Peete and me could use the methods we've already got to find out where that car's already been.'

'Oh, I like that even better,' Leo said. 'Tell me more.'

'Wait. My phone is ringing.'

'Let it ring,' Leo said, but Sarah had already opened and answered.

Delaney walked into the workstations and said, 'I've got a couple of hours away from the bureaucrats. Tell everybody to come in here and bring me up to speed.'

'Delaney wants to talk,' Leo told Sarah

when she closed her phone.

Jason said, 'Let's tell him our ideas about the car, too.'

'Wait, now,' Leo said. 'I'm not going to go in there and hype your idea till I know what's in it.'

'Don't worry. It's an idea for how to catch a thief,' Jason said. 'Who's maybe a murderer, we're starting to think.'

Leo raised his eyebrows and stared, still unwilling to move, till Jason gave him a don't-try-my-patience look he must have learned from his mother, and said, 'Trust me, OK? Isn't that what you always say to me?'

Leo sighed. 'All right,' he said. 'Promise you won't get me into any crazy shit, now.'

When they lined up in front of him, Delaney said, 'Where are we, guys?'

Sarah said, 'We think we're getting close to something hot. We just sent a Toyota Camry to impound that we believe contains evidence of where the credit union money went.'

'Hell, you say,' Delaney said. 'Whose car is it?'

'Used to belong to Frank Martin. Gifted to Joey García after Frank's death.'

'What kind of evidence?'

'Trash. Receipts if we're lucky.'

'What's that going to prove?'

Jason said, 'Not entirely sure till I talk to the owner of a wildcat car service place called JR's down in the south end. Chico says that's where he always takes it.'

'Chico who?'

'Chico García. Joey's older brother. The car's been stored in his yard off and on since Frank died.'

'But this mechanic is the one you need to talk to? What are you going to ask him?'

'For starters, how come he gets paid to do first-rate regular maintenance on one of the most beat-up cars I've ever seen still running? What does he do to keep it going, and does he have any ideas about where it's been?'

'So you think Joey's, what, taking money out of town?'

'Or moving it around some way, yes,' Sarah said.

'You think he has some action going that involves the missing money from the credit union and Frank's death?'

'Isn't that the thought that springs to mind?'

'Maybe.' He looked at them hard. 'Why are you so excited about the stupid kid brother who can't do anything right? I thought you told me he could just sit in jail while we sorted this out.'

'So did we,' Leo said, coming in like the

string bass under the wailing horns to beef up the melody, 'but now we're getting worried because some members of this felon's family are beginning to make noises about coming up with the bail to get him out of Pima County.'

'He wouldn't be the first home invader who ever exercised that privilege,' Delaney said. 'Why is this one a crisis?'

'He has no job here and has never maintained a home. He drifts around.' Leo stayed up to speed on all details of current cases by careful reading of each day's case logs. 'If he's done what we begin to suspect, he might be motivated to drift away to Mazatlan, where they tell us he has many cousins – especially if he finds out we're sniffing round.'

'Guys,' Delaney looked at his watch, 'what are you proposing to do?'

'Go after this wildcat mechanic and make him sweat a little. Chances are he's undocumented and we can get him to tell us what he's been doing to the car.'

'And then?'

'Maybe he chats with his customers. If so he could have some idea where Joey's going, which must be where he's stashing money.'

'The troublesome kid is beginning to look like our chief suspect? This is quite a switch.' He didn't buy their idea all at once; he made them go over, in detail, what they expected to find and why they thought they could get JR to tell them what they wanted to know. He admonished them, 'Tread lightly. Even Republicans are starting to love immigrants now if they're Hispanic and look like they might vote any time in the next fifty years.'

Then he urged them to remember every hour they were spending on the three García cases was inevitably going to cheat some other investigation down the line, 'because I don't print the money, you do understand that, don't you? I only get it to spend it after I sit in committee meetings and beg like a starving dog.'

But finally he said, 'All right, go for it. I'll be in meetings again this afternoon.' His frustration boiling over, he added briefly, 'I told them today that this has got to be the last day. I was hired to do police work. But right now the city council is hell-bent on combining some patrol functions with the suburbs, and they think they can't be deprived of my wisdom. But keep me informed, please. Text me if anything changes.'

The three of them came out of his office feeling moderately jazzed. But in a few steps Sarah remembered something and started to turn back.

'What is it?' Leo said, alarmed.

'I meant to tell him that I think Tracy's

getting close to the message too, and ask if I can keep him till he finds it.'

Leo wrapped a long arm around her shoulders and held her close. 'Work it out with Elsie,' he said softly, into her ear. 'Let the man eat his lunch; don't pester him after you just won a round. Aren't you ever going to learn boss management?'

The shop was ill-equipped and shabby, converted from a two-bay garage that had once had two gas pumps in front and been called a 'filling station.' It had been abandoned years ago by the corporation that now, in much larger and shinier venues, operated 'convenience stores' that sold gas out front and rows of noxious snacks in shiny wrappers inside.

The pumps were gone, and much of the glass that had fronted the station had been replaced with plywood panels. The mechanic who rented the site didn't need much light inside, anyway; he mostly used the building to house the van where he kept all his tools. He did all his repair work in the weedy yard behind the building, in the shade of the mesquites that grew untrimmed around three sides of the lot. The street side of the lot featured a cracked driveway and a crumbling curb, and there was no sign that flaunted the name of the proprietor.

The entire operation was amazingly close to clandestine, in plain sight in the bright city of Tucson but not, somehow, at all noticeable.

The sunshine was intermittent today, covered often by surly gray clouds left over from last week's storm. Temps were hanging in the fifties, and a cold breeze occasionally gusted, throwing dirt against the windshield with a noise like sleet.

Leo had stayed behind with the money problem. Sarah and Jason had persuaded Oscar to join them on the hunt for the mechanic. 'You're the one who knows cars,' Jason had said. 'We need you for this, buddy.' A kind of bond had formed between the two of them yesterday afternoon in what Jason was now calling 'Chico's Little Shop of Horrors.'

Sarah had not been able to find JR's Auto Repair listed in any directory of Tucson services, so Jason and Oscar had done some free-form snooping around the neighborhood, using Jason's recent experience in the bar on Flowing Wells as a paradigm. 'Schmooze,' he had told Oscar. 'Shuffle around grinning like a doofus. Talk about the weather.'

Sarah had agreed to circle the four-block area, looking for mechanics with no logos or waving detectives, whichever came first. On her third circuit Jason had broken off a conversation with a muscular hot-dog vendor in a hairnet and jumped in the Impala, looking cheerful.

'Not many frills in this neighborhood, but there's a lotta nice folks around here,' he'd said. He'd learned the mechanic's name, Juan Rodriguez, and his address. 'My man here on the hot-dog wagon says he's a good little guy, just trying to get along and feed a couple of kids.'

Oscar had been waiting for them in front of a strip mall that included a doughnut shop, a massage place, a wild bird store, a used bookstore and a unisex hair stylist. At the stylist, he said, he'd scored a nice chat with a beautician named Tammi.

'You get any tips about your appearance?' Jason had asked him. Alone among the male detectives in Homicide, Jason seemed amused by Oscar's reputation as a devastating lover of women.

'Tammi recommends a varsity side cut this year.' After Oscar had expressed strong interest in the Mad Men styles she showed him, he'd asked her if she knew the mechanic working on a car in the weedy lot down the street.

'Tammi says she's known him for a while – his name is Juan and he's a big favorite of the girls in the unisex shop. He's very courteous when he comes in for haircuts. But he's not making any moves or anything, she says. Apparently his wife doesn't get her hair cut – she's got about a yard of beautiful hair in a long braid. "You should see them in the store when they go shopping for groceries," she said. "He treats her like a queen."'

'Well, shit, then,' Jason had replied quickly. 'Why don't we just kick his door down and kidnap the wife till he gives up the skinny?'

Oscar had raised his eyebrows and looked at Sarah, who'd said, 'Jason's having a little trouble accepting reality today.'

Parked at the crumbling curb in front of JR's place, they watched the mechanic raise the hood on a sunburned Dodge pickup and lean in for a look.

Jason stared through the windshield a few beats and said, 'I'm already starting to not like this caper.'

'We're not going to hurt him,' Sarah said.

'Uh-huh. Just threaten is all.'

'If he's as close to the edge as this place looks, we won't even have to do much of that.'

'It still smells like police brutality to me if it scares him enough to make him run.'

'You do remember we're chasing a murderer?'

'We haven't even proven that yet.'

'We will.' She turned some of his own ammo on him. 'Trust me.'

They agreed on a simple plan, agreeing it was subject to revision at any moment.

'I'd like to do this as easy as we can,' Sarah said. 'Do you mind starting the conversation in Spanish?'

'Not a bit,' Oscar said. 'Good idea.'

When they were ready they walked together across the lot and introduced themselves to Juan Rodriguez, whose eyes took on the opacity of chunks of coal as they showed him their badges.

'The people in this neighborhood speak very highly of your skill and your honesty, Juan,' Oscar said, in Spanish. 'Do you speak English?'

'*Un poco*,' he said, and then in English, 'If you go slow?'

'*Bueno*.' Oscar switched between English and Spanish and translated Juan's answers so both sides understood the conversation. 'We have come to ask you about a certain car, *un auto particular, entiendo*? We do not wish to harm your business. If we can get some information about this car, we'll be gone.' He gestured, and Jason showed him a picture of the Camry. He studied it briefly, and nodded. 'You recognize it?'

'*Es possible*. It looks ... familiar?'

'Juan, have you worked on this car in your

shop?'

'Perhaps. I work on many cars.'

A sudden gust picked up sand and threw it in their faces. Sarah said, 'Could we buy you a coffee, *Señor*? Is there someplace near-by where we can talk comfortably out of this wind?'

'You want to talk? Only that?'

'Exactly.'

'I have no one to leave here,' he said. 'Can we just talk in the shop?'

He had only one chair, which he offered to Sarah. The three men perched around her in the gloom on sawhorses and a work-bench. Jason, Sarah saw, had already begun to temper his sympathy for Juan somewhat, because of his dread of the dust in the shop. He touched the surface of the bench he'd been offered, looked at his fingertips and leaned carefully on the edge while he put the picture of Joey's old Toyota back in the envelope and read out the license number.

'*Momento,*' Juan said, and stepped to a row of plastic file boxes on a rickety shelf. No computers in this garage, but he kept neat records; he found it right away. 'Yes, I know...' He scrunched his eyes in concen-tration and came up with some words, 'I have ... to work ... on it.'

Sarah said, 'And is this the person who brings this car to you?' Jason slid a mug shot of Joey out of the envelope.

Juan's eyes registered momentary surprise when he saw the telltale gray drape around the shoulders that guaranteed equal status to all arrestees. But his face never changed from expressionless as he said, 'Yes.'

'You understand,' Sarah said, 'we are Tucson city police.' They had agreed not to mention Homicide yet. 'We have no interest in your documentation and the license under which you operate here.' She paused, aware that her denial conveyed a powerful threat. 'We only need to know how long you have been servicing this car and what maintenance you do on it.'

The interrogation that followed was conducted almost entirely by Oscar, who besides being bilingual was a car buff and had spent years in Auto Theft. In alternating Spanish and English, with pauses, he teased out the details of the work that kept Joey's old car on the road, and translated it for his team, with Juan himself interjecting at points in shaky English.

'He has no interest in how the car looks, as you have seen,' Juan said, 'and he does not have much money of his own. But the person he works for requires him to make occasional trips out of town, so he puts hundreds of miles on the car each month. He comes to me for basic maintenance, so he won't break down out there on the road.' As he grew more relaxed, Juan's English, somewhat suspiciously, seemed to improve.

'I noticed that the car looks better under the hood than anyplace else.'

'Yes. It's an old car but a standard make, you know, so I can always get parts. I keep the gears lubricated, the brakes tight. I keep the engine clean and the oil fresh. Also, I rotate the tires and keep them balanced, and I recently replaced the whole set.'

'I noticed that too. You ordered and installed them?'

'Yes.'

'Where does he go, do you know?'

Juan shrugged. 'Not exactly. Somewhere near Phoenix, it must be. Sometimes I have to dig out the front floor, just enough so I can work. That guy, he is a pig, you know? The trash in the car is all food – candy wrappers and fast food bags. But the receipts are from Chandler or Mesa.'

'Does he pay you each time you service the car, or—'

'Not exactly. He brought money along the first time he came to me, and then he wanted to run a...' He looked at Oscar and said a Spanish phrase.

'A charge? A tab?'

'*Si*, a tab. He said that his employer wanted to see the charge. But I said that I cannot run a tab, I deal only in cash. So now he brings a deposit every two or three months, and when I work on the car I give him a bill and show him how much credit he has left. When it gets down to around fifty dollars I show him and he brings more money.'

'The deposits, Juan.' All the detectives leaned forward as Oscar asked the next question. 'Are they cash or a check?'

'Cash.'

'And when you replaced the tires? Did you order those?'

'Yes. After they paid a deposit.'

'They?'

'Well.' Juan licked his lips. 'He says someone else is paying.'

'But you haven't seen that person?'

'No.'

Sarah said, 'And so far you haven't lost on the deal? He's paid for everything he's used?'

'Yes.' He nodded, gratified by this indication that someone understood his greatest anxiety. 'But each time I hold my breath a little, because the arrangement seems a little ... irregular.'

'But on the other hand they're good business, huh?'

'Yes.' A tiny shrug, balanced between resignation and fear, and then he tried to put a Chamber of Commerce spin on his risky life. 'All my customers are good business. Good people here!' He smiled the ghost of a boosterish smile, and then went back to watching them carefully.

Driving back to the station, the three of them batted the question around – who's the 'employer' who pays the bills on the car?

'You think maybe it was Angela who got the money after all?' Sarah said, turned sideways in the passenger seat while Jason drove. 'But why would she "employ" Joey?'

'And if Joey then killed *her* and took the money, why was he doing a home invasion just to score a couple of cameras and an iPad?'

'But if he doesn't have the money,' Oscar said, 'what's all the travel about?'

'And if he does have the money,' Jason said, 'who's his employer now that Angela's gone?'

'Maybe there is no employer,' Sarah said. 'Maybe it's one more dodge for him to hide behind. Have you noticed how fast everything Joey touches slides out of control?'

They went back and clustered around Leo's desk, telling him about their interview with Juan and what they'd learned about the wildcat auto-repair shop.

Leo couldn't seem to stay focused on what they were saying. Presently Sarah realized he was just waiting for them to stop talking so he could tell them about his afternoon. The bank examiners had finally given him a full explanation of how they thought the theft was done. As he talked, Sarah realized it still wasn't really settled.

'The truth is there's still some question about how much money is missing. Nobody's ever been able to prove exactly how much he took because they've never been able to find out where he put any of it.'

'Then how do they know he took any?' Sarah said.

'Well, because the three charities he was banking for all tell the same story: Frank always picked up the money after one of the events – the bake sales, the ball games, the Thursday night bingo games – and took it to the credit union and made the deposit. It was very casual, a system left over from years ago when Tucson was smaller and so were all these organizations. Not proper procedure but he'd been doing these crummy little jobs for so long, all the things nobody else wanted to do, and he did so many favors for so many people, they just took it for granted.

'Then one day the new bank examiners for the whole state came in and looked over the accounts and said, "This isn't right, you shouldn't be handling these little two-bit accounts in the first place. And besides, there should be at least two people counting and signing off on everything." So Frank got kicked upstairs, as it were, to work at being the comptroller his title had been saying he was all along. And two members each from the food bank, the Kiwanis, and the Royal Order of Elks had to take on the job of depositing the money from their special events.

'They all complained bitterly about losing Frank's helping hand, for a while. But then a funny thing happened – they noticed that their take went up and stayed up. After a while they compared notes. Then they started talking to some of the members who were accountants and lawyers, and pretty soon they went and talked to the president of the credit union, and we had that simmering scandal about missing money that went on for months.

'They had no way of knowing how much was missing, but they got together and worked out an estimate of somewhere between seventy and eighty thousand dollars, depending on how long they thought he'd been skimming.'

'While you and I and Will,' Sarah said, 'were busy chasing the Snakes and the Worms.'

'Right. Ridding Tucson of the terrible

plague of illegal drugs. Wasn't that a whooping success?'

'Well, it was what we were tasked with doing. Because, you said it yourself, the credit union scandal wasn't our case until Frank Martin offed himself.'

'With a stolen gun,' Jason said. 'That turns out to be part of a haul in a home invasion burglary almost certainly done by Joey García.'

'Whose car was being maintained by his employer?' Sarah looked at her teammates. 'I'm sick of this circle. I'm going to go see how Tracy's doing.'

THIRTEEN

'Ah, here comes my favorite lady sleuth,' Tracy crowed, snapping his braces. 'I was just coming to fetch you, dear lady.' He was back in first-rate fettle, bowing from the waist, beaming with all his zits aglow.

'You look as if you ... did you? Oh, fan-freaking-tastic – you found it, didn't you?'

'Of course I found it. I thought you said you were going to give me something interesting and fun to work on. This was just routine.'

'Oh, stop. You found it in Angela's email? I don't under*stand* that! Ollie said he searched through her inbox and trash, and—'

'It wasn't in Angela's email – it was in Ed's.'

'What?'

'Well, isn't that where you wanted me to look? It was his message.'

'But Ollie said Ed didn't have an email account on this machine.'

'Ollie just looked at the file system. He didn't find a folder for Ed in Documents and Settings. He didn't know to look at the user accounts. When I saw there was a user account for Ed but no files, I looked in the recycle bin. I found Ed's user folder and restored it and after that it was child's play. I just logged in as Ed – he had no password either. Sheesh, cavemen on computers!'

Sarah scratched her head. 'Recycle bin?'

'Yeah. Angela must have deleted the whole folder.'

'But if it was deleted how come it was recycled?'

Tracy looked skyward and said, 'Oy. Where did I leave my handy brain-brightener? Let's see if you can wrap your mind around this not-very-difficult concept: it's true that in the sordid realm of solid waste you must decide to trash or recycle; either/ or, as Kierkegaard was so fond of saying.'

'Dear me.'

'Yes. But in Geek World, the system gods decided it was safer to make the button that says it's Delete but doesn't really delete anything at all. Thus saving your hard work from your poor ignorant and fallible self, you see? So until you also empty your recycle bin, each of those bits you delete from your hard drive waits around to see if maybe, after you start running around the room shouting obscenities and kicking the wall, you might come to your senses and reach down and grab it back. Isn't that compassionate?'

'Gosh, yes. It would be even kinder if they'd explained it to me, just once, ever.'

'Oh, it's in there, in the instructions all you wooden-heads can't be persuaded to read. Can we quit talking about how I did it so I can tell you what you really need to know?'

'Oh, yes. Please.'

'The email says it's from Frank Martin but I'm sure it was sent by somebody else.'

'You are? How?'

'The display name was the same, in the inbox, as for all the other emails that came from Frank. But when I opened the message, I noticed a difference. Frank's email address was "frank.r.martin." But this one message was sent from "frank.r.r.martin."'

'Oh, flaming hot spit.'

'Eee, please, dear lady. No need to get gross.'

'Sorry. But I see how this could work. The eye just slides right over the extra r, doesn't it? Ed wouldn't have noticed the difference.'

'Yes. And no one ever looks at the return address – you know who sent it when you open it. Anyone can make a new email address. And this shrewd person, whoever he is, realized that Ed Lacey was not going to spend a lot of time scrutinizing the email address, particularly on a message as devastating as this one.'

'And he knew that we see what we expect to see.' She gazed at the shoddy old ceiling of the support staff room and mused, 'I was right. He may be very foolish but he's not stupid.'

'Who?'

'Hmm? Oh, I better not say yet. Tracy, you just moved the ball a long way down the field.'

He made a face. 'Disgusting epithets are not enough for you? You have to use sports metaphors too?'

'I was trying to give you a compliment – but let it go. Can you print me up a copy?'

'Well, I wanted to ask you about that. I try not to change a machine while I'm working on it for you. But it doesn't look like there's ever been a printer driver installed on this machine. So what I thought I might do is take a screenshot of the open email, save it on a thumb drive, and print the jpeg on my own machine. Would that be good enough?'

He had lost her at 'printer driver.' Sarah took a deep breath and said, slowly, 'I really don't care how you do it. I need a paper copy of that email that shows the "wrong" address visible, and a copy of another of his emails that shows the "right" address. Can you do that for me?'

'Give me ten minutes and I'll have them

on your desk.'

Walking back to Delaney's office, she chuckled contentedly, thinking about what he'd found for her. But by the time she'd reached the door of Delaney's office, she'd started to think about the questions that still remained.

She told the detectives what Tracy had found, and then asked them all, 'Why would anybody do that? What would anybody have to gain by tormenting Ed Lacey that way, pretending to be his uncle?'

'I can't even imagine,' Delaney said, 'but before we try to answer that, I wish you'd find out for me how the message got into Eisenstaat's case file, and from there to the newspapers. I can't believe Ed Lacey volunteered information as personal as that. That wasn't his style at all.'

'I'll see if I can find the name of the information officer who handled the case,' Sarah said. 'He must know how the papers got it, at least.'

She caught Pam, the information officer of the day, in a rare moment of calm, checking case files at her desk. She was surrounded by bright pictures of her gleefully grinning grandchildren, playing games and crawling on their dad.

Subject entirely to the whims of fate, information officers had to take calls at all

hours. Officers nearing retirement liked
the assignment because they logged a lot of
overtime, and retirement pay is based on
their take-home in their final years. Except
for that advantage, though, the job was
sometimes so hectic that it was known as a
marriage-breaker and younger officers
generally avoided it.

'We keep a log,' Pam said, 'and it's almost
all we keep on this machine, so I think it
goes back ... yeah, five years. Give me the
name again?'

She found the entries for Frank Martin's
death – the report of his discovery in the
car, and a couple of follow-up reports, the
first of which featured the 'farewell message.' Each report was signed by the information officer who had transmitted the
information to the media. The report that
included Frank's message was signed, in a
clear, firm hand, 'Mary Leary.'

'Huh,' Pam said, puzzled. 'When did
Mary have that job? Must not have lasted
long. I sure never worked with her.'

'She doesn't have it now?'

'No, Mary's got a morning shift on patrol
at West Side. You want her phone number?'

Mary Leary answered from her squad car
and agreed to meet at a Wendy's on Camp-
bell.

'You bet I remember the Frank Martin

case,' she said, sipping her coffee. 'I was subbing for Kelley Pease that week. Two information officers got sick at once and when my sergeant asked me to take it for a few days I jumped at the chance to try the job. Shee, I handed it back to Kelley when she got back and said, "You can have my share of this, Baby."'

'It was too hard?'

'It was all pretty stressful, but it was that Frank Martin case that convinced me never to put in for the job. Suicides always seem like the saddest cases to me. And then when I looked at the next of kin and saw it was Ed Lacey's uncle – he was at the academy when I was in training. He was one of the Red Men, the guys you have to fight! And remember how you start out hating the Red Man's guts—'

'That's mostly fear.'

'Well, rightly so – they can reduce you to just jelly if they want to, and then you're history, out of there. But then those trainers, if they see you're willing to try, can help you so much – and nobody was ever kinder or more considerate than Ed Lacey was about helping. He was a wonderful teacher. So when I saw that it was his uncle we found dead in front of the Sears store, I thought, as a courtesy, I should call him and ask if he wanted to comment for the story I was about to release to the media. He answered at home, and the poor guy had just opened that email message from his uncle. He was simply, you know, devastated.'

'It's so hard to try to comfort,' Sarah said. 'You don't know what to say.'

'Yeah, but this was ... different, somehow. At first he couldn't seem to talk, he kept choking. But then he kind of sucked it up and said, "Mary, I want you to be sure you report his final message exactly the way I give it to you." And he read out that first sentence, something about "I didn't take the money." I did my best to copy it exactly, but he was kind of sobbing at the same time, and then he dropped the phone. I heard some coughing and groaning, and then his wife picked up the phone and said, "Who is this?" I gave her my name and told her, "Ed was trying to give me the message he just got from his uncle, but I guess he broke down."

'I told her he seemed anxious to get it quoted right, and asked her if she could just forward the message to me. And she did, and I gave it to all the reporters.'

Mary's face was a mask of regret. 'I have never seen anybody so close to apoplectic as Ed was when he found me here the next day. He kept yelling, "I told you to report it just as I read it to you!"

'Do you know what it's like to have a Red Man mad at you? I mean, I didn't *think* he'd actually beat me up, but I wasn't sure. I kept remembering the first time I saw him in that big red helmet, beating on me just enough to make me look like a turkey. And the thought does cross your mind that if he wants to, this man is just an awesome fighter; he could put a hurt on you you'd never forget. I couldn't understand why he was so angry; after all, he'd told me to give it to the press. It wasn't till later that I realized he had just read me the first sentence and it was Angela who gave me the whole text.'

'Why do you think he was so upset about the second sentence?'

'I suppose he thought the first sentence proved his uncle wasn't guilty, and then the second sentence seemed to imply that he was. He was probably going to change it slightly.'

'So you got the message only from Ed's email? Not from Harry Eisenstaat?'

'Who?'

'Our investigating officer, the one who attended the autopsy.'

'Oh, him. I never could get him on the phone. After I got the case assigned I called him and left messages, but he never called me back. So I just called around and picked up the info from the first responders and the coroner, and pieced the story together myself. You can't wait, you know – you have deadlines.'

Sarah went back to Delaney and said, not meeting his eyes, 'Looks like we had it backwards, boss. The information officer didn't get that message from Harry. Harry must have copied it out of the paper.'

On Wednesday the weather brightened and so did Delaney. He had slipped his chain at the city council and was back, he said, to doing what he knew best. So he marshaled the crew and told them, 'No more Mr Nice Guy. I want that money found now. Leo, why can't we turn it over to the bank examiners? They've got all the clout they need to look at accounts.'

'They've already swept records in the five-state area for accounts belonging to every permutation of Frank Martin,' Leo said, 'and every possible version of Ed or Angela Lacey. And so far, we haven't come up with another suspect to offer them. We've no leads on who Joey's "employer" might be.'

'I've got an idea,' Ollie said. 'Ask them to try that other name Angela had for a while – her first husband's name. It's in the case notes.'

'Oh, and why don't we try searching on her Polish name?' Sarah said.

'That won't work,' Leo said. 'You need a social security number to open an account.'

'That's right,' Delaney said. 'Is it possible Frank gave the money straight to Joey? He'd take it, wouldn't he, if he could get it?'

'Oh, in a heartbeat, the way I hear it,' Sarah said. 'But why would Frank risk his career to steal it and then give it to Joey? There's no way that makes sense, is there?'

'I can't think of one,' Leo said.

'Let's get Joey in here in the box and make him tell us who's paying for those long rides. Unless everything he said is a lie, if we find his employer, we ought to find the money.'

'Fine, I agree with that. Soon as we're done here, Sarah, you get on the horn with Pima County and arrange to have him transported.'

'The message,' Oscar said. 'Why would anyone do such an evil thing as to send Ed Lacey a fake message when his uncle just died?'

Jason said, 'Isn't there some way to hack on that email address, to see if it made any purchases, or—'

'I like that,' Delaney said. 'Ask Tracy. And Ray, you stick around here, will you, so you're available to go in the box with Sarah when she gets Joey up here? I've got about a million messages to catch up on now, but let me know when you've got him set up,

279

Sarah. I'll monitor outside.'

Sarah called Admin at Pima County and placed a request for transport for Joey García. The officer who took the call said, 'Hold one second, I think I saw—'

He came back on the line a few seconds later and told her, 'Joey García made bail late yesterday and was released at eight-fifteen last night.'

Sarah held her breath until the red cloud of rage that had formed in front of her eyes dispersed. When she was fairly confident of keeping her voice reasonable she said, 'Who secured the bond, do you have that information?'

He gave her the name of a bondsman she knew slightly. She called his office in the jail and asked who brought the bail money.

'His mother,' the bondsman said. 'Teresa García.'

'She can't drive herself right now,' Sarah said. 'Who brought her in?'

'Um ... I think she said it was her daughter.'

'Which one?'

'No idea.'

Sarah called each of them and got no answer, then called Chico, with the same result. Feeling as if she might be going to explode from frustration, she hurried into the ladies' room to splash cold water on her face. When she came out she walked into Delaney's office and told him their prisoner was loose.

'Damn,' Delaney said. 'I thought you said you were going to get the bail amount raised.'

'Leo tried. Judge Kahler said she had already set it at the maximum amount allowed. She was trying to teach him a lesson.'

'Seems like he's not getting the message,' Delaney said. 'What's the fallback plan?'

Sarah, looking horrified suddenly, said, 'The mechanic.'

'The wildcat who worked on his car? How can he help you?'

'He can't – but I think we better help him.'

'How?'

'We should find him and tell him his customer's out of jail.'

Delaney popped his eyes and said, 'Why?'

'He didn't want to have anything to do with us, but we muscled in on his life and made him talk about that Toyota.'

'So?'

'So three people are dead and we think it's all about the money, don't we? I think we better tell that guy his prize customer is out of jail and probably armed and quite possibly dangerous.'

'Oh. OK, give him a call.'

'No cell phone, boss. No computer. This

guy's off the grid and barely feeding his family.'

'Sarah,' Delaney said, looking at his call-back list, 'what do you want?'

'We gotta go find him, talk to him. He probably ought to fix cars at another location for a while.'

Delaney sighed. 'We have a great deal to do.'

'This guy's smart and he's connected down there. If we make him a friend he could help us. Jason and Oscar can find him fast – they did before.'

'All right.' Delaney waved her away. 'Then talk to the arresting officer for that last break-in Joey did. See if there's any other charge he can come up with, so we could issue a warrant for a fresh arrest.'

'Oh, I like that. Thanks, boss.'

When she told Jason, he said, 'See, I told you we were going to mess up that poor guy's life.'

'Blame me all you like after you find him,' Sarah said. 'But right now will you hustle your butt down across Valencia and find that guy? I'm getting hives.'

She was tackling the fresh pile of messages that seemed to be spontaneously proliferating on her desk when she answered her ringing phone and heard a voice yell, from some outdoor space filled with traffic noises, 'Is this Sarah Burke? Right. This is Sam Rollins at the impound yard.'

'Yes, Sam?'

'Yeah, well, your name's on the charge slip so I thought you better know. Somebody cut the padlock off the backyard gate last night, and that old Toyota you sent me yesterday is gone.'

'Is that the only vehicle missing?'

'Yup. So I guess you know who's to blame, huh? And, hey, probably we should be grateful he left the chain-link fence alone – I'll just replace the padlock and I'm good to go. But I think you're looking for a Camry and the man who owns it, both.'

'Yeah, looks like we gotta go around again. Thanks, Sam.' She ran and told Delaney, who said, 'Well, there's our new charge. Will you write up the warrant? I'll put out the Need to Locate, city and county.'

'What about Border Patrol? We think he's a flight risk.'

'Right. Soon as you finish that warrant call them, give them all the information on the warrant and ask them to turn him around if they find him.'

They got busy, and soon every car in Tucson and Pima County was looking for the Camry, and had a copy of Joey's last arrest photo in the car.

In the middle of all that busy work, Jason

called Sarah from the weedy lot in front of the inconspicuous repair shop.

'We're looking in the front window,' Jason said. 'The ceiling light is out and the door is locked. The van he kept his tools in is gone too, and all those file boxes where he kept his records. Looks like our boy's an old hand at this – he knows when to take a powder.'

'Did you ask around the neighborhood if anybody's seen him?'

'Of course. Tried the neighbors on both sides. Talked to Ulysses, the guy in the hairnet that calls himself the *chef de cuisine* at the hot dog stand. Oh, and you know that unisex hair styling shop where I told you all the girls had big eyes for Oscar yesterday? He got so charming in there a few minutes ago I almost fell in love with him myself, but they don't have a word of advice for him today. Nobody down here wants to talk to us now – they all say, like, "Juan who?" We're poison in this part of town.'

Sarah ate lunch at her desk, answering emails and fielding calls. When she walked into the break room to make tea she found Leo sitting there, watching a rerun of an old Barney Miller show on his iPad. She stood by him through a couple of eruptions on the laugh track, till he finally peeled his eyes away and said, 'What gives you the right to interrupt my lame-brained lunch break, which helps me maintain my sunny disposition the rest of the day?'

'Don't know if you've heard,' she said, and started to tell him about the bail-out.

'I know about the bail-out,' he said. 'Anything else?'

She told him about the Toyota stolen from impound. 'What does that suggest to you?'

'Flight. Or a mission. Maybe there's still some money to retrieve? You know,' he closed his iPad and stood up, looking energized, 'there's one very simple thing we haven't tried. What if there's an account somewhere in the name of Joey García?'

Sarah did a modified light-up followed by a quick douse. 'Would he dare?'

'A man who breaks into houses and steals guns for resale to drug lords is not risk-averse.'

'So are you going to ask your examiners to scan for it?'

'Damn right.'

'Don't forget, his legal name is José. His social security account must be in that name.'

'Middle initial?'

'Mmm. Don't know. Can't you start them looking while I try to find Teresa?'

'Is she missing?'

'I don't think so but she hasn't answered her phone lately. In fact, I'm not getting any answers from anybody in the García family, and they haven't called me.'

'Why should they?'

'They just did the one thing we agreed they wouldn't do, get Joey out of jail. You'd think they might like to explain what they have in mind.'

'Have you forgotten we're the police? People lie to us, make excuses and hide things. You want a nice friendly explanation of something, call your mother.'

Ignoring his advice, Sarah called Pilar, who was no more friendly than usual but at least answered the phone this time. She denied having delivered her mother to the bail bondsman, and was immediately angry at her mother for reneging on her promise to leave Joey in jail.

'She told me this time it would be different. But when he whines to her she always gives in. It makes everything I do for her seem pointless and stupid.'

'I'm very sorry to tell you there's another problem.'

'What now?'

'Well, you know, we impounded his car yesterday.'

'I didn't know, obviously. Why?'

'We showed probable cause to suspect it

was involved in a series of home invasions.'

'Probably was. So?'

'So last night he cut the lock on the impound gate and took back the car. He's at large somewhere in Tucson now, and we have to find him before he does any more damage. You're saying you haven't heard from him?'

'No.'

'If he does call you, will you let me know?'

'Yes. But he won't. He might call Cecelia, but he won't call me.'

'All right. Do you know where your mother is now?'

'Actually, I do. She has a monthly appointment at a spa where she gets a massage and body wrap. It takes all day and she enjoys it a great deal. I delivered her there this morning, and I'm due back at five to take her home. Just think – she let me take her there and never said a word about getting Joey out of jail. When was she going to tell me, I wonder?'

'I need to know what name Joey has on his social security number. Do you think it's all right if I call her there?'

'You bet. Why should she be all relaxed and happy in her aloe wrap when the rest of us are dealing with the results of her foolishness?'

'Good. May I have the number for her

spa, please?'

'Actually, why don't you just give me yours?' Pilar said. 'I'll see to it that she calls you – it will be my pleasure.' She hung up, still fuming, leaving Sarah wanting to beg for a little mercy for Teresa. But there was no time; Oscar and Jason walked onto the floor just then, talking to each other and then to Sarah.

'We stopped at Chico's place on the way back,' Oscar said. 'He says Joey called him last night, asking for a couple of phone numbers in Mazatlan. Anything we can do to keep him from going there?'

'Plenty,' Sarah said, and told them about all the processes under way. 'We need to capture the rest of that money, which must be what he's going for. Unless he's already across the border without the money. But we think he's going to try to get it, and then make a run. So we'll try to get him at the border.'

Her phone rang then, and Teresa said, 'Oh, Detective, my daughter says I have done such a foolish thing. But you know, he's my baby...' She made a small, painful sound and began to cry. Through sobs, she finished, 'You can't just ... turn your back ... on a person you love.'

'I understand, Teresa. But right now ... I need to know what name he uses on his social security account.'

'Social security? What's that got to do with anything?'

'We think he's got some money he's hiding ... money that isn't rightly his, you understand? And that he's got it in another town, in a bank, under his birth name. Does he have a middle name or initial?'

'José *is* his middle name.'

'Oh?'

'Yes. We named him after his father. But then, it was awkward having two Vicentes, always together. So for convenience we called him by his middle name, José. And then when he grew up a little he wanted to be called Joey instead.'

'But his social security card reads Vicente José García?'

'Yes.'

'All right. Thanks for calling me, Teresa, I'm sorry I had to interrupt your spa day. Don't worry now, I know you did what you thought was right.'

'I know I have no right to ask, but ... if you arrest him again, will you let me know?'

'Yes. I'll be in touch, Teresa.' She ran to Leo's space, found him on the phone and stood in front of him making time-out signals. He said, 'Hold one,' into the phone. Then, to her, 'What?'

She waved a paper under his nose, saying,

'I have the name you should search for.'

He said, into the phone, 'Gotta go. Talk to you later.' He grabbed the paper she handed him, read it and caroled, 'Oh, yes, baby!' as he dialed the bank examiners' number that, by now, he had memorized.

Walking away, she looked at her watch and said, aloud, 'Four o'clock, though. Rats!'

Ollie popped his head out of his cubicle and asked her, 'What's wrong with four o'clock? Perfectly good time, almost quitting time.'

'That's what's wrong with it. The bank examiners have all gone home, probably, so they won't start scanning the state for Joey García's account till tomorrow. And by then he'll have the money in Mexico, what do you bet?'

'Don't we have a wants order on him at the border?'

'Sure. You didn't get the memo about the system not working to perfection? He'll find some way to slip through the net.'

'Sarah, this case is making you gloomy and paranoid.'

'Yes, it is. What is it with this guy? He makes so many dumb mistakes, but yet he always seems to stay one step ahead of us.' She didn't say, 'Of me,' not wanting to own the failure. But that was how it felt, as if she had inadvertently engaged in *mano-a-mano* combat with Joey García, and he was winning.

Till the next morning at six a.m., when Delaney called and said, 'Well, we found Joey García's car. Joey's in it, and he's dead.'

FOURTEEN

'Luz told me I'd find him in this part of town,' Sarah said. A sign across Speedway said, 'Elegant Junque,' and another advertised, 'Cash for Gold.' The strip mall in the next block included a tattoo parlor, some factory close-outs and a motorcycle repair shop. Off-track wagering was featured in the nearby bar, and if that didn't suit there were four more bars within easy staggering distance. 'She was right. This is Joey's natural turf.'

The Toyota was parked on a small bridge across the ditch that ran along Arcadia Street. Tall cottonwoods and scrap underbrush grew all along the ditch, so the car was hard to see until you were almost on top of it. The patrolman who found it in the dark said his lights just happened to reflect off the one spot on the rear bumper that wasn't too dirty to reflect anything.

Delaney was worried about the big traffic jam he was sure was going to form along the narrow shoulder on the Arcadia Street side

292

as soon as all the techs and detectives got here. 'I don't want anybody getting hurt here,' he told Sarah. 'Why don't you go park in that empty parking lot behind the bar that's over there on the other side of the ditch?'

Sarah parked behind the bar and walked back to the bridge, where the photographer was already busy taking pictures of the car. The rear of a fingerprint specialist protruded from the driver's-side doorway, and a DNA tech was leaning into the car from the other side. Both of them kept readjusting the portable lights they'd clipped onto the doorframe. It was very dark on the bridge; the trees blocked out the street lights and the bar had only one small light burning over the door. But the DNA tech said, 'I'm smelling a lot of sweat on the passenger's seat. I'm going to swab this side really well and maybe I'll do you some good. Damn, the light is tough, though!'

Sarah said, 'You want me to hold the light for you?' and did, for a couple of minutes. But it proved so difficult to fit two sets of arms in the small space that before long the tech said, 'Nah, lemme clip it again, it's easier.'

Delaney was pacing the Arcadia Street side of the bridge, catching detectives as they arrived and telling them to go back out onto Speedway and come in and park in the lot behind the sports bar.

'Plenty of room over there right now,' she heard him saying. 'They won't be open for several hours.' He told the patrolmen who were stringing crime scene tape, 'Tape it up straight across the street side, good and tight over here. Two strands so we can keep everybody out. And then on the other side of the ditch, the parking lot side, make a big half-circle, will you? Give us a little room to work.' He put the officer with the posse box at the top of the half-circle on the parking lot side, and spent a lot of time at the beginning motioning everybody around to that side to sign in.

He and his detectives had to wait, anyway, for the photographer and other crime-scene specialists to finish. So although they had arrived in the gray dusk of a winter dawn, it was full light by the time Sarah got a look at Joey García.

The big surprise was how little there was to see. He looked even less dangerous slumped over his steering wheel in dirty canvas pants and a ragged sweater than he had in an orange jumpsuit, and he also looked undamaged. Except for the lack of a pulse, waxy skin and staring eyes turning milky, he might have been just catching a snooze. He was slumped forward with his head resting on the steering wheel, turned to the right as though he'd been watching something out the passenger's-side window. There were no visible marks or scars; no blood showing and no signs of a fight.

He had been prepared to have one, they discovered, after the photographer was finished and the ME arrived. It was Greenberg, this time, with his transport van following right behind. As soon as he'd confirmed the presence of death and had a cursory look, he recruited a couple of patrolmen to help his driver get the body out of the car. Greenberg never took on any of the grunt work if he could possibly avoid it; he was saving his honed-to-the-max body for finer things, and was especially careful with his hands.

Stretched out on the gurney, with his dimpled face ablaze in a red sunrise, Joey looked like somebody who'd had a momentary seizure or shock and ought to be revived at once. But the doctor was matter-of-factly shining light in his eyes and taking his temperature, and while he was getting ready to strap him down the detectives, gloved up and intent, got busy patting him down and checking pockets. He had a fully loaded Glock Nine in the cargo pocket of his pants and a Walther P22, also with a full magazine, in an ankle holster strapped to his right leg.

It wasn't an arsenal but it was a lot more than most people carried with them to a bar, especially after you added in the switchblade in his jacket and the box-cutter that slid out of a special pocket with a Velcro closure sewn onto the left leg of his pants. Joey had been loaded and locked, ready to go into battle, but there was no sign that he had used any of his weapons.

He had an old leather wallet, very dirty, in his back pocket. It held just over two hundred dollars in cash, an Arizona driver's license and no credit cards.

While four men hoisted the gurney into the van, Delaney talked to Greenberg, asking him for the earliest possible autopsy for this victim. 'Unless something obvious shows up when you get him undressed,' he said, 'this is going to be one for you and your lab guys to figure out, isn't it? So sooner is better, don't you think?'

'Sure,' the doctor said, 'but I don't run the place, you know. I'll try, though – I'll let you know.'

Ollie took charge of disarming and listing the weapons. The rest of the detectives, as soon as the lab technicians would let them have it, swarmed the Toyota, wanting to see it clearly before it was towed again to impound. There was nothing in the backseat but a fleece jacket and an empty grease-stained carton with the remains of a burger and fries. A ratty, soft-sided suitcase stuffed with clothing, a cardboard box of shoes and underwear, and another with a radio, camera and a few batteries took up the storage space behind the seats. The glove compartment held the vehicle documents that belonged there, and nothing else.

What the Toyota didn't hold, that they could see, was any money.

Greenberg phoned Delaney within the hour with a time for the autopsy next day. Sarah took the observation job, even though it once again required her to work on Friday. She had been the first detective on the scene, it was her turn to do an autopsy, and she welcomed the chance to watch Greenberg discover what killed Joey.

'No big mystery about what killed him,' Greenberg said, once he had the body open. 'This guy died of suffocation.' He showed her the red spots in the lungs and inside the eyelids. 'Not strangulation – no marks on his throat. Nothing fancy about the means, either. See here? It appears he met his end inside a used plastic garbage bag.' He showed Sarah the morsels of lettuce and cooked egg he had just found in Joey's airway. 'That's just about the ultimate insult, isn't it? You don't even get a clean garbage bag to die in? Jeez.' He thought a minute before he said, 'You know, I found some lettuce in his hair earlier, and I just figured it was a result of his messy eating habits. But now I think that might have been left by the murder weapon, too.'

'Is it here somewhere – do you still have it?'

'What, the shred of lettuce? It's in the garbage,' Greenberg said. His nose twitched. 'I'm not going through *that*.'

'OK. Has he got a bruise on the back of his head?'

'Not on the back. On the right side here, all around this ear, above and below – he's pretty tan, but do you see the discoloration here on his jaw? How'd you know to ask me that?'

'Angela had one on the back.'

'Ah, yes, the hanging victim that gave Cameron so much anxiety.' He was already feeling competitive towards the new doctor, Sarah saw. 'Yes, well, this is very similar, in a way, I suppose, but there's no attempt to disguise it as strangulation. All he shows in the way of marks is this bruise, left by a fist or some other device, that held the bag tight till the victim stopped trying to breathe.'

'You would think,' Sarah said, 'that he'd have put up a monumental struggle, wouldn't you? And in that confined space in the front seat – why isn't everything all torn up?'

'Because of this,' he said, and showed her the taser marks on the right shoulder. 'He was immobilized.'

'Just like Angela,' Sarah told her team when they reviewed the autopsy on Monday. 'I think we can forget all the conjecture about suicide in her case.'

'So now we're looking for the murderer that did them both?' Delaney said. 'I thought you were all looking to hang this one on Joey's buddies in the bar.'

'Well, we all liked that better in the beginning,' Jason said. 'Nice and clean, and it fits his character – he got some money, came back to Tucson and started partying in a favorite bar, bragging to his mates, "So long, you suckers with jobs, I'm off to Mazatlan to play in the sun." And one or two of his buds decided to get some of that cash he kept flashing.'

'I still like it,' Delaney said. Then, looking at Sarah, he said, 'But you don't want to settle for that, huh?'

'I'm bothered by the similarity to Angela. The taser marks and the suffocation – that's not a typical crime in Tucson. We live in a city awash in guns, and most of the mopes just go ahead and use them when they want somebody gone.'

'That's right,' Leo said. 'And there's something else she's right about. It's in the report – the tellers at that small branch bank in Mesa get to know their depositors, and they say Joey made all the deposits into that savings account, and all the withdrawals that came out of it. The last withdrawal he made cleared the account – that was on the morning he died.'

'I read that report too,' Delaney said. 'So?'

'We know he never held a steady job in all those years, so where did the money come from if not from Frank and the credit union here?'

'He's got a record of small crimes he got caught at. We don't know how much thievery he was able to do in between without getting caught.' Delaney obviously wasn't convinced.

'That would be occasional money, though,' Leo said. Working with the bank examiners had given him a clearer feel for this case than the rest of the team. 'Joey's deposits were systematic, between fifteen hundred and two thousand a month for about four years. He'd have to have fantastic luck to get a steady income like that from fencing electronic toys and jewelry.'

'You make it all sound very logical,' Delaney said, 'but Joey is dead, the money has disappeared, and we don't have anything that proves he ever had anything to do with

Frank or the money Frank supposedly stole.'

'Still,' Leo said, 'we can't just walk away from a string of four violent crimes in one family and say we don't have a clue.'

'I'm not saying we should. I'm saying what are we going to do next? I want to hear,' he looked at his detectives, 'what's left to do that we haven't done?'

'Well, we have the DNA sampling that was done on the car,' Sarah said. 'We won't have the results for some time, but—'

'And when we do it may all match Joey García,' Delaney said. 'Let's not pin our hopes on *that*.'

'I'd like to go up to Mesa and interview each of those bank tellers,' Leo said. 'It's a small bank and they remember things.'

'I agree,' Delaney said. 'Anybody else?'

'That laptop we gave to Tracy,' Ollie said. 'Where is it now?'

'Back in the trunk,' Delaney said. 'The kid's been good about remembering that.'

'OK if I check it out again?'

'Sure. Anybody else?'

'I want to talk to a couple of people at the jail,' Sarah said. 'Maybe Joey, you know ... *said* something.'

'Good. Why don't you do that? Now, here's what I want. Ray, just for the hell of it, go back to that block on Speedway where we found Joey. Must be four or five bars on that block, plus a couple of antique shops, good places to move some used merch, right? Stroll around there today, talk to the folks, take along the picture, see if anybody remembers Joey. Watch their eyes if they say yes, and see how many lies they tell right after that.

'And Oscar, pick up the tool kit we keep in Lost and Found and go back to the impound yard. Pull the Toyota out into an open spot and tear that sucker apart. Joey didn't get much time to enjoy that last pile of money, so most of it's gotta be someplace. See if you can find it in the car. Maybe, come to think of it, you ought to have some help with that.'

'I'll do it,' Jason said quickly. 'I'm cool with Toyotas, put myself through Pima College selling used ones.'

'Good enough. Go for it.'

You'd think he gave them a week off with pay, Sarah thought, watching Jason and Oscar charge off the second floor with their eyes alight.

Sarah phoned the jail, found Greta in the admitting section and got her to agree to a short interview in one hour's time, perhaps with coffee if things broke just right. She cleared her desk and stopped by Ollie's workspace on her way out.

302

'What are you looking for on the laptop?' she asked him. 'Is Tracy helping you?'

'Tracy's gone back to high school, where he probably does not enjoy perfect rapport with his teachers. He's going to be working here a few Saturdays this winter, he said, but not many because the college hunt is getting serious. So before he left I got him to show me a couple of those conjuring tricks he was using to pull stuff out of the laptop. I don't have specific goals, I just want to nose around in there and see if I can act enough like a teenager to find something. It'd be cool if I got some idea about what the late Angela Lacey was finding out about just before she got so rudely interrupted.'

'What a good idea,' Sarah said, in a voice so full of fake admiration Ollie stopped checking his email and gave her his equally fake Alfred E. Neuman grin.

'I can put my toe in my ear, too,' he said. 'What do you want, Sarah?'

She told him about Marjorie Springer's remark about Angela's 'research.'

'She asked me that day, "You think maybe she found something?" But then, you know, there was so much else to do ... I never got back to that. Would you take a look for a folder conveniently labeled, oh, I don't know, "Angela's Deadly Research"?' She smiled at him.

'Sure. Happy to – making a note, "Angela's Deadly ..." There! Now will you go away and leave me alone for a long time? Because I'm not very good at this yet, and I don't want you listening when I have to call a high-school boy and ask for advice.'

The freeway was full of drivers behaving as though they had just received word that this was the last Monday of the year for getting work done. Wide awake and feeling her jaws throb, Sarah pulled off on Silverlake a few minutes later and parked to the right of the jail. She took her time walking in across the brick pavers – the weather had returned to Resort Special, and the sun on her back felt like a cure for traffic and other forms of stress.

Greta Wahl apparently felt the same way – she walked out to the desk to greet Sarah, said they'd better skip coffee today and suggested they sit outside, 'I like to get out of this air-conditioning once or twice a shift if I can.' A compact, tightly organized woman with no outstanding features, she somehow exuded confidence and authority so completely that, in the potentially chaotic surroundings of the admitting section, her presence alone was sufficient to calm the room.

She'd read the report of Joey's death. 'I have to say I'm not surprised. His temper was out of control. But I'm glad you called me – you reminded me of something I meant to tell you.' She tapped her upper lip a couple of times, thinking.

'It was two days, I think, before his mother bailed him out. Joey had been brought up into the front section to make a phone call. You know the arrangement? They can have all the phone calls they want, but they all have to be collect calls, there aren't any coin boxes on the phones here. We don't have to monitor calls, in fact we're not allowed to – that's supposed to be the advantage of this pod construction: they're never in direct contact with the outside so they don't have to be monitored for visits and phone calls.

'So I wasn't monitoring but I was working on the same floor and couldn't help over-hearing. Joey had trouble getting his call through, it sounded like the person he was calling didn't want to accept charges, and he got enraged. He was screaming into the phone, "You better take my call, bitch!" I was just going to call the floor guard to have him taken back to his cell when it went through.

'There were a few minutes' fairly quiet conversation, and then he blew up again, yelling that he wasn't going to sit in this place – this hellhole, he called it, can you imagine? About Pima County! I was just thinking, *wait till you start doing real time in Florence,* when he went berserk, screaming that this person better get him out of here, because "I got plenty I can say about you and if I start to talk you're gonna be in here with me!" Somebody said something back, also loud, and Joey yelled, "Damn right it is, you think you're the only one knows how to threaten?" And then the guard came and took him away.' Her nose twitched. 'Took two guards, actually. He was out of his mind, raving and kicking.'

'Greta, could you tell if he was talking to a man or a woman?'

'Well ... he called the person on the other end, "Bitch." Of course, some people say that to men now, but ... I didn't think Joey was gay, did you?'

'No.'

'So it was probably a woman.' She stood up. 'That's all I've got, and I'd better get back. Hope it helps.'

'Wait,' Sarah said. 'There's a record kept of the numbers called, isn't there? Must be.'

'Yes. And there's a sign on the phone that warns that numbers are recorded, so ... You can get a print-out of the numbers in that time-span, is that what you want?'

'Sure is. Do I need a subpoena?'

'No. If the call was privileged, like to a doctor or lawyer, maybe, but this wasn't that kind of a call.'

'So ... I just call the phone system?'

'Got your notebook? I'll give you the number to call.' She wrote, frowning in concentration, and handed the notebook back.

'Hey, I owe you one,' Sarah said. 'Thanks, Greta.'

'Glad to help.' She walked back inside at her street-cop pace, fast but not hurried, the consummate steady hand.

Sarah went back to South Stone, looking forward to telling Delaney what she'd found. He was in his office, on the phone. He was on the phone every time she checked for the next hour, and then jumped into the elevator and disappeared for the rest of the afternoon.

By then she didn't want to talk to him because she was involved in describing what she needed to a bemused quite new employee of a telephone system she didn't understand. The girl was polite and wanted to help, but was completely out of her depth; she kept saying, 'Why don't I check on that and get back to you?' Feeling like a not-very-great Wallenda on a slender wire over a canyon, Sarah finally talked the nervous girl in the anonymous distance into passing this call on to her superior. She'd evidently been cautioned in some business school that she should deal with the public as best she could and not be passing rude strangers along to her boss all the time. When Sarah suggested she could put her own chief of police on the line if need be, she decided to opt for the smaller risk.

Once the transfer was complete, though, and Sarah had an experienced, competent woman on the line who understood what was necessary, the whole thing went on greased wheels. When she learned Sarah felt some uncertainty about the date, she said, 'I can go for a day before and a day after the day you think it was, and it still won't be a very long list. Collect calls – they're kind of a pain, you know. They don't make so many.'

Sarah told her where to send the fax, and she said she'd call when it was on the way.

Ollie had stuck his head in her workstation once in the afternoon. He'd looked pleased with himself and he'd had his mouth open, ready to tell her why, but she'd waved him off. She'd been deep in the conversation that had persuaded the young girl to transfer the call to her superior at the time, and could not risk pausing for even one second.

When she finally had her list of numbers on the way she went by Ollie's desk to tell him what she'd done. He waved *her* off then, muttering, 'Found something hot.'

Nobody else had come back by the time

she checked out and went home, rubbing her ear thoughtfully, hoping what she'd done would be enough.

'You look tired,' Aggie said, at dinner.

'We live in a world of interlocking systems, you know that?' Sarah said. 'And no matter how many systems I learn, there's always going to be a new one popping up that will make everything I know stop working.'

'Is that what makes you tired?' Denny said. 'When I'm tired, like tonight, it's because I swam so hard in gym and I have too much stupid homework.'

'Your Aunt Sarah lives in a much more rarified world,' Aggie said. 'We probably can't hope to understand a thinker at her high level.'

'Or a mother who ridicules her own child when she's down, that's pretty hard to understand too. You want to watch a rerun of *Battlestar Galactica* after the dishes?' she asked Denny.

'You bet. Can Grandma watch too or are you two having a fight?'

'It's not a fight,' Aggie said. 'More like a joust, to help Aunt Sarah keep her sense of humor limbered up.' She looked very tired herself, Sarah realized with a pang. When her mother began to stack her dishes, a thing she never used to do at the table while she was still sitting at it, Sarah touched her arm and said, 'Sit still, you cooked. I'll get this.' When the dishes were done, they all watched one short episode of an old saga and went early to bed.

Sarah felt much brighter in the morning, and observed that the rest of the crew sitting around Delaney's desk also looked as if they found their jobs rewarding and life worthwhile. *All of us in a good mood at once? Is the moon blue?*

Delaney said, with a glint, 'Oscar, you have some pictures to show us?'

'Yes.' He had an old corkboard set up next to Delaney's desk with a sheet over it. He got up now, proud of himself, lifted the sheet and twirled it away like a bullfighter. On the corkboard he'd pinned copies of the digital shots he'd taken yesterday, which showed, in succession, the steps by which a Toyota Camry could be reduced to a pile of spare parts. The last shot was of the bare chassis, off its wheels, surrounded by its mounds of rubble.

'Amazing old car,' he said. 'Motor could go another hundred thousand easy.'

'Now tell us what you found?'

Standing together by the cork board, Oscar and Jason said, in unison, 'Absolutely nothing!'

'The money's not there,' Delaney said. 'Now, Leo, you?'

'It's not in Mesa anymore either,' Leo said. 'As we know, Joey drew out the last of it – a little over nine thousand dollars – on the morning of the day he died. I've spoken to the bank tellers and it looks like he's been drawing it out a little at a time for years. It was up to almost ten times this much at the tipping point, three years ago. Then for some reason he quit depositing and started taking money out, one or two thousand at a time.'

'So nothing new there either. Now Ray, did you get anything from your stroll around the neighborhood?'

'Met a drinking buddy in one of the bars,' Ray said, 'who had heard Joey talk about money a lot. He discounted most of it as tequila talk, but he said it always seemed to center on the idea that Joey was coming into a nice piece of cash, he was going to be a lot better fixed pretty soon.'

'But nothing definite?'

'No. I went in two places that sell used merchandize – you know, it's a fine line be- tween junk and antiques in this town. They both said they buy things that look ready for resale, and base that judgment on what they're already selling. It doesn't seem to get any more scientific than that. They might have bought a few items from Joey over the years – nothing steady.'

'See, just what I said, occasional money,' Leo said.

'OK. Who's next?'

Sarah told them the story of Joey's enraged phone call and her efforts to get the number. 'I haven't got the list yet, but it should be along any minute.'

'And you like this phone call a lot,' Delaney said. 'Why?'

'Because of the part about the threat,' Sarah said. 'I think it explains the one thing we've wondered about all along.'

All the heads in the room swiveled in her direction, eyes of all colors staring at her as Delaney said, 'Oh, really? Only one? Which of the many things I have wondered about does it explain, Sarah?'

'Well, you know – haven't we said, all along, why would Frank do this? He was a good employee all those years and got along all right on what he earned. Why would he suddenly start to steal? Especially if he wasn't going to spend it on himself? Doesn't that suggest blackmail?'

'Yes,' Delaney said. 'But how do you blackmail a man who only does favors for people? Ollie, you're bouncing around in your seat, all of a sudden. You got an idea, or just an itch?'

'I found Angela's deadly file,' Ollie said.

'What?'

'I asked him to look for a file we've called "Angela's Deadly Research,"' Sarah said. 'It was just a— Marjorie told me she was looking up things, and she was afraid she might have found the item that got her killed. What did she actually call it? The file?'

'Ed's Life,' Ollie said. 'It's got that geneology she told you about – Ed's father and grandfather, their sorry lives and history of alcoholism. She put all his triumphs as a man in there, too – his awards and merit raises on the police force. This was just for her own satisfaction – she didn't open this file until after he died.'

'OK. Anything else in it?'

'There's a small story copied from the middle pages of *The Star* – old, over forty years ago – about a Boy Scout leader being dismissed from the leadership of his pack because a parent accused him of molesting her son. No charges were filed because the accused simply resigned and did not protest the charge.'

'My God,' Oscar said. 'Don't tell me it was Frank?'

'Bingo,' Ollie said.

'So that's the secret he'd pay to keep covered up,' Delaney said. 'Do you think it was Angela putting the arm on him?'

'I don't think so,' Ollie said. 'This file was opened just a few weeks ago.'

'That's what she said at lunch, Oscar, remember? Said it was something to do after dinner when the game show was over and she still wasn't ready to go to bed. It was just a flippant remark but it sounded bitter and true, a new widow discovering that evenings alone were long. She was so edgy with us that day – no wonder, now we know what she was hiding.'

'Yes. I think she had just found out about Frank – why would she start a file about something she'd known about for years?'

'Why would she start one and then delete it?' Ray said.

'Oh, well, this Angela was actually almost as computer savvy as Genius Geek, I think,' Ollie said. 'She retrieved this file several times. There's another little folder in this section that contains her diary. She didn't make daily entries, it's more like a personal blog post – she wrote when she had something to say. And one of the things she had to say was that she kept getting a strong feeling she was being stalked. Whenever she found something in the apartment she thought was out of place, she'd delete the Ed file for a while.'

Sarah's phone chirped and she stepped outside and answered it, to hear a secretary say that the list was on its way. While she waited for it, she called Greta Wahl and thanked her for playing an important part in the chase that was now underway.

The bell rang on the fax machine in the hall. When she saw it was for her, Sarah had a momentary feeling of ease, of sunny open spaces reaching toward an end point. She harvested the list of numbers and walked it into Delaney's office, saying, 'Here we go, guys, I got it.'

All the detectives leaned around her, running their eyes down the listed numbers. They didn't know the exact time of the call they had to find.

'There it is,' Sarah said, pointing. 'Just as I thought. Cecelia.'

FIFTEEN

Sarah drove the car when they went to pick her up. Oscar asked to ride in the second seat, saying he thought he could coax her into co-operating.

'OK, if you think so,' Delaney said, getting that look again, *Oh, yeah, Oscar and the ladies.* 'Be a whole lot better for her if she does.'

'And for us, too' Sarah said, when they were under way. 'Who wants to stage a fight in a beauty shop?'

'She would never do that,' Oscar said. 'She's too proud.'

They had talked to the owner of Desert Cuts, confirming the payments Cecelia had been making – a thousand a month for the last four years. 'Another two months and she'll own it,' the woman said.

'Really? The whole place for fifty thousand?'

'The chairs, the dryers – and the business I have built up, that's all it is. I don't own the building – she will still have rent to pay, same as me.' The shop owner's name was

316

Lois, she was from Iowa, and she had bought in to Cecelia's story about saving her tips.

'A hundred percent!' she insisted. 'Of course I believed her – why wouldn't I?' She had brought her asthmatic son to the desert because she had heard the dry air would be good for him – 'The other big lie I believed! Oh!' She mopped her face, which perspired freely when she was agitated. 'We got here just in time for dust storms and global warming. Hell's bells, a couple more years and this town is just gonna dry up and blow away completely!'

On the phone, Sarah had persuaded her to come to South Stone early in the morning before the shop opened. 'And don't tell anybody where you're going. Not even a whisper, you understand?' Sarah said. 'Extremely important!' She was less concerned for the investigation now than for the welfare of the shop owner.

Lois was devastated when she learned that the sale would not go through.

'I've made all my plans,' she wailed. 'I was going to move back home!' She grew fixated on the notion that someone might expect her to repay some of the money. 'It's all I have to retire on,' she said, and then realized, with a fresh gush of tears, that she would not be retiring any time soon.

Sarah said she wasn't going to be the one who decided anything about the money, and promised to let her know where to go to talk about that. 'But tell me,' she said, getting that warm feeling around her solar plexus that signaled a strong hunch growing, 'that nice haircut Angela got in your shop just before she died – did you do that one yourself?'

'Yes. Because she asked me to,' Lois said, preening a little. 'She said she'd been told I was the best haircutter in town. She paid extra to have me do it after hours, too. Said she couldn't get away from the store during our regular hours, and she needed to spruce up to be in a wedding. She certainly did need a haircut – she was a mess before.'

Ollie had found the appointment noted in Angela's diary, along with the ironic comment, 'The ad says, "Do your head a favor, take it to Desert Cuts.". So I did. Very satisfactory!'

Angela's diary had disposed of the pedophilia charge succinctly, too. She wrote, 'I always knew beyond question that Ed hadn't been abused sexually – he was a wonderful lover, thought sex was terrific – used to say I was the best treat he ever had. And he adored his uncle. He could be a headache, but whatever that Scout's mother had wrong in her life had nothing to do with

Frank.'

Sure she was asking the right question, Sarah said, 'Did you tell her you were selling the shop?'

'Didn't have to – somehow, she knew all about it,' Lois said. 'She asked me what I was going to do after Cecelia took over the shop, and I told her I was moving back home. I'd promised Cecelia I wouldn't tell anybody till the deal was complete, but when Angela asked me like that, I was so happy I just told her all about my plans. Oh, dear, you don't think— I mean, I didn't think it was so surprising that a member of the family would know what Cecelia was doing. Do you suppose I—' Thinking she might be put in the wrong for talking out of turn, she began to cry again. All in all, it was a damp morning at headquarters. It took a lot of time, but eventually Sarah assured her she was not at fault. Lois did a hasty repair of her makeup and went back to her shop.

They had found all the money Cecelia had stashed around her house – easily enough to cover what Joey had withdrawn the day he died. Oscar and Jason had gone to the house yesterday with a subpoena while Cecelia was working, and found it. 'It was mostly in those pots by the front door, where I said we should look first,' Oscar said. 'In cans for that fancy Brazilian coffee she liked.'

Even better than the money, from Sarah's point of view, was Angela's purse, which they found, carefully oiled and nested in an old towel, in a bottom drawer. 'She just couldn't resist it,' Oscar crowed. 'Women and purses, isn't it amazing?' They'd put it all back where they found it and swore they left no tracks – they didn't want her to bolt – but the knowledge that the money and the purse were there put an edge on the day.

'When I saw that she had put plants in those pots,' Oscar said, 'but in smaller pots that she hung inside with hooks – that's when I knew.'

They went in the shop to get her, Wednesday morning, carrying the warrant for her arrest. She was working with a customer, halfway through a haircut; she looked up when the bell sounded on the door and smiled when she saw Oscar. Her smile grew more tentative when Sarah walked in behind him. And when she spotted the backup car that the rules called for, parking at the curb with two patrolmen inside, she knew she was cooked. She laid down the comb she was holding and asked him, quietly, 'Did it have to be you, Oscar?'

'I came to make sure it went as easy as possible for you, Cecelia. If you will step outside with me we will read you your rights out there before we put the cuffs on.'

She tossed her great mane of hair, sniffed once and took off the apricot-colored smock, that matched the towels and hairbrush handles in the place. Looking in the mirror, she pushed her hair around a little and wet her lips. Then she picked up the hair dryer she'd been working with and hit Oscar a solid whack in the gut that bent him double, threw the dryer in Sarah's face and bolted for the door.

Sarah caught her just before the door closed. The two backup patrolmen leaped out of their car at once and helped her get the cuffs on.

Oscar had debated, on the way to the shop, putting cuffs on Cecelia, saying he didn't think it was necessary. But Sarah had said, 'This woman has killed two people that we're sure of, let's not underestimate her.' So she had her cuffs ready, and made sure they were good and tight, and put on the hard way – arms in back, uncomfortable almost at once and worse as time went on, and once in the car making it impossible to lean back in the seat. Before they put her in, though, Sarah left her standing in cuffs in front of the shop a few minutes. Several of her best customers registered shock when they saw her there, listening as Sarah read her Miranda rights off a card she kept clipped in the glove compartment.

When Cecelia was secure in the backseat, with a patrolman standing guard on either side, Sarah went back in the shop and said, 'Ready?' to Oscar, who had just got up off the floor with as much dignity as he could muster. He was still having some trouble getting his breath, and was having a lot of loose hair brushed off him by a helpful haircutter. He got back in the passenger seat of the Impala and never spoke another word to Cecelia, then or later.

Sarah put her in Interview I and stepped outside to check with her interview partner. Cecelia had been wearing only a sleeveless top under the smock – it got pretty hot in the shop – and the whole crew of detectives had gathered around the video picture now. They were all trying to maintain professional decorum – Delaney was there. But watching her heaving bosom in the low-cut top, as she tried to adjust her generous backside to the tiny stool, and seethed over being cuffed to the restraint strap on the table, the men clearly found quite diverting.

'It kind of makes you think of Sophia Loren in one of them early pirate pictures, don't it?' Jason whispered.

Sarah said again, to Ollie this time, 'Ready?' They had the list of questions, drawn up yesterday afternoon, and they went through them dutifully. How had she

learned of Frank's being accused of pedophilia? Did she know it was a false charge,
or did she believe it? When did she threaten
him with disclosure, and what did she say?
Did he protest at all, or give right in? Did
Ed know about the accusation? Did he
know she was extorting money from his
uncle? How did she get Joey to help her with
Angela's murder? 'We know you could not
have hung her in the closet without help,
Cecelia, was it Joey who helped? Did he do
it just because you paid him, or did you have
something on him too? Did he help you
with Frank's murder as well?'
Cecelia denied everything. She declared she
had never received any money but her own,
hard-earned income that she stood on her
two feet and earned. She didn't know what
they were talking about. If Joey had something funny going on with a bank, that was
Joey's doing – she couldn't be expected to
keep track of her crazy-ass brother. Why are
you talking about Frank's murder when
everybody knows he killed himself?

They talked at cross-purposes like that for
about an hour. When the transport vehicle
arrived they stopped talking and two fresh
officers, who had been warned to watch her
every move, took Cecelia away to the Pima
County Adult Detention Center.

'I thought there was one second there,

when you asked that last question about who helped her with Frank's murder, when she almost said, "No!" kind of indignantly,' Delaney said. 'Like maybe she did that one all by herself and was proud of it and didn't want to share the credit.'

'I thought I saw that too,' Sarah said.

'Holy Moly,' Ollie said. 'That's really sick.'

'Well, you can watch the video,' Delaney said. 'See what you think.'

'I think I need a cup of coffee first,' Ollie said. They all went in the break room together, poured coffee and sat quietly staring at it for a couple of minutes. Finally Delaney said, 'OK, what did you all see in that interview?'

'Total denial,' Sarah said. 'She feels no guilt at all for having wrecked her entire family. She saw a way to get something she wanted, she took it. She still feels entitled to it.'

'That's right,' Leo said. 'This broad is never going to break down and confess. We gotta get her with solid evidence.'

'I think so too,' Delaney said. 'So how much have we got?'

'Well, the money in the pots is pretty good,' Oscar said. He was proud that he had found the money in the pots.

'It's not enough, though. Not even close to what they claim is missing.'

'But along with what was paid to the shop owner, it is,' Ray said.

'Yeah, but money's so fungible,' Leo said. 'Even a so-so defense attorney can show a jury we can't prove it's the bank's money.'

'Even a so-so State's attorney can convince them innocent people don't hide their money in flower pots,' Ray said.

'But what we really want to prove is the murders,' Delaney said. 'Which ones look the most promising, do you think?'

'I think we're pretty close on Joey,' Sarah said. 'There's the threatening conversation from the jail that Greta overheard . . . and we've got the record of the phone call, the number that led us to Cecelia. For Frank, there's the gun he was supposed to have used to kill himself – we know Joey stole that. There's Frank Martin's car – we can get Chico to tell how Cecelia maneuvered for Joey to get that.'

'Hey, yeah,' Jason said, 'and we've got the tapes Oscar and I made when we interviewed the shade-tree mechanic who worked on the car, so we can prove he was making regular trips for his "employer" – Cecelia was obviously pulling the strings there.'

'And I can match that up with the withdrawals my bank people will testify Joey made,' Leo said.

'Close,' Delaney said. 'But what bothers

me is that we can't prove how Cecelia could get Frank to steal money for her . . . that seems pretty shaky to me.'

'Well, I remember something Angela told me,' Sarah said. 'She said that after she married Ed, there was nothing Frank wouldn't do to keep her happy – she said it seemed to be very important to Frank to see Ed happily married.'

'Yeah, so?'

'Well, I think Frank must have been afraid, all those years while Ed was growing up, that somebody would dig up that old story about the Boy Scout mother's complaint, and take Ed away from him. I think Ed was Frank's reason for living, after his wife died, and Cecelia must have realized that he'd always do anything to protect that relationship.'

'You know,' Jason said, 'we've all noticed how secretive these people are. Why don't we talk to Chico and Luz again? Maybe they will admit they were covering up for Frank Martin all these years. If Angela began to suspect something about the money once she found out about Frank and ask questions . . . that would get Cecelia on her case, huh?'

'This whole story's going to be an easier sell if we can line up the forensics for any one of these murders,' Ollie said. 'If any of the DNA they lifted out of Joey's car matches Cecelia, she'll be toast.'

'That's right,' Sarah said. 'And what about Angela's apartment, and everything we took out of it? If Angela was right that Cecelia was snooping through her stuff, there's a very good chance she might have left some DNA – and it didn't occur to us to ask for that comparison at the time.'

'All right,' Delaney said. 'So we're all inclined to keep digging, right?'

'Absolutely,' Sarah said. 'And suspicion of murder one . . . she won't be eligible for bail, will she?'

'No.'

'So maybe she'll get sick of sitting in Pima County and start to make deals,' Jason said.

'Somehow I doubt it,' Delaney said. 'Let's get back to work.'

Sarah heard Ollie, later that day, tell Leo, 'You know, it's surprising how little satisfaction there is at the end of a long hunt like this one.'

'Yeah,' Leo said, 'you keep turning over rocks, and the worms that crawl out keep getting uglier. So after a while you think, *what's the use?*'

'Makes you understand what happened to Harry Eisenstaat, huh?'

'You see me turning into Harry Eisenstaat,' Leo said, 'shoot me.'

SIXTEEN

Delaney didn't seem to suffer from any feelings of anti-climax. He made a point of talking to the chief about the case, that week while the story of Cecelia's arrest was running in *The Star*. And one afternoon he gathered his crew in front of his office so the chief could shake everybody's hand and congratulate them on the excellent teamwork that had cracked this very troublesome case.

Oscar Cifuentes wasn't singled out for any special praise, but he certainly wasn't excluded, either. Delaney placed him in the center of the row and made sure the chief got his name right. Sarah asked Leo later that day, 'Have you noticed that Delaney seems to be getting friendlier towards Oscar?'

'Yup,' Leo said, 'getting creamed with a hair dryer in the beauty shop turned out to be the luckiest thing that's happened to Oscar in some time.'

'How did you ... I never told anybody

about that,' Sarah said.

'Come on, Sarah,' Leo said. 'You had two backups in a patrol car there that day and this is the police department. Did you really think they'd keep it to themselves?'

'But why does it make Delaney feel better about him?'

'He's never going to admit that's what it is. He says Oscar's finally catching on to team-work.'

'Well, he is. But he's been doing that all along.'

'I know. But having the great lover get punched out by a woman makes it easier for the boss to see it.'

'Jeez, Leo, that's just ... pitiful.'

'Please, Sarah, can we stop this conver-sation before we each start saying sexist things? This is a very good week for me and I don't want to be cross about anything.'

'All right. Why is this a good week?'

'My son's in the current crop of recruits and this is their final week of class. He's just received official word that he's on the list to graduate next Friday.'

'Leo! You dog! Why didn't you ever tell me?'

'Because he threatened to kill me if I told anybody where he was until he was sure he was going to graduate. All along he's been seeing other kids flunk out and he got terribly afraid he wouldn't make it.'

'Oh, you must be just bursting with pride!'

'I never thought there was any doubt at all but I could never convince Tom. He said, "You're my dad, what else are you going to say?"' Leo laughed. 'God, it's going to be good to have all that angst out of the house.'

'Listen, can we come and watch? I'd like to bring Denny, too – she's getting kind of interested in what we do for a living.'

'Sure, if you ... are you sure? You've seen it so many times before, haven't you? And it's pretty dull stuff, you know, speeches and all that.'

'I know. And I always love it.'

Aggie didn't think she was up for that much standing and walking, and Will opted to stay home too; he had a project going and said he'd heard enough speeches, he thought, to last him for the rest of his life. So Sarah drove and Denny watched the red-tail hawks sailing on thermals over the desert.

They got good seats. It was a beautiful clear day, with a little breeze. The class marched in proud single file, with their own guidon leading the way. The American and Arizona flags were posted by the podium, and stirred lazily in the breeze as the crowd sang the national anthem. There were speeches and prizes, and a judge to administer the oath of office. Then the recruits stepped forward one at a time to receive their badges, and Tom Tobin, slim and handsome, received his from the chief who had recently congratulated his father on a job well done. Sarah turned to smile at Leo and saw that he and his wife were holding tight to each other's hands as if they feared falling down, and both had tears in their eyes.

The class marched out as the audience stood and clapped. Sarah put her arm around Denny's shoulder then and said, 'Did you enjoy that?'

'Oh, Aunt Sarah,' Denny said. 'Oh, wow. Did you see the parents' faces? They were all crying!'

'Well, they were so happy.'

'They were beyond happy. They were plotzed. It was beautiful!'

They drove home toward the good little pork roast Will had said he was going to cook 'in Denny's new gadget.' Denny was silent for the first couple of miles and then said, 'Do you think I could do it?'

'What? Make it through the police academy? Of course you could do it if you made up your mind to. It's hard, though, so I would urge you to consider everything else available before you decide.'

'I will. Everything else is going to have to

brighten up, though, if it wants to compete with that. Do you think Will Dietz would be offended if I offered to make the gravy?'

'What?' Sometimes Denny's lightning changes of pace still left her behind. 'No, I shouldn't think so. Why?'

'Because he is a very good person and I would never want to hurt his feelings, but he is really an awful bust when it comes to making gravy.'

'Ah ... well, I suppose it's not the worst flaw a man could have.'

'Not at all, especially if he lets me make it instead. Oh, Aunt Sarah, do you really think I could do that?' She spread her arms out, toward the soaring hawks, toward all the beautiful possibilities out there.